THE CHALET SCHOOL DOES IT AGAIN

ELINOR M BRENT-DYER

Girls Gone By Publishers

COMPLETE AND UNABRIDGED

Published by
Girls Gone By Publishers
4 Rock Terrace, Coleford, Radstock, Somerset, BA3 5NF

First published by W & R Chambers 1955
This edition published 2012

Cover design by Ken Websdale
Typeset in England by Books to Treasure
Printed and bound by CPI Group (UK) Ltd, Croydon, CR0 4YY

ISBN 978-1-84745-145-3

Prunella wrenched off her coat and, before anyone could prevent her, had climbed the railings and dived ...

CONTENTS

MAKING FRIENDS AT THE CHALET SCHOOL

(All page numbers apart from references to *The Chalet School Does It Again* are from Chamber hardback editions)

The Chalet School Does It Again contains a prime example of a theme which recurs at intervals throughout the Chalet School series: that of the girl who forms a friendship with a fellow-pupil considerably older than herself. Examples of such friendships are used in a variety of ways to further plots and characterisation, and that of Len and Prunella, although only ever lightly sketched in, is significant both in this book and in the overall development of Len and her triplet sisters.

There are of course different kinds of friendship, and where there is a big gap in age it would be easy to imagine that we must be talking about hero-worship rather than a friendship of equals. EBD does portray this, as something quite normal and to be expected, although needless to state, any form of sentimentality is heavily stamped upon. A good example would be Jack Lambert's admiration of Len, beginning in *A Leader in the Chalet School* and continuing through the subsequent books:

> "Len Maynard is dormy prefect for Pansy and Jack has latched on to her ever since she came—Jack I mean. That's the why of all this. Come and sit over here, Jane, and we'll do what we can for you."
>
> "Only," put in another girl, "we must make it plain to you that Jack is not foolish—what you call 'soppy'—about Len. In this school, we do not like such things. But Jack asks many questions and Len can answer them. If they are in different dormies, it will be difficult for Jack, you understand."
>
> *Jane and the Chalet School* p15

But this sort of attraction, though useful in providing role models as well as opportunities for the condemnation of soppiness, cannot be considered true friendship. And it is not what we are dealing with here: Len feels no particular admiration for Prunella, even after they have made their peace with one another—they just 'click'.

Going back to the early years of the Chalet School, it might be supposed that in the first few books, when the school is so small that pupils of all ages learn together or are divided into sets according to ability, girls would quite naturally mingle and make friends across the age range. It is interesting, therefore, that while Joey—accustomed to the companionship of her much older twin siblings—gets on well with everyone from the prefects down to the youngest in the school, her closest and longest-lasting friendship group is the Quartette she gradually forms with Frieda, Marie and Simone, who are much her own age. She does become close to other girls, notably Juliet and the Robin and to some extent Stacie, all older or younger than herself; but here the friendship blurs into family relationship, as all three become part of the household at the Sonnalpe and end up somewhere along the scale from friend to sister. So even at this early stage, a friendship which steps

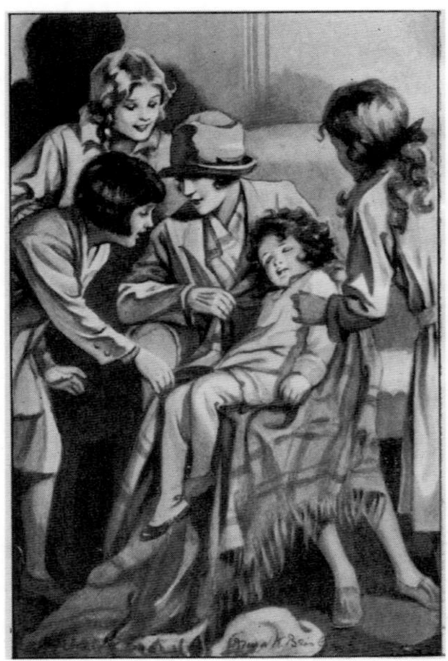

outside the age group needs an added factor if it is to endure.

As the school grows more forms are introduced, and in *The New Chalet School*, with its huge influx of new girls from the former St Scholastika's, we see the effect this has on established friendship groups.

> [Miss Wilson] began to read at once in a clear, rather deeply pitched voice, and the girls listened eagerly, for, with so many new girls, it was plain that there must be big readjustments in forms.
>
> They were right. They had begun the year with two Sixths and two Fifths. Now there were to be two Fourths and two Thirds as well. The result was that certain little coteries in those forms found themselves broken up, and pulled long faces over it in private. Alixe von Elsen, for example, who could generally be relied on to keep things lively, found that she had been promoted to Five B, while Kitty Burnett and Emmie Linders, two cronies of hers, were still in Four A; Joyce Linton, another of their gang, had been moved up into Five A, so Alixe had not even the satisfaction of being with her.
>
> *The New Chalet School* p79

However, class divisions are not necessarily organised according to age. In EBD's world 'removes' to a higher class are given on merit and attainment, and thus the friendships we see being split need not be between girls of different ages. In the example above, Alixe and Emmie are both thirteen (both were stated to be twelve the year before, in *Exploits*), while Joyce, we know, is fourteen; Kitty's age may best be described as elastic. But there is no great difference here. The pattern is maintained that as a general rule, the girls gravitate towards their contemporaries—as one might expect, considering the huge amount of development in both maturity and interests which takes place during the teenage years.

This is not to say that no two friends of different ages are ever in the same form, but rather that their being together in class need not be the cause of their becoming friends. Margot Maynard and Emerence Hope do eventually end up together in Inter V in *The New Mistress at the Chalet School*, but their friendship is by then of long standing. Joyce Linton and Thekla von Stift take advantage of being in the same form to combine in some very unpleasant behaviour, but their mutual attraction predates their knowledge that they will be together. In fact, Joyce's friendship with Thekla is the result of a calculated choice on her part; each wishes to make use of the other, and there is no suggestion that either particularly likes the other. We see the first seeds of this when the empty-headed Joyce is beginning to feel her way towards the popularity she craves:

> 'Don't you like [Thekla]?' asked Joyce inquisitively, as her work brought her up to them in time to hear Marie's remark.
>
> 'She is not like the rest of us,' said Marie shortly. 'Bring some more chairs, please.'
>
> It was quite plain that she was going to say no more, and Joyce shrugged her shoulders and went to do as she was told. But her curiosity was aroused, and when Thekla had finished unpacking and returned to the room, she looked at her consideringly. She was rather impressed by the elder girl's supercilious airs, for Joyce was empty-headed

> enough, and Thekla's evident feeling of superiority made her think that here was someone who would be worth knowing. She looked at her again, and then turned to watch Marie as she set chairs for the Staff. Joyce had been the prettiest girl in her old school, and had thoroughly enjoyed queening it. She was by no means delighted to find on her arrival at this school that there was a girl who could certainly rival her in appearance. That it should be one older than herself made it no better. Joyce had had experience of the way in which younger girls run after older ones, and she was not content to be second.
>
> *The Chalet School and the Lintons* p63

In contrast to this deliberate, self-serving alliance, Margot's friendship with Emerence is the result of an instantaneous and violent attraction, based no doubt in part on a recognition of a similar bent towards mischief and an impatience of conformity. As Mary-Lou Trelawney puts it, 'They practically rushed on each other the first moment they met. Deep calling to deep, I imagine!' (*Theodora* p119). Len's and Prunella's reaction to each other on the other hand is rather one of instant antagonism, and again this is entirely true to life. Readers of romantic fiction will be well acquainted with the storyline of 'woman meets man, hates him, fights him at every opportunity and ultimately falls into his arms', but this can and does happen in friendship as well as in love.

> Later on in the day, it seeped through to them via Betsy Lucy and Sue Meadows what the something was that had upset Len's equilibrium. Despite all the rest could say and all Len's own protests, Prunella

> insisted on calling her by her full name. No one else ever did it unless she had been thoroughly naughty and Len hated it. At that age, she loathed her stately name and much preferred its shortened form. She had put up with Prunella more or less quietly for the few weeks that had passed, but that morning, her patience had snapped and she had treated the members of Primrose dormitory to a display of temper that even Margot could hardly have bettered.
>
> p72

It comes as a surprise to their classmates, therefore, when the two become bosom friends and remain so through several books, although ultimately they have to recognise that there is little scope for such a friendship in the realities of school life (*Theodora* p110).

Another notable age-disparate friendship, that of Mary-Lou Trelawney and Clem Barrass, begins differently again as we see them getting to know each other during the holidays before they, entirely unexpectedly, end up at the same school (*Three Go to the Chalet School*). Their friendship is cemented by the coincidence of their being placed in a two-bed dormitory in their first term; their attempts to get into the same form nearly result in brain-fever for Mary-Lou, but fortunately Clem's home circumstances allow them to continue and develop the bond during school holidays.

Samaris and Samantha on the other hand, in *Two Sams at the Chalet School*, not implausibly form an initial bond based on their both being new girls together in the middle of the school year, plus the similarity of their names.

These oddly-assorted friendships also progress to quite different endings. Len's and Prunella's, as we have seen, dwindles in response to the practicalities of their situation. Mary-Lou and Clem, like Joey and the Robin, are able to maintain their friendship as it morphs almost imperceptibly into a family relationship—to all intents and purposes they become sisters. With Sam and Samaris this is taken a step further: like so many of the more solitary girls in the latter part of the series, they discover an unexpected family relationship; they are not sisters, but they are 'kin', and to this they are tempted to ascribe their unexplained attraction. As Sammy says, "I guess if you're blood kin it makes all that much difference." (*Two Sams* p195)

Margot and Emerence on the other hand make things work for them by sheer force of willpower. They too make an abortive attempt to get into the same form when they first meet, but this is forcefully dealt with by the powers that be (*Changes* p91). Their friendship, however, is a constant throughout the early Swiss books, although the fundamental self-centredness of Margot's side is not fully shown until *Theodora and the Chalet School*, when she nearly shipwrecks on the acceptance of a highly unsuitable parting gift from her bosom friend. The dynamic within the triplet bond, and the strain put upon it by developing outside friendships, is beautifully drawn, and it is entirely appropriate that it should be Mary-Lou, herself experienced in a wide variety of friendships (contrast the all-inclusiveness of the Gang with the closeness of her bond

with Clem, and the little vignette we are shown of an instinctive 'clicking' with Betsy in *Does It Again*, see p53), who is able to intervene and help them to understand themselves and each other.

Margot and Emerence's friendship is probably the most fully developed of these examples. From the moment when they meet, right through their many turbulent and ill-judged escapades, to the point at the end of the series when Margot actually visits Emerence at her home in Australia, they never waver in their devotion to one another, and while Margot certainly learns from the incident in *Theodora*—and retains her clock as a lasting reminder of her own selfishness (*Theodora* p215)—her determination to get her own way is still strikingly evident in *The Chalet School Triplets* when the Australian invitation arrives, and Margot spends a good chunk of the first two chapters enlisting her sisters' support, with apparently no thought for the possibility that they too might have liked such an opportunity. In fact EBD notably avoids the kind of didactic moral which she might have drawn, showing (as she herself might have said) 'cause and effect' within the relationship, but including no cliff-hanging episodes, no redemptive illnesses, just good, believable, true-to-life situations and reactions. When Emerence does fall over a cliff in *A Chalet Girl from Kenya* it is Jo Scott, not Margot, who rescues her.

These friendships, then, may dwindle and fade; they may persist into adult life; they may become transformed into a sisterly bond, as happens to Mary-Lou and Clem when Mr and Mrs Barrass's wandering lifestyle and ultimate premature decease lead to Clem's becoming to all intents and purposes a member of the Carey/Trelawney household. Or they may come to a more violent end, as is the case with Joyce and Thekla, and it is interesting to note that as their unholy alliance breaks down, the difference in their ages suddenly becomes more important:

> With her tossed golden curls, her sleepy blue eyes, and her bare feet, [Joyce] looked very small and young, and the girl who had summoned her in calm defiance of all rules, looked very much taller and older. 'What d'you want, Thekla?' asked Joyce, yawning drowsily. 'And whatever time is it?'
>
> 'That is no matter,' said Thekla. 'I wish to speak with you, Joyce. Come to that window, and we will sit behind the curtains.'
>
> [...]
>
> 'It is this,' said Thekla, paying no heed to what the child said. 'I wish that you shall not be friends with Jo Bettany, for I hate her, and she shall not be friends with you.'... Thekla's cold grey eyes grew colder, and her face set in hard lines. 'It is that you are *my* friend, and I do not wish that you should friends with that horrible girl be,' she said. 'Do you hear, Joyce? I am older than you, and have the right to guide you—'
>
> *Lintons* pp239–40

This episode results in the expulsion of Thekla and the at least partial redemption of Joyce, although the latter never fully attains to the standard of the ideal Chalet girl. Her friendship with this older girl has been entirely negative in its effect. And this brings me to another point.

Examples of age-different friendships do, as we have seen, occur at several stages of the series, but this is not a case of an author re-using an old plot strand and doing it to death for want of fresh ideas. The theme is actually used very differently in different situations. Such a friendship may be good for the protagonists (for example, Clem Barrass and Mary-Lou

Trelawney) or definitely destructive (Thekla and Joyce); or it may be intrinsically neutral (Len and Prunella; Margot and Emerence), but used to allow an exploration of the personalities of both parties as the friendship develops. It is always rooted in character and cirucumstance—we have already seen how Joyce and Thekla are drawn together by their more unpleasant attributes, while Mary-Lou's and Joey's solitary childhoods, surrounded by grown-ups, make it natural for them to relate easily to older girls.

It is interesting therefore that two of the Maynard triplets choose older friends when they first step outside the closeness of the triplet bond. This may be in part because their same-age needs are satisfied by each other, so that they are looking for something different when they move beyond the family unit. Len's choice of Prunella perhaps reflects her old-for-her-age attitudes fostered by the responsibility of being the eldest of (at this stage) eight, together with the maturing effects of their time in Canada. In Margot's case, the separation from her immediate family in *The Chalet School and the Island*, added again to the couple of years she spends in Canada, have produced a surface sophistication superimposed on a fundamentally babyish attitude to life, and this seems well matched to Emerence's older years and spoilt-child upbringing.

(Of course all three Maynard girls are stated to have had best friends in Canada, but we never see this and it is apparently mentioned purely to underline Margot's carelessness in not keeping up the friendship, as compared to her sisters. Prunella and Emerence are the first friends actually to 'happen' within the series.)

Con, much more of a loner, and with a rich life of the imagination, forms no such bond but is sufficiently aware to recognise this for herself. Her pairing with Odette seems more convenient than rewarding, and as such is sufficiently true to life: how many of us in our own schooldays have 'gone around' with someone with whom we had little in common, rather than be left with no one to play with? Although Con's motivation seems rather to be one of compassion:

> Con was by way of being friendly with her, mainly because she felt sorry for her, and brought her with the others as much as she could. Odette had made very few friends, even after two terms.
>
> *Theodora* p145

Much of *Theodora* is spent in analysing the conflict between the closeness of the triplet bond and the natural desire to move beyond it, experienced in different ways by the three concerned, according to their different characters. The way is paved for this in many ways, not least by the accounts of their beginning to form outside friendships. That between Len and Prunella, though never a main theme and not even referred to very often, is nonetheless a significant part of their story. It is short on actual episodes but forms part of a wider exploration of their characters, particularly that of Len. Like the other age-disparate friendships within the series, it is firmly rooted in observation. EBD knew girls.

Ruth Jolly

PUBLISHING HISTORY

The Chalet School Does It Again was first published by W & R Chambers in 1955 and was reprinted in 1956. It had a full-colour dustwrapper, unsigned but probably by D[orothy] Brook. We have used the dustwrapper illustration on the front of this GGBP edition, and the spine is shown on the back cover. There was also a black-and-white frontispiece by D Brook, which we have reproduced. No further impressions or editions were published in hardback.

The Armada paperback edition was published in 1990 and, as far as is known, was not reprinted. This had a cover illustration (see opposite) by Gwyneth Jones.

The first Girls Gone By edition was published in 2002.

Text

For this GGBP edition we have used the text of the original hardback edition, which contained a number of errors, typesetting and otherwise. See 'Errors in the First Edition' for details.

Clarissa Cridland

Elinor M. Brent-Dyer
THE
CHALET SCHOOL
DOES IT AGAIN

THE CHALET SCHOOL DOES IT AGAIN

by

ELINOR M. BRENT-DYER

CONTENTS

THE CHALET SCHOOL DOES IT AGAIN

Chapter I

A Queer New Girl

LEN MAYNARD shot down the stairs, giggling wildly at every step she took. She reached the bottom, turned right and raced along the corridor, through the wooden passage that linked up the chalet which formed one of the school's Houses—Ste Thérèse de Lisieux, to be accurate—with the main building. This had once been a luxury hotel, but tourism had drifted away from the Görnetz Platz and the proprietor of the hotel had been very glad to dispose of his property to the Chalet School Company.

Once in the main building, Len dropped into a more sedate pace, though she still giggled as she went. She reached a door which she opened just wide enough to allow her to slide in, and closed it behind her. About a dozen girls were in the cheerful room, all chattering eagerly, for this was the first full day of term and everyone had plenty to say about the Christmas holidays now, alas! behind them.

Someone saw Len and gave an exclamation. "Len Maynard! I wondered where you were. Are you three really to be boarders this term?"

Len nodded. "Hello, everyone! Had decent hols? Oh, good!" as half a dozen voices informed her that their holidays had been more than decent. "O.K., Connie. You've got it in one. We three are boarders for the rest of our school-life."

Connie Winter, a mischievous thirteen-year-old, with wicked, blue eyes shining in a face freckled like a plover's egg, grinned. "Seems rather weird when you live just next door."

"I know. But Mother says that if the winter here is anything like the winters in Tirol—and she jolly well knows it is because this is the Alps and so is Tirol—then we can't risk missing days on end because of storms and blizzards. And once we start in as full boarders, we may as well keep on. So there you are!"

"Good!" a thin girl possessed of a sharp, fair prettiness, broke in before any of the others could comment. "Which dormy are you in? Not ours, I know."

"I'm in Primrose—over at Ste Thérèse's. Con's in Wallflower over here and Margot's planted out in Gentian at St. Hild's. Jolly mean of Matey, isn't it? But she always *did* separate us, if you remember."

"Primrose? That's one of the new dormies, isn't it?" A stocky, young person of twelve joined in. "How many are you and who's dormy prefect?"

"Seven of us and Betsy Lucy's our pree. so we're lucky that way, anyhow," Len giggled again.

"What's the joke?" Connie eyed her curiously.

Len swung herself up on the table in the middle of the room and gave vent to a whole series of chuckles. "Oh, my dears! We've got the weirdest thing in new girls I've ever seen in my life!" She spoke as if she were at least thirty and the rest were suitably impressed.

"A new girl? But how is she weird?" the thin girl demanded.

"You wait till you see her!" Len was swinging her crossed ankles. Her curly, chestnut hair was all on end, thanks to her wild rush, and she kept breaking into little gurgles. "Oh, she's definitely not your cup of tea, Emerence—at least, I can't imagine it. If you come to that, I don't know whose cup of tea she'll ever be here. Not mine, at any rate!"

"How d'you mean?" Emerence asked, puzzled. "Do go on and tell us something, Len, and don't sit there giggling like a village idiot!"

"Village idiot yourself!" Len retorted amiably. Then she pulled herself together. "She's out and out the primmest thing you ever saw."

"Huh! That's nothing new to us," Emerence replied. "What about young Verity-Anne Carey? *She's* prim enough for anything!"

"Mother says Verity-Anne isn't *prim* exactly. I mean, look at the things she says—*and* gets away with! Mother says she's more precise than prim."

"Oh? Well—yes; perhaps she's right. But what's the difference, anyhow?"

"You'll know when you see our latest," Len replied darkly. "She's not in the least like Verity-Anne."

"But how do you know? You've only just seen her, haven't you?" interjected a boyish-looking individual whose flaming, red hair was cropped short.

Len turned wide, violet-grey eyes on her. "I've been showing her how to put her things away. Matey was unpacking her when I went past and she yanked me in and told me to go upstairs with her and show her how drawers and closets had to be kept."

"What's her name?" Emerence asked.

"Prunella Davidson. I should think she's about fourteen, so I don't suppose we'll see an awful lot of her. She's safe to be in one of the Uppers. She's rather pretty," she went on consideringly. "She's got yards and yards of brown hair that she wears in two enormous plaits and she's a bit bigger than you, Isabel. And the way she *talks*!" Len stopped to giggle again. "She says 'Do you not?' and 'Have you not?' and she quotes proverbs—she does, honestly! When I was explaining about the way we have to arrange our drawers, she said, 'Quite so! A place for everything and everything in its place. I quite understand. Most appropriate!' I nearly bust in her face!" And Len broke into peals of laughter at the recollection.

The members of Junior common-room received this information with dropped jaws.

"You're trying to pull our legs," Connie said accusingly when she had got her breath again.

"I'm *not*! She honestly does talk that way and that's exactly what she said."

"Help!" Connie pretended to swoon into her neighbour's arms and was jerked to her feet with unfeeling promptness.

"Stand *up*, you silly ass! *I'm* not going to hold you up, so don't think it." Charlotte Harrison turned back to Len. "What else did she say, Len?"

"Well, she approves of our cubeys. She said," and Len broke off to gurgle again, "'that one so frequently wants a little privacy'. She did say just 'zackly that!"

"Cripes!" gasped Emerence. "She must be crackers!"

They all agreed with this. Whoever had heard of a girl of fourteen demanding privacy? They gave it up and turned to something else.

"If she's fourteen, how is it she's in the same dormy as you?" Charlotte asked.

"We're a mixed dormy," Len explained. "There's Betsy to start with—and she's sixteen—"

"You said she was dormy pree. She doesn't count," Isabel said quickly.

"P'raps not," Len agreed, unperturbed. "Well, there's me, and I'm eleven. Then there's Sue Meadows who's fourteen, too, and another new girl called Virginia Adams who *looks* about fourteen. And Nesta Williams who's twelve. I told you it was a small dormy."

"No smaller than lots of others," Emerence told her.

Isabel Drew had been counting on her fingers. "I thought you said seven of you? That's only six—unless you're counting Betsy in."

"I wasn't. Prees. never do count in," Len responded. "I'd forgotten. We're to have Nan Wentworth this term." Len suddenly looked grave. "Did you know her mother died these hols? Just after Christmas it was. That's why Matey's moved Nan in with our lot. She said she thought she'd probably rather not stay in Poppy. There's twelve of you there, isn't there, Frankie?"

Frankie—otherwise Francesca Richardson—nodded. "Twelve of us and Dorothy Watson and Nora Penley. Not really, Len? Oh, poor Nan! I'm awfully sorry for her." She looked anxious for a moment. "I say, we—we shan't have to—to *say* anything to her, shall we?"

"Matey said not unless she says anything about it first. She's just a kid, you know," went on Len who was a good ten months younger than Nan Wentworth. "She's to stay on at the school. I heard Daddy telling Mother that it was the best thing for her. Her father's in the Navy, you know, and he's hardly ever at home. There's only her granny and *she's* done nothing but cry since Mrs. Wentworth died. She's awfully old, too. Daddy said Nan would be far better off at school and he meant to tell Commander Wentworth so. Oh, and Mother told me to see that we were all nice to Nan, but not to fuss round her."

Emerence, who was the eldest of the group, nodded. "*I* see. It would sort of keep on reminding her. We're to be just ordinary, but *nice* ordinary."

As this was exactly what Mrs. Maynard had meant, Len nodded, "You've got it. That's what Mother meant." She pricked up her ears. "Someone's coming!" She turned round to face the door as it opened to admit Matron, beloved and feared of all the girls, together with someone who was unmistakably after Len's description.

"Girls, this is Prunella Davidson. Look after her, please," Matron said. Then she fixed Len with an icy glare and that young lady slid off the table in a hurry. "Tables were not meant for sitting on, Len."

"No, Matron," Len murmured, flushing red.

"Then don't let me catch you doing it again, please. Emerence, run along to Senior-Middle common-room, please, and tell Mary-Lou I'm ready for them now."

Emerence said very properly, "Yes, Matron," and departed. Matron followed her out, shutting the door firmly behind her and the dozen or so members of the Junior-Middles were left with the new girl.

Len went up to her. Good manners had been drilled into all the young Maynards from their earliest days, even if the tradition of the school had not been that new girls were to be looked after and helped to feel themselves part of it as quickly as possible.

"We're all Junior-Middles, Prunella," she said, "and I expect you'll be a Senior-Middle. But Matey's sent for them to unpack so I s'pose she felt you'd rather be with someone than all on your own. Come on, and I'll tell you who we all are."

Prunella regarded her gravely. "Thank you. You are most kind," she said politely. "You told me in the dormitory that you are Helena Maynard, I think?"

"I'll bet she never did!" Isabel muttered to Charlotte who was next to her and her boon companion. "Len hates her proper name."

Len herself was replying, "Oh, but no one ever calls me that! I'm always 'Len'."

Prunella smiled indulgently at her. "But when one has a proper name it is surely better and wiser to use it and not descend to babyish abbreviations?"

Len looked baffled for a moment. Then she evidently decided to ignore this and proceeded with her introductions. "This is Frankie Richardson who's in the B division of Lower IV."

Len had turned to Frankie as she spoke and the eye hidden from Prunella drooped in a wink at that young woman. Prunella "rose" as they had expected.

"Oh, surely not!" she exclaimed, in shocked tones.

"Oh yes; everyone calls her that," wicked Len replied, her eyes dancing. "And this is Connie Winter—in my form." She went on, reeling off the names and, where she could, giving shortened forms of them. The rest backed her up. Even Isabel Drew never flinched when solemnly introduced as "Izzie Drew"—a form of her name never used before.

By the time she had finished, Prunella was looking both startled and bewildered—and small blame to her! However, she said, "How do you do?" most properly to the owner of each name. Conversation languished when this was ended. It was revived by the new girl.

"And this is your recreation room?" she said, gazing round approvingly.

"Our *common*-room," Charlotte replied rebukingly. "This is the Junior common-room. The Upper Fourths are Senior-Middles and have their own and so have the Fifths and Sixths. Of course, the prees. use the prefects' room."

"I see. A really excellent arrangement," Prunella approved.

The younger girls gaped, but before they could say anything, there was a clatter of feet outside and then the rest of the Junior-Middles irrupted into the room, led by a girl who, despite her flood of golden curls, was unmistakably Len's sister.

"Well, here we are!" she proclaimed in bell-like tones. "We three are full boarders this term! Isn't it nifty?"

"Len's just been telling us," Isabel said. "And it's no use looking for Emerence. Matey collared her for errands."

"She would! Oh, well, I'll see her soon."

"In the meantime, this is a new girl called Prunella Davidson," Len said. "This is one of my sisters, Prunella—Margot. And here's the other. She's called Con."

"Constance—or Constantia?" Prunella asked with a little smile.

Con, as dark as Margot was fair, stared at her. "Constance, of course, but no one ever calls me that," she said firmly. "We've got a new girl in Wallflower, called Virginia Adams. She told Matey they called her Virgy at home, though."

"Don't blame them," said one of the newcomers. "Virginia! Help! What a mouthful!"

"Well, it's better than 'Ginny'," said someone else. "We've two news in Pansy—both French. One's Suzanne Élie and the other's Andrée de Vienne. I say! We look like growing again, don't we?"

"Mary Woodley's not coming back," put in a third.

There was a chorus of exclamations at this. Len finally made herself heard above the rest. "Not coming back? Why ever not? She didn't say anything about it last term."

"Don't suppose she knew—then. Her father's got a job in Australia—Tasmania, I think. Isn't Launceston in Tasmania? They're off next month. My Auntie Joan lives next door to them in Newbury. She and Uncle and the cousins came to spend Christmas with us and when we were having tea, she said, 'Well, Heather, you're losing *one* girl from the Görnetz Platz. The Woodleys are off to Launceston in February. Well, never mind. As soon as Lesley and Anne are old enough they'll be coming to join you, so they'll help to make up'."

"Who're Lesley and Anne?" Isabel Drew asked.

"My cousins—Auntie Joan's kids. It'll be years before they

come, though," Heather added. "Lesley's only seven and Anne's four. They're not bad—for kids, that is."

"Are they anything like you?" Connie asked sweetly.

Heather giggled. "Just exactly like! One morning, Auntie made us line up and then she said to Mummy, 'Did you ever see anything to beat it—all exactly alike? Aren't they *monotonous*!' And the boys—my brother Martin and Auntie's Peter are just the same, too."

The door opened to admit Emerence who had escaped from Matron at last and she and Margot fell on each other promptly. As both had the reputation of being thoroughly naughty girls, it was a friendship that no one encouraged, but that didn't matter to the pair. When they had finished exclaiming, Charlotte gave Emerence the latest news.

"I say, Em, Mary Woodley's left—gone to Australia."

"Bad luck for Australia," grinned Emerence who came from there herself. "I never did like Mary Woodley." Then she looked round. "Where's Prunella Davidson? Oh, there you are! I met Mary-Lou Trelawney just outside and she told me to take you to the office. Miss Dene wants to see you. Come on!"

A curly-headed individual gave a shriek. "I've got to go and fetch two news called Virginia and Truda. I forgot about it till you spoke, Emmie. Out of the way, Nora!" She burst through the little groups standing about and shot out of the door.

"Just like Elsie Morris!" Emerence said with a grin. "She'd forget her head if it was loose! Come on, Prunella. Can't keep Deney waiting!"

Prunella followed her into the corridor, across the wide entrance hall and to a door which stood slightly ajar. A very clear, pleasant voice was heard.

"Then that will be all, you two. Truda will be in your form, Elsie, but keep Virginia—what is it, child? Oh, you want to be

'Virgy', do you? very well—Virgy, then, with you until someone comes from Upper IVA for her. I know Matron has that crowd for unpacking. You'd rather be with the younger Middles than in the common-room by yourself, wouldn't you?"

"Yes, please," said a fervent voice.

"Run along, then. If the new girl, Prunella Davidson, is outside, Elsie, send her in, will you?"

"Yes, Miss Dene." There was a pause. Then Elsie's voice came, "Curtsy, you two. We always curtsy here, you know."

The door was opened wider in time for Prunella to see Elsie rising from a bobbed curtsy which the other two were imitating. They came out and, as she passed Emerence and her charge, Elsie said, "Miss Dene is ready for Prunella now, Emerence."

Emerence nodded. She touched Prunella on the arm. "Come along. This is the office." Then, as she led the way in and bobbed her curtsy, "I've brought Prunella Davidson, Miss Dene."

Miss Dene, a slim, fair person, immaculate from her gleaming, brown hair to the tips of her pretty slippers, gave her a smile. "Thank you, Emerence. Will you wait in the hall? I won't keep Prunella more than a few minutes."

Emerence replied, "Yes, Miss Dene," very properly and went out, shutting the door behind her and Prunella was left alone with the school's secretary.

Miss Dene, formerly a pupil at the school and for many years a member of its staff, gave the new girl a friendly smile. "So you are Prunella. Come along and sit down."

Prunella left the door where she had been standing quietly and came up to the big desk. Somehow her grown-up air had vanished and it was an ordinary, rather shy schoolgirl who faced the pretty secretary. Miss Dene indicated a chair nearby and Prunella sat down and regarded the toes of her slippers in silence. The next moment, she had forgotten them, for Miss Dene had taken up a bunch of exam. papers which the new girl recognized as her own. She felt a sudden qualm. Had she done well enough to go into one of the Upper Fourths or was her fate to be with the younger girls?

"These are your papers," Miss Dene said. She unclipped them and glanced over a printed form, filled in with various handwritings. "I see that your general subjects are well up to standard for your age. Your French is marked *Très faible* and you seem to have done no German. Your Latin is weak, too. Your art is marked excellent but your needlework is very poor." She looked at it for a moment while Prunella went hot and cold by turns. Then Miss Dene looked up and smiled again. "Miss Annersley says that, with the extra work everyone has in languages, she thinks you ought to be able to manage to work with Upper IVB. You will have extra coaching in German, French and Latin which should bring you level with the rest by the end of the term. As for your needlework, we can safely leave that to Mdlle. I see that you are to take extra art but not music." She laid the bundle aside and smiled at the girl again. "Well, that's settled. Now tell me—I may as well know at once—do they call you 'Prunella' at home or do they use a shortened form?"

This was the time for Prunella to inform her as she had done Frankie and Co. that when one had a proper name not to use it was foolish. She did nothing of the sort. She replied meekly, "I'm always 'Prunella', Miss Dene."

"I don't wonder. It's a very pretty name—and what's more, I believe it's the first time we've had it in the school," Miss Dene told her. "Very well. 'Prunella' it shall be. And now, the sooner you meet your own form, the better. Just a moment." She pressed a button at the side of her desk and a bell shrilled very faintly from the hall. It was evidently a recognized signal, for a minute later, the door opened and Emerence appeared.

"Come in, Emerence. Prunella will be in Upper IVB. Will you

take her along to Senior-Middle common-room and see if you can find anyone to take charge of her? Matron should have finished with some of them by this time. Try to find Clare Kennedy or Maeve Bettany or someone like that. Send whoever it is to the common-room—or no; go and send them here. Prunella can stay with me till whoever it is turns up. Off you go!"

Emerence went off. When she had gone, the secretary turned again to the new girl. "I thought you'd rather not be alone in a big, strange room, Prunella, and it may take Emerence a few minutes to find someone. I know Matron is busy with that set at the moment." She paused a moment. Then she went on, "I wonder if you've been abroad before?"

"Not exactly," Prunella replied, meanwhile looking the picture of a demure, well-behaved schoolgirl, with her long plaits dangling over each shoulder to her lap and her hands folded under them. "I was born in Singapore, though. I don't remember anything about it. We went to Australia when I was two and when we left Australia, we went home to England. I was seven then and I've never left England since."

"Then you've done no ski-ing or sledging, of course? Those are joys to come! You'll enjoy them, I know. You'd be a funny girl if you didn't. This is likely to have to be our winter-sporting term, for with the deep snow we can't have any other games." Miss Dene broke off as there came a tap at the door and called, "Come in!"

A slim girl of fourteen or fifteen entered. Her smooth, black hair was parted in the middle and tied back from an oval face lit by a pair of very dark Irish-grey eyes. With her straight features and sweetly meek air, she looked nun-like in the extreme. But, as Prunella was to find out, Clare Kennedy was not Irish for nothing.

"You sent for me, Miss Dene?" she said in a low, very sweet voice.

"Yes, Clare. I want you to take charge of Prunella Davidson who will be in your form. Prunella, this is Clare Kennedy who is form prefect of Upper IVB. She will look after you until you feel your feet and tell you where to go and what to do. Take her along, Clare, and find someone to tell Nan Herbert to bring Joy Williamson and Chloë Yeates to me."

"Yes, Miss Dene," Clare said. She turned to Prunella who had stood up. "Will you come with me, Prunella?"

Prunella prepared to follow her, but Miss Dene checked them for a moment. "I nearly forgot, Clare. Prunella is in Ste Thérèse's—in Primrose. That's next door to you, isn't it? You *are* still in Jonquil, I suppose?"

"Yes, Miss Dene." Then the nun suddenly vanished and became an ordinary schoolgirl as Clare asked eagerly, "Oh, Miss Dene, do you mean we've grown so much this term that we've had to open new dormies?"

Miss Dene laughed and nodded. "We have indeed. I quite expect we shall find that we have to open two or three others next term, too. Now run away. I've a great deal to do and very little time in which to do it. Be off!"

Clare curtsied and led the way. Prunella imitated her with a deep, formal curtsy which made Miss Dene open her eyes rather widely though she said nothing. But when she was once more alone and before Nan Herbert of Lower V came with her two charges, she went to a filing cabinet, riffled quickly through the files and finally took from one a letter which she read thoughtfully.

"I—wonder!" she said to herself as she replaced it and shut the drawer. "I really do wonder!"

Chapter II

Upper IVb

ONCE they were outside, Clare turned to the new girl. "Come on!" she said briefly. "Oh, and before I forget, unless we're sent for to the office or the study, we're not supposed to show our noses in this part of the house. *We* use the back corridors and the back stairs."

Prunella gave her a startled look. "I fear I do not understand," she said.

"Well, you see," Clare explained as they crossed the wide entrance hall, "visitors come this way, of course, and it would look rather awful if shoals of girls were skitin' about in every direction at all hours of the day, as you'll admit. So, as I just told you, we never use the front part of the stairs and so on. Oh, and another thing. Except for first and last day, we aren't supposed to talk on the stairs or in the corridors—only in our common-rooms and form-rooms. Sure, 'twould mean too much row altogether! First and last day, though, rules don't count. However," she added cheerfully, "'tis yourself will be finding out all about it before long. If there's anything bothering you, come to me, of course, and I'll explain with all the pleasure in life. Turn round this corner. Now then; here we are!" She opened a door and ushered Prunella into a long room, bright with light, since someone had switched on the lights and drawn the gay, cretonne curtains across the windows.

Clare slipped a hand through Prunella's arm, steered her into the room and shut the door behind them. Then she walked her captive over to a throng of girls clustered together in a corner between the great porcelain stove and one of the windows and said, “Pipe down, everyone! I’ve brought us our new girl. This is her!”—with a sublime disregard of the rules governing the verb “to be”—“Shove up, Babs, and let the poor creature sit down, can’t you?”

A fair-haired, blue-eyed girl of Prunella’s own age, looked up. “*Barbara!*” she said, rebuke in every intonation. “I told you last term that I wouldn’t answer anyone who didn’t call me by my proper name and I think you might remember! If you do it again, I’ll start in and call you ‘Clarry’!” she added with a sudden chuckle.

“You do!” Clare retorted threateningly. “Sure, that’s one thing I won’t put up with at all, at all, and so I tell you!”

“Well, you just remember to call me ‘Barbara’!” was the lightning riposte.

“I agree with you,” Prunella remarked with gracious patronage. “If one has a Christian name, surely one should use it and not stoop to babyish abbreviations?”

The jaws of all those near enough to hear dropped. There was a startled silence. Then a mischievous-looking girl said, “Well, I can understand that Barbara doesn’t want to be called ‘Babs’. But let me catch any of you addressing me as ‘Francesca’ and you’ll know *all* about it!”

“Don’t worry! Life’s a lot too full at school for us to bother with all your syllables,” declared a copper-curled young woman who was balancing miraculously on the extreme end of a bench on which four others were crowded. “You’ve been ‘Francie’ ever since you came and ‘Francie’ you’ll remain to the bitter end!”

“I should hope so!” Francie returned.

Before Prunella could make any remarks, a short, plain girl with a good-humoured face, broke in, “I’m Ruth Barnes, Prunella.

And this—this *thing* that's squashing me to a jelly is Jocelyn Fawcett. Do get up, Jos! These chairs weren't made for two. Get a seat of your own, can't you?"

Jocelyn chuckled. "There wasn't another in this corner when I came in. But anything to oblige!" She jumped up and went to drag a big wicker armchair up to the circle while Ruth stretched with an exaggerated sigh of relief. "*That's* better! You must have bones of iron. They were digging into me at every point!"

"That's the worst of being a scrag," observed a pretty girl sitting next to Barbara. "I'm Dora Ripley, Prunella, and the rest of us in this sardine-tin are Dorothy Ruthven next to me, Christine Dawson and Caroline Sanders."

"And I'm Heather Clayton," put in another girl who was sitting opposite the "sardine-tin". "Now you know all of us—Oh, that ginger object on the end of the bench is Maeve Bettany."

"Anyhow, *that* isn't all of us," Clare remarked as she perched herself on a nearby table. "What have Sue Meadows and Sarah Hewitson and Betty Landon done to be wiped out so completely, the creatures? Where are they, by the way?"

"I have already met Susan Meadows," Prunella observed. "She is in the same dormitory as I am."

"But her name isn't Susan," Barbara said with a wriggle that nearly dislodged Francie. "She's plain Sue—christened that way, I mean. She said so last term."

"Dear me! How very remarkable!" Prunella said primly.

"Oh, I don't know," Maeve returned while the rest gaped. "It's a name all right and quite pretty."

There was a pause after this. No one could think of anything to say. Prunella looked round for a chair, saw one at the farther side of the room and went to carry it over to the group. By that time, Clare had pulled herself together.

"Have you ever been in Switzerland before, Prunella?"

"No," Prunella replied gravely as she sat down. "But I was born in Singapore and I have lived in Australia."

"Have you the basket of the gardener's son? No, but I have my aunt's new gloves," Maeve murmured rapidly to her nearest neighbour who choked audibly.

"Australia? That's where Emerence Hope in Lower IVA comes from," Ruth said hurriedly. "Have you ever met her?"

"Not until I came here. She took me to the office to see—Miss Dene, I believe she was called," Prunella returned. "Australia is quite a large place, you know. In fact, it is a continent. We lived in Brisbane."

Ruth subsided, crushed, and Jocelyn intervened. "That's in Queensland, isn't it? Oh, then you wouldn't be very likely to meet. Emerence lives in Manly, a suburb of Sydney, when she's at home."

Maeve, seizing a moment when Prunella was not looking, patted her hands gently together at this. Jocelyn was keeping her end up, thank goodness!

"Which school were you at before you came here?" Francie asked.

"I was at a preparatory school in the town where I lived with my grandmother until my parents came home from Africa," Prunella replied.

Everyone was silent. As Clare said to Barbara later on, "You simply can't think of a thing to say to anyone who talks like the worst kind of French exercise!"

Prunella glanced round the stunned group, a queer glint in her hazel eyes. Not that anyone saw it or would have understood it if they had. The new girl asked a question in her turn. "I presume this is where we are intended to pursue our avocations? A really charming room!"

No one was very sure what "avocations" were, so no one

answered. Then Barbara said rather feebly, "Er—er—this is where we spend our free time when we can't go out. Er—have you any hobbies, Prunella?"

"I am interested in drawing and painting, but I fear I shall have little time to spare for them," Prunella responded. "I find that my French and German are considered to be far from adequate and I must endeavour to improve them."

Again the talk fell flat. Dora murmured in an aside to her bosom friend Dorothy Ruthven, "What an *awful* creature! She talks like her own great-granny!"

"I wonder if she can spell all those long words?" was Dorothy's reply.

Ruth made an effort. "Oh, but we aren't allowed to swot in our free time. Anyhow, you needn't worry. The whole staff jolly well see to it that we don't get a chance to do anything *but* improve in modern languages!"

"Indeed?" Prunella spoke with real interest. "Might I inquire what methods they use to accomplish that?"

They nearly fell over themselves in their efforts to enlighten her.

"Two days a week we mayn't speak a word of anything but French from the moment we wake up until the moment we go to bed," Barbara told her.

"And the same goes for German on two other days," Ruth added.

"We speak English on two other days—which is hard lines on the French and German girls in the school—if any!" Maeve contributed her share. "Still, they have the two days of their own languages, so it pans out equal in the end."

"When you write comps. and essays, you have to do them straight into which ever language it is that day." This was Dorothy's share. "All the lessons are taken in that language, you see."

"Even maths.!" groaned Jocelyn.

"*And* gym and games!" Clare wound up for them. "You simply can't *help* it soaking in when you have to go at it like that. I wouldn't be worrying, Prunella."

Prunella had listened to all this in stunned silence. However, by the time Clare finished, she was her own woman again. "Dear me! How truly interesting! At that rate, I can quite imagine that even the dullest pupil must learn something during the term. An excellent idea! On the principle, I presume, that when in Rome one must do as the Romans do! A truly admirable arrangement!"

It was their turn to sit stunned. Whatever sort of a school had this weird new girl come from? But perhaps it was her home that was responsible for the way she talked. They gazed at her, fascinated. Then the door opened and the three missing members of the form came in to be followed by a crowd of other girls led by a masterful-looking young woman of about fifteen with keen, blue eyes and long, light-brown plaits dangling on either side of a pink and white face that was full of character.

Clare stood up with an involuntary sigh of relief. "Oh, Mary-Lou!" she said. She went across the room. "I'm thankful you've come!" she muttered. "We've the oddest new girl you ever saw!"

Mary-Lou grinned at her. "I've just heard Len Maynard on the subject," she muttered back. Then, aloud, "So you've a new girl, too? *We* have four, but three of them are French. They're at the office, at the moment."

"Well, come and meet Prunella," Clare urged. She tucked her hand through Mary-Lou's arm and drew her towards the chair where Prunella was sitting, looking round with an air of calm assurance that almost dazed her fellows. "Prunella, this is the Head of the Middle-School—Mary-Lou Trelawney; and here's Prunella Davidson."

Prunella stood up and held out her hand. "How do you do?" she said primly.

Mary-Lou, who had been on the point of welcoming the newcomer in her own breezy fashion, waggled the hand limply with a mutter that might have been anything. For once, the wind had been taken completely out of her sails.

"All unpacked?" Barbara asked as the group broke up into little coteries of threes and fours and the girls began to stroll about the room.

Mary-Lou nodded. "The last hanky in its case and my drawers looking immaculate. Matey saw to that all right! How long they'll *stay* like that, is another matter. What about you?"

"Oh, I did mine yesterday. The Welsen crowd began two days earlier than us and Vi and I came back with Nancy and Julie and stayed with Auntie Jo for the two days. I got mine done yesterday when you lot were still in the train. I say, I've some news for you all!"

"What about?" demanded a charmingly pretty person of Mary-Lou's age.

"My cousins the Ozannes—Vanna and Nella. They're leaving at the end of this term."

"What? But they're only seventeen, aren't they?"

"No; eighteen last October. They're six months older than Julie Lucy and ten months older than Nancy. They *were* to have had a year at Welsen, but Uncle Paul's got a job in Singapore and they're all going out in April, so Vanna and Nella are leaving."

"What about their brothers?" demanded someone else.

"Oh, *they* won't go," said a girl who had come to stand beside Barbara. "Mike's not halfway through his training and Bill's in Germany, doing his National Service."

"But they're only in Upper V!" Jocelyn exclaimed.

"Oh, well, you know what they are! Aunt Elizabeth says it's

as far as either of them is likely to get and they may as well stop being schoolgirls and go out and be company for her. She doesn't really like the idea very much, but it's a jolly good job for Uncle Paul, so they're going."

"What do *they* say about it?" someone asked. "Have they said anything to you, Vi?" Vi, who was quite the prettiest girl there, as Prunella noted, laughed. "They don't know. Vanna says it'll be fun to see the East, and Nella says she'll get out of maths., anyhow. But I rather think they're a bit fed up about it."

"Well, it's news all right," Mary-Lou said. Then she turned to Prunella. "Have you been to the office yet? Oh, but of course you must have as you know which form you're in. Seen over the place by any chance?"

"Thank you. I have seen my own dormitory, of course, and this room and another like it with younger girls," Prunella replied gravely. "If I may ask, what else is there to see?"

"Lots!" they informed her. "There's Hall and your form-room and the Speisesaal—"

"I beg your pardon?"

"Speisesaal—German for dining-room," Mary-Lou said breezily. "We're in the German part of Switzerland. Well the name 'Oberland' would tell you that. Anyhow, we use lots of German expressions."

"She'll see the Speisesaal in a minute now. The gong will sound for Kaffee und Kuchen in a moment," put in a girl whose English was just touched with a pretty Scots accent. "But we ought to show her Hall and the Honours Boards. Have we time?"

She was answered by a deep, musical throbbing which rang through the corridors and everyone was on her feet at once and forming into lines by the door.

"Half a tick!" Clare exclaimed. "Let's find where Prunella is sitting."

She ran across the room to a big board hanging at the far end, scanned it keenly for a moment and then came back. "O.K. She's between you and Caroline, Francie. Look after her, will you, seeing she's not at the same table as me."

She took Prunella by the arm and pushed her gently into line between Francie and Caroline.

"I'll give an eye to her, Clare," Francie said kindly. "We always march in in our table places, Prunella, so that there's no scrambling round the tables. O.K., Mary-Lou. We're ready now."

"Lead on, then," Mary-Lou said amiably. "Oh, and I know rules don't really count to-day, but we'd better not talk too much as we go. Matey's somewhere around and she's pretty well hairless, anyhow, there's so much to do."

Warned by this, the girls stopped their chatter and laughter and the long line marched out of the room, down one corridor and half-way along another where a big double door stood open, a babble of talking coming from it. They entered and Prunella saw that they went round to take their places in proper order. Then she looked round the Speisesaal and approval beamed from her face.

It was a long, rather narrow room, with tables running down it in three lines. One stood across the head and one across the foot. The one at the head was empty, but the others were covered with gaily-checked cloths. Plates piled high with crusty bread covered with pale, sweet butter alternated with others holding fancy bread-twists and small cakes. Dishes of a richly-dark jam flanked them and small plates with a cheerful blue and yellow design stood at each place. One big sideboard between the door by which they had entered and another further up were laden with cups and saucers to match and on a table at one end stood a huge coffee-urn from which a slight girl of seventeen or eighteen was rapidly filling cups which she handed to two others who bore them to the tables and set them by the plates. Between two of the three windows at present curtained, stood another table from which a girl with a long, reddish pigtail was pouring hot milk. Three other girls were putting plates piled high with white, dully-glistening oblongs of sugar on each table. It was not in the least like any other dining-room Prunella had ever seen, but it was very gay with its bright lights and coloured cloths and Prunella noted that it was summer-warm, thanks to another of the great porcelain stoves set at one end.

The Senior-Middles were followed by an even longer line of Juniors and when the last girl had taken her place, the coffee distributor left the urn and went to the empty table. Prunella had time to see that she was a handsome girl, with a thick mop of black curls. She wore the school dress for Seniors—a well-cut gentian-blue skirt with cream shirt-blouse and the school tie and blazer. She struck a bell which was the only object on the table and at once the long rows of girls stopped talking, folded their hands and bent their heads.

"Grace!" the Senior said; and then repeated a brief Latin Grace after which she returned to her duties at the urn and the rest pulled out their chairs and sat down.

A pleasant-looking Senior arrived with a tray laden with steaming cups which she set down at the head of the table and the girls began passing them down.

"We always have Kaffee und Kuchen by ourselves," Francie explained as she offered the new girl a plate of bread-and-butter. "Oh, the prefects are here, of course, but they sit together at the bottom table and they don't interfere unless we start yelling our heads off. Try some of this jam, Prunella. It's black cherry and scrummy!"

"Thank you." Prunella helped herself to the jam and found that Francie had spoken truly. Then she sipped at her cup and nearly dropped it in her surprise. “Why, it’s *coffee*!” she exclaimed in a completely natural voice.

“Well, of course it is. What did you think Kaffee und Kuchen mean?” Caroline asked cheerfully from her other side. “Coffee and cakes, my dear! Don’t you like it? You can have hot milk if you’d rather. Shall I ask Clem for a cup for you?” She half-turned, nodding towards the red-haired Senior who was looking round to see if everyone was served.

Prunella had recovered from her surprise. “Thank you, Caroline. That is very kind of you, but I like coffee and I do not care for hot milk. But, considering what time it is, I anticipated tea.”

Two or three of the girls who had not been privileged, so far, to meet this extraordinary new girl, stared at her way of talking, as well they might. Caroline grinned before she said placidly, “No tea here. We have this milky coffee for brekker—er—I mean Frühstück and—er—Abendessen.”

Prunella guessed that the last word meant supper, so she asked no questions. In any case, a bespectacled young person was leaning forward and asking eagerly, “I say! Do any of you know when the Welsen panto is coming off?”

“Not the foggiest,” Francie replied. “Not for a week or two anyway. They’ll want to push in a few rehearsals after the hols. Probably the Head’ll say something at Prayers. She said last night that there was lots to tell us only we were so late she would only let us know the really important things—like Mary-Lou being the Head of Middle-School. I say! Look out, Pen! You’ll have your cup over if you lean across like that!”

“And *will* Matey talk!” Pen said sadly as she sat up.

“You bet she will—beginning of term and a clean cloth!” Francie returned with a grin. “Anyhow, you don’t want to start off with a fine, do you?”

"I do not!" Pen was positive on that point.

"Well, then sit up and don't be an ass! More bread-and-butter, Prunella, or will you have a twist. They're jolly good."

"Thank you, I should like to taste a twist. They are new to me." Prunella helped herself and then asked, "Pray, what do we do after our meal?"

"Well, no prep, of course. We only arrived last night and we've been unpacking and settling in most of the day. Oh, we've had two walks—one this morning and one this afternoon. To-morrow we'll have short lessons in every subject so that the staff can give us prep. Then come Saturday and Sunday and we start fair on Monday."

"We'll probably dance," someone from the other side of the table said.

"That's the most likely thing—after we've changed," Caroline agreed. "It'll be early bed to-night, anyhow, we were so late last night."

"What's that about bed?" demanded tall Clem who was passing them with a cup of milk for someone.

"I just said we'd be sent to bed early because we were so late last night," Caroline explained. "Oh, Clem, do you know when the Welsen panto's coming off?"

"Not I! No one's said anything that I've heard of. I don't suppose it'll be much before the beginning of next month, though," Clem said. "Here, Monica, take your milk."

She handed over the milk and returned to the table near the top door where the prefects had congregated and the Middles were left to their own devices. Prunella bit into her twist and as she ate it decided that it was delicious. As she made a good meal, she reflected that this school certainly gave you no chance to feel out of things. Francie and Caroline named odd girls to her and saw that she was well supplied throughout the meal. Both girls were kept busy chatting to the others, but they turned from time to time to address remarks to her and even tried to draw her into the conversation. Prunella replied primly and precisely, more than once causing one of her new companions to be momentarily bereft of breath at her manner of expressing herself. But she had no neglect to complain of.

When Kaffee und Kuchen ended, everyone seized her crockery, knife and spoon and carried them to an enormous trolley where two prefects piled everything quickly and safely, as she noticed. When it was full, sides of wire netting were pulled up and it was wheeled out of the room, the crockery rattling but secure. It was all done with the utmost speed and ten minutes after the girls had said Grace, the tables were cleared and they were filing out to their common-rooms.

"Dressing-bell will go in a minute or two," Clare Kennedy told Prunella when they were safely in their own abode. "That won't worry you, though. You're changed already."

"Matron told me to change when I had finished unpacking," Prunella replied.

"I expect she did. Oh, well, we shan't be long. There are heaps of mags on the table over there and *some* of them are English. The others have gorgeous illustrations, too, so you can amuse yourself all right till we come back. Then I expect we'll go into Hall for dancing and games."

A bell sounded at that moment and the girls in their tunics raced to line up. Mary-Lou, who seemed to take her duties as head of the Middle-School very seriously, brought them to order almost at once, repeated her warning about making little noise in the corridors and on the stairs before she marched them off and Prunella was left to herself.

She made no attempt to look at the piles of magazines Clare had pointed out to her. Instead, she went to one of the windows and pulled back a curtain. A young moon was rising and the skies were clear and starry. The snow lay white beneath the cold light and all the shadows were clear-cut and black. She stood looking out for a minute or two. Then she swung the curtain back into place and turned round.

"It's better than I thought," she said aloud. "So far, anyhow. But I'm jolly well going to show them all and that's that!"

She went over to the magazine table and chose one and when the rest came down, ready for the evening in their gentian-blue frocks of velveteen with muslin collars and cuffs, the new girl was sitting demurely turning over the pages with a keen eye for the delightful illustrations of a Swiss magazine.

Chapter III

The Fourths are Intrigued

"HELLO, Mary-Lou! What does it feel like to be a Head—even if it's only Head of the Middles?"

Mary-Lou, wrapped up to the tip of her nose for the morning walk which took place every day that was fine enough at this time of year, turned with an infectious gurgle. "Hello, Betsy! I didn't hear you coming. Oh, it's all right. Matter of fact, I can't say I feel at all different. It's just the look of the thing. I must say it came as a shock first night when the Abbess announced it. I nearly fell through the floor from shock!"

Betsy Lucy leaned against the wall of the corridor. She was a sixteen-year-old, no taller than Mary-Lou who had shot up into a leggy creature after being sturdy not to say stocky for the first thirteen years of her life. Betsy was in the habit of describing herself as the Plain Jane of the family. Actually, there was something very taking about her puckish face, with its sparkling, brown eyes, crooked mouth and very slightly tip-tilted nose. But, as she was wont to point out, when your eldest sister is the image of a handsome father and your younger one is a howling beauty—"Kitten's too small to say what she'll turn out," she generally added—a face like hers was plain enough in all conscience!

"I certainly can't claim Beauty," she had said once, "so I must do my best to acquire Brains!"

"Brains aren't acquired, either. They're something you're born with or not," her chum, Hilary Wilson, had pointed out. "Still, your work's not at all dusty," she had added kindly.

During the previous term, Mary-Lou and Betsy had encountered each other at odd intervals and, to quote the latter young lady, they had rather clicked. Both had much the same interests and, if Mary-Lou was a good year the younger in age, she was quite as grown-up in other ways, the fruits of being an only child brought up by her mother and grandmother in a quiet village. Betsy, on the contrary, was third in a family of six, the eldest being her sister Julie who was Head Girl of the school and the youngest their small sister Katharine, who was only six. Betsy was a very normal girl, with the outlook to be expected from a member of a large family. Mary-Lou, on the other hand, still shocked people by her trick of treating grown-ups on a perfect equality. She was never rude and rarely cheeky, but it took a good deal to overawe her.

Now, as Betsy leaned against the wall and settled her shawl more comfortably, she asked, "What's all this talk that's going round about a new girl among your lot who talks like her own great-granny?"

Mary-Lou gave a gurgle. "That just about describes it. Name's Prunella Davidson and if they'd called her Prunes and Prisms they wouldn't have gone far wrong!"

Betsy's brown eyes widened. "Really? Worse than our one and only Verity-Anne?"

Mary-Lou frowned as she considered this. "No: she's not in the least like Verity-Anne," she said finally.

"Not? Then what are you talking about?"

"It's rather hard to explain. I mean, Verity-Anne *was* like that—I mean it's really part of her. Know what I mean?"

Betsy nodded. "Oh, yes; I see what you're getting at all right. Prunella isn't, I suppose?"

"I—wonder. She talks as if she'd walked straight out of Jane Austen—no; further back than that. Fanny Burney might be nearer it—"

"Fanny Burney?" Betsy gasped. "What on earth d'you know about *her*?"

"Well, I've read *one* book of hers. I was stuck in my bedroom these hols. for nearly a week with a terrific head-cold. Gran said she wasn't going to have everyone else infected; not if she knew it! So there I was. I read most of the time. There wasn't anything else to do. When I'd finished all my own books, I went along to Mother's room and the only thing I could see was *Evelina* so I bagged that. Not bad, though it took some reading."

"I'll *bet* it did!" Betsy spoke in tones of deep conviction. "Really, Mary-Lou, you are the limit!" She stopped short as a sudden thought struck her and her jaw dropped. "Are you telling me that she says things like, 'La!' and 'Lud!' and—and 'Stap my vitals!'—for I don't believe you!"

Mary-Lou went off into peals of laughter at the thought of the stilted Prunella indulging in such expressions. "'Course not! Oh, Betsy, what an ass you are! All I meant was that she talks most primly, never uses slang, and flatly refuses to call anyone by a short form of their names. She's driving Len Maynard completely wild by always addressing her as 'Helena', f'rinstance."

"And does she call you 'Mary-Louise'?" grinned Betsy.

"Well, as she's in B, I don't see too much of her and now you mention it, I don't remember that she's ever called me anything but 'you'," Mary-Lou said.

"Nameless!" Betsy giggled. "Poor you! But I suppose," she added teasingly, "that she can hardly call the Head of Middle-School by her full name if she doesn't use it normally."

"Actually, I don't think she's ever had much reason to speak to me," Mary-Lou said, ignoring the gibe. "But we have General

Lit together and the odd thing is that she isn't nearly so prim in form as she is out of it. If you ask me," concluded that shrewd observer, Mary-Lou, "a lot of it is put on—*and* for a reason. But what the reason is, I can't tell you."

Betsy was about to reply to this, when Prunella herself appeared, clad like themselves in big, blue coat with crimson pixie-hood and shawl and nailed climbing-boots. Like them, she carried an alpenstock, for the deep snow had been frozen hard and was glassy in surface.

"Hello!" Mary-Lou saluted her. "Aren't the rest ready yet?"

"Almost so. I have no doubt they will be with us shortly," Prunella said in a prim voice. "Miss o'Ryan detained us beyond the ringing of the bell and thus we are I regret, somewhat behindhand."

Mary-Lou choked back a giggle as Betsy goggled at this weird specimen speechlessly and asked, "But where's everyone else? I was having massage for my ankle—I sprained it rather badly last term so I have to go for remedials every day. But what's happened to the rest of A?"

"I cannot be certain, but I think I heard Clemency Barrass remark to Rosalie Way that the milk had not come at the proper time and the cook was unable, therefore, to heat it punctually," Prunella replied.

Nothing more was needful, for at that moment, there was a clatter of feet and the rest came swarming out of the Splasheries where they had been changing as fast as they could for the walk. Betsy was claimed by Carola Johnston who had "bagged" her as a partner before Prayers and Vi Lucy came to drag Mary-Lou into line. The Head of Middle-School paused long enough to inquire if Prunella also had a partner and, on hearing that Barbara Chester had asked her, promptly went off with Vi who contrived to look enchantingly pretty, even in their unbecoming if cosy winter outfit.

Left to herself, Prunella turned and saw Barbara coming towards her.

"Come on!" she said in French, which was the language for the day. "Miss o'Ryan and Miss Armitage are waiting for us outside, so hurry up!"

"J'ai attends pour vous," Prunella replied with an execrable accent.

"Eh bien, maintenant j'y suis," Barbara returned in the pretty, fluent French which so many of her form envied. She took the new girl's arm and led her out to the path where the two mistresses, very trig and smart in their ski-ing outfits, were skirmishing round, making sure that every girl had a partner.

The Lower Fourths had congregated at the other side of the house and had already set off along the road to the Sanatorium and the Seniors were in the front drive, waiting for a note the Head had asked them to take to Mrs. Graves, once Hilary Burn and a very popular Old Girl and P.T. mistress, now the wife of Dr. Graves who was on the staff at the Sanatorium. Most of the seniors had cherished a warm affection for their former mistress, so they were delighted with the commission, though it meant very brisk walking, since the Graves's chalet was two-and-a-half miles away.

The thirty-odd girls who made up the two Upper Fourths set off from the side-door and walked smartly down the path and out at a small entrance on to what was known as "the high road", though it badly needed re-surfacing and was, to quote Dr. Maynard, Head of the Sanatorium, a very second-class road indeed. Arrived there, they turned left at a word from Miss Armitage and made for the long motor-road that wound through the mountains down to the plain.

It was a glorious day, bitterly cold, of course, at that altitude, but with a bright sun shining down, turning the frozen snow to a glittering whiteness that meant the wearing of coloured glasses as no one wanted snow-blindness.

"The weather really has been gorgeous since we came back," Barbara said to her partner by way of starting up a conversation. "Let's hope it keeps on. If we get any blizzards, it means being stuck indoors and that *can* be an awful bore."

"So I should imagine," Prunella responded. "Pray, what do we do in such circumstances?"

"Oh, we do extra lessons to make up for what we miss in weather like this. Then we have gym and dancing and things like that for exercise. But I'd a lot rather be out—though *not* in a blizzard," she added. She had had a minor experience of what snow can be like in the Alps during the previous term and she had no wish for another.

"Indeed?" Prunella paused a moment before she added, "I can understand that gymnastics would furnish us with no little exercise; but surely dancing is hardly adequate?"

Barbara gaped at her for a moment before she pulled herself together sufficiently to reply, "Not ordinary ball-room dancing, perhaps. But we do country dancing and you get all the exercise you need in that. You wait till you've had a go at 'Old Mole' and followed it up with 'Goddesses' and 'Picking up sticks' with 'Sellenger's Round' to wind up with and you'll find all you want is to sit down somewhere and get over your aching! I know!" she added darkly.

"Ah, I comprehend now," Prunella said with an indulgent air. "You mean dances like 'Sir Roger de Coverley', I presume?"

Barbara muttered an agreement and the conversation lapsed as it had a habit of doing when Prunella took part in it. Barbara was casting about in her mind for something else to say and Prunella was gazing at the snow-clad mountains, heaving austere shoulders against the pale, blue winter sky with a real delight.

Presently they came to a tall house and, with a sigh of relief, Barbara waved towards it. "That's Freudesheim where the Maynards live. Dr. Maynard is Head of the big San. at the other end of the Görnetz Platz, you know."

"Do you mean the father of Helena Maynard?" Prunella inquired.

"And Con and Margot," Barbara nodded. "Did anyone tell you they are triplets?"

"Yes, Sue Meadows told me so. A most unusual thing, I should imagine. Pray are there any more of the family?"

"I should just think there were!" Barbara exclaimed. "There are the three boys—"

"Pray are they also triplets?" Prunella inquired.

Barbara giggled. "What a ghastly thought! No; they're singletons, as Auntie Jo says. Then there are the twins—they're just babies. Perfect ducks, both of them and as wicked as they come, especially Felix. Felicity has only spasms of being bad, but Felix is a demon *all* the time."

"They are your cousins, then? I had no idea of that."

Barbara laughed. "Not real cousins. But we've known Auntie Jo and Uncle Jack all our lives and we've always called them that and the Maynard crowd call Mother and Daddy Aunt and Uncle, too."

"Oh, indeed."

Barbara was too much interested in her subject to notice the crushing reply. She went on, "I wish you could meet Auntie Jo. She's smash—er—awfully decent."

Before Prunella could get out the rebuke for using slang that she meditated, Miss o'Ryan called out, "All right, girls! You may break ranks now. Keep together and don't be getting too far ahead or lagging behind. And don't yell too much, either."

They broke ranks promptly and Barbara, by dint of bustling

her partner along, contrived to catch up with her cousin Vi Lucy, and two or three more of what were known as The Gang, of which she herself was a proud member. She had made a martyr of herself and taken Prunella for a partner, but she saw no reason why the others should not take their share, too. A walk was very boring if you had a partner who wet-blanketed almost everything you said!

"Auntie Jo hasn't been over to see us yet," Vi observed when six of them were walking in a bunch. "I wonder why?"

"Oh, I expect the twins have been cutting teeth or something," Mary-Lou said airily. "All the same, I wish she'd come. It's ages since we saw her—not since last term. The hols. *were* queer with no Plas Gwyn to go scooting over to at intervals."

"Horrid," put in a small, very dainty person. "Mother and Gran missed Auntie Jo a lot, too."

Verity-Anne Carey was not only Mary-Lou's great friend. Commander Carey had married Mrs. Trelawney in the previous summer and the two girls called themselves "sisters by marriage" in consequence. Verity-Anne was not in the least like Mary-Lou, being tiny, very quiet and retiring, and what Matron called "a mooner"; but those who knew realized that while the elder girl looked after her "sister" and saved her from endless "rows", it was Verity-Anne who acted as a brake on some of Mary-Lou's wilder flights.

Prunella now remarked, "I understand that Mrs. Maynard is quite an important person in the school from various remarks I have heard."

"She jolly well is," Vi returned. "And then there are her books," she added vaguely.

"Her books?" Prunella repeated. "Does she own a lending library, then?"

Their shrieks of laughter nearly brought a sharp reprimand on them, but Miss Armitage was restrained by her partner, who murmured, "Sure there's no one about to mind. Let the creatures enjoy themselves, Cicely!"

Prunella looked rather offended at this reception of her innocent remark. Vi saw it and hastened to put things right. "Sorry, Prunella, but it did sound so mad! Of course Auntie Jo doesn't run a lending library! She wouldn't have time. What I meant was her own books—the ones she writes."

"I see." Prunella's brow cleared. "So she is an author? And what books has she written, if I may ask?"

"Oh, piles!" This was Vi. "You *must* know them, Prunella! There's *Patrol-Leader Nancy*, and *Tessa in Tirol*—"

"And *Werner of the Alps*—that came last Easter," Mary-Lou put in.

"And her Christmas one—*Buttercups and Daisies*, a Guide story," added Lesley Malcolm, a fifteen-year-old with a clever face. "That did make me homesick for *our* Guides, but the Head hasn't said anything so far so I suppose we aren't restarting them just yet."

Prunella had had *Buttercups and Daisies* herself for Christmas. She turned a startled look on Lesley and said as any other girl might, "But—but that was written by Josephine M. Bettany! I've read it and I lo—liked it very well," with a sudden recollection of her present rôle. "Indeed, I have read several of her books. They are really very interesting, though I think it a pity that she puts in so much slang. English especially for schoolgirls, should be pure and undefiled."

One or two choked at this and Lesley, who had scarcely met Prunella hitherto, stared at her with dropping jaw.

"Oh, *gosh*!" Barbara muttered to Vi who was next her. "What can one *do* with such a creature?"

But Mary-Lou had given the new girl a look of deep consideration before she replied, "No modern girl would read them if they weren't written in—in modern idiom. You couldn't expect it."

"And what a grievous pity that is!" Prunella exclaimed. "Do you not think so?"

But Mary-Lou had had enough. "Not in the least," she said coolly. "People must talk like their neighbours or else other folk will think there's something wrong with them. Oh, I don't say slang can't be rather mad and some of it really is ugly. But on the other hand, a lot of it is frightfully expressive. Besides," with a sudden memory of a lesson Miss Annersley had given them during the previous term, "language, like everything else, goes on growing. If it doesn't, it becomes dead. Anyhow, the people in Aunt Joey's books are just like real people and there's precious few real people nowadays who go around talking as if they'd just had a session with *Elizabeth Bennet* or *Evelina Belmont*!"

"With *who*?" Vi demanded. *Elizabeth Bennet*, she recognized. Upper IVA had read *Pride and Prejudice* as their prose literature the previous term and most of them had enjoyed it. Perhaps one reason for that was that Miss Annersley had arranged some scenes from it for them to act when it was their turn to be hostesses for the Saturday evening. But both Mary-Lou and Vi had really enjoyed the story, although Mary-Lou had been moved to remark that a more ghastly set of snobs she had never met anywhere! But *Evelina* was new to them.

"*Evelina Belmont*—heroine of *Evelina* by Fanny Burney," Mary-Lou explained. "It's a priceless book, Vi. *Evelina* is really the child of *Sir John* and *Lady Belmont*. But he left them when he found that she—*Lady Belmont*, I mean—hadn't really a fortune though he'd thought she had. *Evelina* goes to visit some friend in London and goes into Society with a capital S. Everybody falls madly in love with her, even though she has some ghastly relatives. Then she falls in love with *Lord Orville*, so everyone tries to get her father to recognize that she's his own child—he'd said she wasn't!—and he gives them all a shock by saying that his daughter is living with him that minute. Somehow they find out that the nurse had taken her own baby to him and said she was his. They prove it somehow so he recognizes *Evelina* as his own kid and she marries Lord Orville—and, I suppose, they lived happy ever after!" Mary-Lou finished this masterly résumé of Fanny Burney's great novel with a grin at Vi and fell silent.

"Is it in our library?" Barbara asked, much impressed.

"Sure to be. Ask Madge Herbert if you want to read it. I warn you, though," Mary-Lou added, "that it's toughish going, the English is so grand and elegant."

"The *story* sounds all right, though," Barbara argued.

"It is—if you can put up with the way she wrote. She has Jane Austen beaten to a frazzle when it comes to language," Mary-Lou replied with another infectious grin. "Anyhow, Madge is your best bet if you really want it."

"That is Margaret Herbert, the school librarian, is it not?" Prunella asked, a certain amount of rebuke in her tone.

The rest looked at each other and chuckled.

"That's where your toes turn in," Vi said sweetly, "'cos why? Her name isn't Margaret at all—it's Magdalen."

"The more reason, then, to give up such a babyish abbreviation," Prunella said, her nose in the air.

"Phooey! No one has time for a name like that!" Mary-Lou said flatly. "It's no go, Prunella. You'll just have to take it. More than half of us use shortened forms of our names, and we all talk a certain amount of slang—there's lots that's forbidden, though," she added with a grimace.

Prunella said nothing—and said it very haughtily. In fact, she was so supercilious about it, that she failed to notice a heaped-up pile of snow and went headlong over it before anyone could stop her. They shrieked and rushed to her rescue and she was hauled to her feet with real good-will; but she resented the indignity. Especially when Lesley said, apparently to the wide air, for she addressed no one in particular, "'Pride goeth before a fall'!"

Luckily, Miss o'Ryan chose that moment to call to them and wave agitatedly. Verity-Anne glanced her way and said, "We've got to turn back. Miss o'Ryan is waving like mad at us."

"The sun's gone in," Mary-Lou said placidly. "I expect they're afraid the snow may be coming again. We've had none since we came back. Yes; everyone's turning. Come on, folks! We've got rather ahead."

They turned and ran, warned by the young mistress's urgency. Mary-Lou had been right when she said they were ahead of everyone. They were now some way behind the others. But they soon caught up with them, Prunella, in particular, sprinting swiftly and easily so that when the rest came up with her, Barbara said rather enviously, "I say—you can—run!" Then she stopped to puff and blow.

For no reason that anyone could see, Prunella went darkly red and stalked along beside her unlucky partner in silence for the rest of the way. Not that any of them had much breath for chattering. The mistresses *were* afraid of a fresh fall of snow and they bustled the girls along as fast as they could, every now and then casting anxious glances at the sky which was heavily overcast. Mercifully, they were all under cover by the time the first flakes began to eddy softly down.

Once they were safely inside, they were told to hurry and change and then go to their form-rooms for the current lesson. Mary-Lou was kept busy for the rest of the morning and afternoon and found no time to think out the idea which had come to her during the walk. Prunella and her vagaries faded into nothingness beside algebraic progressions, not to mention art and prep. which occupied the afternoon hours. In addition, the snow fulfilled all Miss o'Ryan and Miss Armitage had feared and came down in a wild, swirling dance so that the lights had to be switched on at the beginning of afternoon school.

It was when she was changing for the evening after Kaffee und Kuchen and talking through her curtains to Vi who was at one side of her that she said, "There's something awfully weird about that girl, Prunella Davidson. I don't believe for a moment that any girl nowadays talks as she does. If you ask me, it's put on for some reason and I'm going to find out what's behind it or my name's not Mary-Louise Trelawney!"

As by this time both Upper Fourths were becoming hugely intrigued with Prunella and her little ways, everyone was interested and said so. They quite agreed with their leader that there was something odd about the new girl, though they were at a loss to say what it was.

"Just the same if she's really got some weird secret," Vi observed as she finished folding her counterpane and laid it on its shelf for the night, "I'm sorry for her. With Mary-Lou on the job, she hasn't a hope of *keeping* it a secret very long."

Mary-Lou finished her second pigtail and tossed it back over her shoulder. Then she asked anxiously, "I say! You don't mean you think I'm prying or anything like that, do you?"

"Talk sense! Of course I don't! Anyhow, we simply *can't* go on with a Miss Priscilla Prim trying to put us all right on everything. She just won't fit in—not with us. You can talk about Verity-Anne, but Prunella could give *her* spades and aces and beat her into fits! You go ahead and find out what's wrong and then we can put it right—perhaps."

"If she'll let us," Barbara put in from the other side of Mary-Lou.

"Well, anyhow, if she calls me 'Viola' once more, I'll throw the first thing handy at her!" Vi said with sudden heat.

Barbara laughed. "It's a lovely name, Vi. You needn't get so mad about it. But I do agree that we ought to do something about it. I'm certain it can't be right for any girl our age to go on acting and talking like her own great-granny! It—it isn't *natural*!"

"It isn't *decent*!" Vi retorted as she left her cubicle to join the line forming at the door. "Well, thank goodness she isn't in *our* form! We do get a rest from her during lessons! But don't any of you lot try to catch her disease. It 'ud be too much of a strain for everyone!"

"Don't you worry," Barbara assured her, taking her place in the line. "I don't think we've a solitary soul who *could*!"

Mary-Lou came out of her cubicle and surveyed them. Their dormitory prefect had not yet come up, being occupied with a German coaching, so she had to take charge.

"Are you all ready?" she demanded. "Cubeys all tidy? Good! Silence! Forward—march! And no more talking till we're in our form-rooms, young Emerence!"

Emerence made a face at her, but left it at that and, as Mary-Lou made an even worse one back at her, honour was satisfied on both sides and Leafy dormitory marched down to evening prep. feeling reasonably pleased with itself.

Chapter IV

THE STAFF ON THE SUBJECT

GENERAL work was over for the day and the Chalet School staff were gathered in their own sitting-room, most of them feeling virtuously that duty was over and they were free to enjoy themselves.

It was a very pretty sitting-room. It opened out of the staff-room proper where school jobs were done. Here, they were supposed to rest. The pale green walls were hung with three or four charming reprints of good pictures and one or two water-colours contributed by themselves. The wide window was hidden at present behind its gay cretonne curtains with their design of poppies and cornflowers. Flowering plants stood here and there. There were comfortable chairs, a round table on which stood a handsome silver coffee service, the pride of Mdlle's heart, and the pretty coffee-cups they had clubbed together to buy. Shelves of gaily-jacketed novels stood against one wall and there was a big, useful closet opposite, where they could keep writing-cases, knitting-bags and other odds and ends. In one corner stood the inevitable porcelain stove which kept the room at summer temperature in the coldest days.

The mistresses, most of them quite young, were scattered about in little groups of threes and fours, drinking coffee and talking hard. Mdlle de Lachennais, the doyenne of the party, sat before the coffee service. Everyone had been served and now she was working on a strip of embroidery intended to adorn a summer dress. Beside her sat Miss o'Ryan, an Old Girl of the school and now history mistress. She was knitting swiftly at an elaborate, lace jumper as she chatted to the language mistress who was also Senior mistress. Not far away, Miss Lawrence, Head of the music staff, was lounging comfortably with the latest thriller. Mathematics and physical training, represented by Miss Wilmot and Miss Burnett, also Old Girls, were having a fierce argument in a corner near the window. At the other side of the room, under a drop-light, sat Miss Derwent, Miss Armitage, Miss Moore and Miss Bertram in the throes of a game of Ten-Rummy at which Miss Armitage was faring very badly, to judge by her frequent groans. Only Frau Mieders and Matron were absent and everyone knew they were having coffee with Miss Annersley and Miss Wilson, Head of the Welsen branch, who had come up for the week-end.

Suddenly Miss Armitage, with a louder groan than ever, tossed down her cards. "Someone else can count them! It doesn't matter, anyway. I'm a long way the worst. I've been left in every single hand!" She stood up and shook herself. "I believe there's a hoodoo on the wretched things! Anyhow, I'm playing no more to-night." She raised her voice. "Mdlle, is there any more coffee left? There is? Oh, good! I need something to buck me up after that—that fiasco of a game!"

She picked up her cup and brought it to the table. Mdlle filled it, asking sympathetically, "But what, then, is wrong, Cicely, chérie?"

"Me—or the cards. Or perhaps it's just general bad luck. Anyhow, I've been left with a practically full hand every time. What have you two been discussing so earnestly—Thanks, Mdlle—all this time? I looked across once or twice and you looked as if you were settling the affairs of the nation."

"We've been discussing that new child in Upper IVB—Prunella Davidson," Miss o'Ryan said, finishing her row and holding up her work to examine it critically.

"That's awfully pretty, Biddy. But it's not for yourself, is it? If so, you've miscalculated the size. It'll swamp you!"

"It's for Jo—her Christmas present," Biddy o'Ryan explained mildly.

"*Christmas* present? Hasn't she a birthday before then? Anyhow, you're somewhat previous, even for that, aren't you? We're only just in February."

"I mean last Christmas," Biddy said with calm. "I didn't get time to do it before, though I had the wool and the needles *and* the design. I gave Jo those on Christmas morning and you could have heard the squawks of her at the summit of the Jungfrau!" She broke off to chuckle softly. "*Was* she mad! She thought I meant her to knit it herself. However, I told her I'd do it this term, so she calmed down and began to plan for a linen coat and skirt to wear with it. Jo's a good plain knitter but, as she says herself, anything lacy is beyond her, the creature!"

"It's really lovely," Miss Armitage said, examining it more closely. "And that soft green is Jo's colour beyond a doubt." She handed the knitting back to its owner. "Oh, Prunella Davidson! What do you two make of that child? I'm worried about her myself."

"Which child?" In a pause of the argument, Miss Burnett had caught the last words and now got up to come over and join in the talk.

"Prunella Davidson, my dear. What do *you* think of her?" Miss Armitage made a long leg, hooked her chair towards her with her foot and sat down.

"Very neatly done," Miss Burnett said approvingly. "What do I think of her? My dear, that's just what Nancy and I have been discussing."

By this time, everyone was taking an interest. All of them were baffled by the enigma Prunella presented. In form, she appeared rather shy, very quiet and more or less irreproachable in behaviour. But all of them at one time or another had been privileged to hear her when she was with her contemporaries and they all confessed that though the Chalet School had had its full share of unusual pupils, it had never had one quite like the latest importation.

"The thing that puzzles me," said Biddy o'Ryan, knitting industriously as she talked, "is how she gets away with it."

"How do you mean?" Miss Derwent asked.

"Well, here's a sample. I had to go to speak to Matron early this morning. She was over in Ste Thérèse's—in Honeysuckle, to be exact—and I had to pass Primrose. The door was open and I was privileged to overhear a specimen of the young lady's conversation when with her little play-mates. It was an eye-opener, I'm telling you!"

"How do you mean?" Miss Lawrence asked.

"Well, Len Maynard had evidently asked for the time, for our young Prunella said, 'I thought, Helena, that you had your own watch? However, I have no objection to informing you that it is now exactly three minutes past seven.' Len gave a squawk and shrieked something about being late for her practice and Prunella said, 'If you make haste, I have no doubt you will be only five minutes late and, you know, "Better late than never"'."

The staff exploded at this. Then Miss Moore said thoughtfully, "Do you know, she treated *me* to a proverb last Saturday morning when I was taking their mending. She hadn't any and I remarked on it and she replied, 'You see, Miss Moore, if ever I see the slightest appearance of weakness in a stocking or a button hanging loosely, I take the first opportunity to correct the weakness. "A stitch in time saves nine", as no doubt you will fully agree.' I gave her a look, for I thought she was trying to play me up. But I'm certain she wasn't. For one thing, although one or two of that crowd looked at each other, it was in exasperation rather than—than on the giggle."

"She irritates me beyond words by the way she always says, 'Will not' and 'cannot' instead of 'won't' and 'can't' like any normal Christian," Miss Armitage put in. "It's frightfully unnatural at her age!"

"Do you know anything about her background, Mdlle?" asked Miss Wilmot who had followed her friend over to the table and was now leaning against it.

Mdlle shook her head. "I know nothing—but nothing," she said. "Besides, for me it is always work in another language and I have not really met her out of lessons." But she looked meditative.

"You'd better make an opportunity," Miss Wilmot said. "You'll get a shock."

"Rosalie Dene's the one to get hold of if we want to know about the kid," Biddy said sagely. "Where is she, by the way? I haven't seen her since just after Mittagessen."

"It's her free week-end and she went off by the afternoon train to spend it in Berne with Frieda von Ahlen," Miss Burnett replied.

"Then we'll just have to wait till Sunday night," Biddy said resignedly. "We shan't see her before then. Frieda will keep her till the last minute."

It was all they could do then and the conversation drifted away from Prunella and her peculiarities to other objects of more general interest. Most of them forgot it for the time being; but next day, some of them remembered when it was revived by an outsize in rows.

It began with Len Maynard coming downstairs in a towering rage. Now Len was a sweet-tempered creature. If it had been Margot, the youngest of the Maynard triplets, no one would have been surprised. She owned a hair-trigger temper, though careful training and perpetual watchfulness on the part of her parents during the early years had brought her to the pitch where she generally managed to restrain herself before the worst happened. Even Con, the second of the three, had been known to flare up on occasion. But of Len, her mother had once remarked, "I don't believe she *has* a temper. If you ask me, Margot got a double share and Con took over what was left. Len was well outside the door when paddies were distributed!"

This time, however, there could be no mistake about it. She arrived in the common-room with flushed cheeks, stormy eyes and so black a frown that it looked as if she were trying to tie her eyebrows into knots. When Isabel Drew asked her a harmless question, she snapped at her with a vim that made the startled Isabel give it up and leave her alone. Connie Winter, less wise, asked curiously, "What's the matter with you, Len? Aren't you well? You do look mad!"

"Mind your own business!" Len retorted furiously.

It was so unlike her, that even Connie the inquisitive was silenced and they went in to Frühstück without anything more being said. Len sat through the meal wrapped in an almost visible flame of fury. The table prefects glanced at her questioningly once or twice, but they, too, said nothing—then. Annis Lovel, however, mentioned it in the prefects' room when they were gathering for mending and letter-writing which always occupied the first part of Saturday morning. Pat Collins backed her up.

"If it had been *Margot*," she said, "I'd have thought someone had upset her applecart. As it was Len, I do wonder what has happened."

"Oh, it'll only be some storm in a teacup," Julie Lucy responded with Head Girl superiority. "Those Middles are always—" she stopped short and looked blankly at the other two. "You *did* say Len, didn't you? Or did I imagine it?" she asked.

"I said Len all right," Annis returned.

"But goodness! If I'd been asked if there *was* a kid in this abode of sin who didn't know what it meant to go off in a rage, I'd have plumped for Len Maynard!"

"So should I. But she was in a rage all right this morning. Sat through Frühstück looking as if she'd go up in a display of fireworks at any moment, didn't she, Pat?"

Pat nodded. "The rest left her so severely alone I imagine she'd given them a taste of it already."

"What on earth can have upset her? If it had been almost anyone else, I shouldn't have been surprised. It's more or less what you expect at their age. But Len!" Words failed Julie at this point.

"Tummy upset, probably," suggested Edris Young. "Ought we to give Matey a hint?"

However, they decided to let that lady find out for herself. It was unlikely that anything so surprising could escape her for long.

Later on in the day, it seeped through to them via Betsy Lucy and Sue Meadows what the something was that had upset Len's equilibrium. Despite all the rest could say and all Len's own protests, Prunella insisted on calling her by her full name. No one else ever did it unless she had been thoroughly naughty and Len hated it. At that age, she loathed her stately name and much preferred its shortened form. She had put up with Prunella more or less quietly for the few weeks that had passed, but that morning, her patience had snapped and she had treated the members of Primrose dormitory to a display of temper that even Margot could hardly have bettered.

It began with Prunella forgetting whether this was the day for turning her mattress. It was unlucky that Len was the first person she met to ask, and worse that she chose to put her query in the form she did.

"Oh, Helena, would you be so good as to tell me if this is the day for turning our mattresses?" she inquired.

Betsy had already left the dormitory, this being her morning for early violin practice, so they were alone for once. Len stopped dead in the middle of the aisle between the cubicles and gave Prunella a glare.

"I've told you till I'm tired that *no* one ever calls me 'Helena'!" she flared. "What's more, I'm not going to put up with it any more. I won't say a thing to you if you can't call me 'Len' like everyone else does! So now!"

"Your baptismal name is 'Helena'," Prunella told her coldly. "I dislike foolish abbreviations and I do not intend to break my rule for you. And permit me to point out that no nicely-behaved little girl ever says, 'So now!' It really is a most ill-bred expression."

For a moment, Len was silent, mainly because she was so angry that the very words seemed to choke her. The rest were looking round their curtains in amazement at the scene and that did not soothe her very much either. At length it came.

"Just you listen to me, Prunella Davidson!" she exploded. "You're only a new girl and a very silly, conceited new girl, or you wouldn't try to come your prim airs and graces over us who've been here for years and years! Anyhow, if you want me to answer when you speak to me, you'll call me 'Len' or do without!"

Sue, as the eldest left in the dormitory, tried to smooth things down at this point. "Len really is right, you know, Prunella," she said in her quiet voice. "Even the staff don't call her anything else. And as her own father and mother chose it, I don't see that you've any right to start in calling it foolish."

"But it *is* both foolish and undignified," Prunella insisted, a sudden gleam in her hazel eyes. "I will have nothing to do with it—"

Len cut across this. "Then you can have nothing to do with me, too!" she retorted furiously. "I'm certainly having nothing to do with you after this! How dare you insult Papa and Mamma by saying things like that?" In her rage, she resorted to the old baby names which the triplets had discarded during the previous year.

Prunella shrugged her shoulders, a gesture which maddened Len even more. "If they do not wish to be thought foolish, they should not act foolishly," she said.

Len gave her another glare. But she still retained enough sense to realize that if this went on, it might end in a full-blown row which would include Matron, if not the Head. For the first time in her life she felt sympathy with her sister who had, as a small child, ended her furies with fits of angry screaming. But you don't do things like that when you are in your twelfth year, Len told herself. She swung round without another word and rushed from the room, slamming the door behind her with a vim that would have brought Matron down on her if that lady had not been busy at the other end of the building.

Nan Wentworth scuttled after her. She was a frail little creature, very timid, and her mother's death at the great Sanatorium at the other end of the Görnetz Platz, had deepened her timidity. She had no wish to be involved in anything, so she ran.

Virginia Adams, one of the four new girls in Upper IVA, also felt that it was none of her business, though she secretly sympathized with Len. She finished stripping her bed and then followed Nan from the dormitory. Only Nesta Williams, who had come with the school from England, remained to back up Sue. She tossed up her cubicle curtains and walked out to join the two girls left standing in the aisle.

"You're all wrong, Prunella," she said. "It doesn't matter what your ideas are, you've no right to try to enforce them as you do. And you needn't talk about Len being ill-bred. You were most frightfully rude to her about her father and mother and there's less excuse for you than for her, seeing you're at least three years older. I can tell you, I'd have had plenty to say if you'd spoken of *my* people like that!"

"So should I," Sue agreed. "Anyhow, Prunella, here's some advice for you. Let other people have their own ideas and try to climb down a little from your lofty perch. It won't do you any good, you know."

The bell rang at that point so Prunella had only time to say disdainfully, "Birds of a feather flock together!" and turn back into her cubicle.

"Go to the door, you folk," Sue said, raising her voice. "Where's Virgie and young Nan got to?"

"Gone already," Nesta told her.

"Silly asses! They'll get into a nice row if anyone catches them!" Sue replied. "Prunella, are you ready? The bell's gone."

Prunella came out, having turned her mattress just in case. Matron was never to be trifled with. Her lips were in a straight line and she made no reply to Sue who had gone to make sure that the ventilators were in the windows and properly fixed before she led them off downstairs.

It did not take the Staff concerned with the Middles long to notice that there were under-currents about that day. Prunella had nothing to say to anyone else and Nesta, whose desk happened to be next to hers, calmly moved it away before she sat down. Sue Meadows was chattering for once, to Maeve Bettany, Barbara Chester and Clare Kennedy with occasional glances at the new girl. Len Maynard was supposed to be writing to her aunt, Lady Russell, head of the Chalet School Trust, but she spent more time staring into space with a face like thunder and had to be continually reminded to go on. She had found time to tell her sisters what had happened and they both looked furious. Margot's blue eyes sparkled in a way everyone knew and Miss Moore, who took them, watched her warily.

"What on earth's the matter with them all?" Nancy Wilmot demanded of her colleagues at large when they were all in the staff-room, busy with mid-morning milk and biscuits.

"There's been an atmosphere like a couple of thunder-storms and a volcanic eruption combined in Lower IVA this morning. What's started it?"

"Oh, we all have off-days," Biddy o'Ryan said, laughing. "If you come to that, the atmosphere of Upper IVB hasn't been exactly peaceful though it's nothing I could be laying a finger on."

"Lack of outdoor exercise," Miss Moore suggested with a glance out of the window where the snow was falling heavily. "This is the third day there's been no chance of their getting out. I expect the confinement's upsetting them."

"It's certainly upset Len Maynard," Nancy Wilmot sighed. "I spent the whole time telling her to get on. Heaven knows what sort of a letter Madame is getting from her!"

"Well, I know nothing about that little crowd," Biddy replied as she set down her empty cup, "but Prunella wouldn't have a thing to do with anyone else in the room. I asked her a question about her mending and the creature just sat and stared vacantly at me till I could have shaken her."

"What's that?" demanded Matron, coming into the room at that moment.

They told her and she looked thoughtful. "H'm! I'd better see them—and anyone else who seems off-colour."

"What's wrong?" the Head asked with a startled look. She generally came to share Break with her staff, but she had been talking to Mdlle and had paid little heed to the chatter of the junior members of it.

"Jack Maynard gave me a call just before I came along to

say that he's had five cases of this forty-eight-hour 'flu notified this morning and he was just off to the Pinosches and he judged from what Frau Pinosch told him that little Konrad was down with it, too."

"What do we look for?" Nancy Wilmot demanded. "I should have said Betsy Lucy wasn't quite the thing. She came to me about some algebra she didn't understand and I very nearly sent her to you on the spot."

Nancy spoke with a certain airiness and Matron fixed her with a look before which she wilted completely. When she considered that the culprit was sufficiently subdued, Matron spoke. "You never did have much sense, Nancy. If you thought Betsy was out of sorts, may I ask why you didn't send her to me instead of just thinking about it?"

Nancy coloured darkly, feeling very much like the naughty girl she had been some years ago at school. "I—I wasn't sure," she stammered.

"Then you *should* have sent her at once and let *me* be the judge. What was she like?"

"Well, she seemed flushed and I thought her eyes looked heavy."

Matron ruminated for a minute. Then she nodded. "After Break, send them to their form-rooms and I'll come down and go the rounds. As for Betsy, it's just possible that in her case it may be toothache. She came to me two days ago for oil of cloves and I noticed that one or two of her teeth needed attention. I put it off for we can't take them down to Interlaken in a storm like this. But it gives me a good excuse. We needn't alarm the girls. I can make a tooth-inspection."

Nancy grimaced. She was never subdued for long. "Poor lambs! I still remember sundry occasions in my own schooldays when you went the rounds, Matey, and I was yanked off to Herr von Francius to be drilled and filled when I didn't even know there was anything wrong."

Matron laughed. "And look what beautiful teeth you have now!" she retorted. She drew her thermometer out of her big apron pocket. "I may as well inspect you crowd while I'm here. Run and fetch me a glass of water and disinfectant and a towel, Biddy. Open your mouth, Nancy. I'll begin with you."

Biddy departed and Nancy meekly put the thermometer under her tongue. However she was perfectly normal and so were most of the rest though Matron frowned a little over Miss Derwent.

"You're up a point," she said accusingly.

Miss Derwent looked alarmed. "Oh, Matey, I'm sure I'm not! Your thermometer must be wrong. I feel as fit as ever I did—not an ache or a pain anywhere!"

"Well, I suppose it's nothing much to go on," Matron said doubtfully. "Mind you come to me if anything like that happens, though."

"Oh, go away and torment the girls!" Miss Derwent cried. "I'm up to the eyes in work just now and I can't spare a week or so just because my temp.'s not dead normal!"

Matron laughed and left it at that. The bell rang and the mistresses fled to herd their lambs to their proper form-rooms where Matron, accompanied by Miss Wilmot, went the rounds, presumably examining teeth. She found very little in that direction, but every now and then, she gave the young mistress a glance and a name was written down on the pad Nancy Wilmot had with her. When she had finished with a form, Matron departed to the next room while Miss Wilmot read out the names she had written and directed their owners to go to San. for further inspection.

Several people bewailed themselves at this, for no one loved the dentist. Betsy Lucy was among them and so were three more from Upper V. Lower V contributed seven to the list and as for the four Fourths, no fewer than twenty-three girls were sent from their numbers—among them both Len and Margot Maynard. Con was pronounced all right.

When Matron had finished, the residue were turned on to badminton in the gym or Twos and Threes and sundry other games in Hall. The victims had their temperatures taken and had to answer two or three pointed questions. The result was announced after Mittagessen when the Head announced to the school at large that forty-eight-hour 'flu was in their midst and anyone who felt in the least unwell was to report to Matron or her form-mistress at once.

Chapter V

Con Creates a Sensation

THE epidemic broke out on a Saturday and, by the following Wednesday, more than half the school had gone down with it. The actual illness was supposed to last only forty-eight hours but, as is the way with any form of influenza, the effects went on much longer. The patients, once they were past the fever-and-aches stage felt weak and depressed, loathed their food and only wanted to be left alone to die quietly—or so Miss Armitage said when Matron urged her to sit up and sample Karen's delicious chicken jelly.

It was on Monday that the shots fell most heavily among the staff and, by Wednesday morning, Miss Annersley and Rosalie Dene had to face the fact that, with over sixty girls still well and of all ages, there were exactly four mistresses.

"If *they* can stand up to it," Rosalie finished pessimistically.

The Head looked worried, but said nothing on that point. She looked down the list of pupils who, so far, had not fallen victim and then wailed, "It wouldn't matter if they were all more or less at the same stage. We could do something about that. But they range from Julie and Madge in Upper VI to half-a-dozen of Lower IVB!"

"And none of the brightest members of that form, either," Rosalie added, looking ruefully at the list. "Well, at least Julie and Madge can be trusted to work by themselves which is so much to the good. The five out of Lower VI can go in with them and they're all fairly responsible people. Suppose we set them tests for this morning? That would settle them all right and Julie and Madge can invigilate."

"Even so, that leaves us with four staff for six other forms," the Head sighed.

"And we can't apply to Welsen for any help. They're riddled with it themselves. Julie Berné was on the phone to me this morning and she says they have precisely three members of staff available—herself, Bill and Violet Norton. The rest, even Gill Culver, are laid out."

"Let me see how many there are in each form," the Head said, recovering herself and holding out her hand for the list. "H'm! This isn't too helpful! Seven of Upper V, including the two Ozannes who never do a stroke of work if they can help it, and that new girl, Jane Worth. Lower V—nine girls. Well, we can put all those together for the morning, at least."

"Twelve of Upper IVA—they don't seem to have suffered as badly as the rest," Rosalie put in. "Then there are ten from B—Come in!" for a tap sounded at the door.

Matron entered with such a long face that Miss Annersley threw out a protesting hand as she cried, "Oh *no*, Matey! Not another! I can't bear it!"

"Who is it this time?" Rosalie demanded practically.

"Biddy o'Ryan and Miss Denny," Matron said tragically. "Biddy has just been to me to confess that she has been very sick and doesn't feel well. I took her temperature and she's 100°! Sally Denny excelled the lot by fainting in the staff-room just now. She should have stayed at home, but she says that she felt she must try to be here as we are so short-handed. She's over 101° and I've put her into my own bed for the moment."

"We must prepare a room for her at once," Miss Annersley said. "She can't take 'flu home to her brother. He's all right again, but there must be no risks so far as he's concerned. There's that little room next to mine, Matey. Have it seen to, will you? Rosalie, we shall have to make fresh plans, I'm afraid."

Rosalie glanced at the pile of correspondence awaiting her. "There's only one thing to do that I can see," she said. "I must give all this a miss and teach to-day. I'll open them when I've a spare moment and see what needs immediate attention. Anything else must wait."

Matron withdrew to attend to her own chores. She knew that she had her hands full to overflowing and could give no help anywhere else. Unfortunately, several of the maids were down, too, so the kitchen was short-handed as well.

"I agree that you must let the correspondence wait," Miss Annersley said when they were alone again. "But have you forgotten that you have to go down to Interlaken to meet those two sets of prospective parents and bring them up?"

Rosalie gave an exclamation of horror. "Oh, *no*! How simply awful! I really had forgotten all about it. Can't we possibly ring them and put them off? No one will be greatly attracted to a school in the throes of a 'flu epidemic!"

"I could ring up the Bollands," Miss Annersley said thoughtfully. "They are staying at the Bären in Berne. But we can't do anything about the Allens except meet them. They're coming from Vienna by train and I've no idea where they're likely to be. They expected to reach Zurich late last night and were to come on from there this morning. Don't you remember we arranged for them all to meet you at the Kursaal about eleven?"

"With all the scrimmage we've had, I'd forgotten every word of it," Rosalie apologized. "Then you'll have to count me out, anyhow. It's an awful nuisance."

"I couldn't agree more." In her agitation, Miss Annersley descended to slang. "This is no time for interviewing intending parents. I really think the best thing will be for you to go down and meet the Allens as we arranged, but tell them what has happened and ask them if they can possibly put off their interview for a few days, at any rate. I'll ring the Bollands myself and warn them off."

She stretched out her hand to the telephone which chose that moment to ring.

"Jo, I expect," Rosalie said. "She hasn't rung up this morning, so far. Luckily, it's better news to-day. Matey told me that Len had slept most of the night and her temp. is nearly normal. She's had a doing, poor brat!"

She picked up the receiver. "This is the Chalet School—Oh?—*Oh!*—She's here and can speak to you herself. Just a moment!" She covered the mouth with her hand and hissed, "Mr. Bolland!"

Miss Annersley took the receiver. "Mr. Bolland?—This is Miss Annersley—Yes?—Oh, *dear*!—I *am* so sorry!—Yes; I know how you feel; we have it here ourselves—Yes; very tiresome. Mercifully, the worst is over in two or three days—Yes; I hear it's everywhere just now—I'm so sorry about Mrs. Bolland—Yes—Oh, of course! Any time will do!—Very well—As soon as she is well again we'll make a fresh appointment if you'll give us a ring. Please give Mrs. Bolland my kind regards and deepest sympathy and say how very sorry I am—Thank you—Yes—I quite agree—Good-bye!"

She returned the receiver to its cradle and looked at Rosalie. "Well, I'm sorry for them. Being ill in an hotel is so dreary. All the same, I'm *not* sorry on our own behalf. We shan't have to worry about them for the next week or so."

"Flu?" Rosalie asked.

The Head nodded. "A pretty sharp attack, he says. Quite a number of the guests are down with it. The management have installed a couple of nurses and have closed their doors for next fortnight—quite the best thing they could do. Well, that leaves us with the Allens. You had better—"

Pr-r-ring! went the telephone again and Rosalie took time to grin at the Head and murmur, "What's the betting it's the Allens who are down now?" before she lifted the receiver and said in her clear, pretty voice, "Hello! This is the Chalet School—Oh, it's *you*, is it, Jo? Now give me a chance and don't go shooting off questions at all angles like that. Margot is practically well again, though she's still on the fractious side as you might expect. Matey says Len had a much better night—slept for five hours on end and then only woke to ask for a drink and dropped off again when she'd had it. The temp.'s down to 99.5° so I expect she'll be more or less herself again by the end of the week."

"When can I come to see them?" Jo demanded frantically. "I know they're well looked after—you don't need to tell me that! But I hate them being ill away from me."

"You can't come just yet. You'll have to get accustomed to this sort of thing, now they're proper boarders. Are your crowd all right still?"

"Quite, thank goodness! How's young Barbara, by the way? I'm responsible for her to Anne Chester, remember."

"Barbara looked blooming when I last saw her and I'm told she ate her usual lavish breakfast. Oh, and Con's quite well so far. She seems to be living in the moon at present. I understand from Mary-Lou that she's writing an epic poem which no doubts accounts for it."

"Are you telling *me*! Con in the throes of composition might as well be blind, deaf and dumb for all the use she is to anybody! And now tell me, when can I see my other two?"

"I'll take over. Give *me* the receiver," said Miss Annersley in much the same tones as Lady Macbeth might have said, "Give *me* the daggers!" She wrested it from Rosalie. "Hello, Joey! This is Hilda. I was in the office with Rosalie, so I know all about your woes. I'm sorry, my dear, but you mayn't come yet. We're as infectious as we can be. Matron has just been in to inform us that Biddy o'Ryan and Miss Denny are down with it now. You have four small children at home and you can't run any risks, especially with the twins and Charles."

"But I want to see them!" Jo wailed. "I *know* they're all right and thoroughly well looked after—after all, I've known Matey the best part of my life!—but after all, they're *mine*! Have a heart, Hilda! Just a wee peep!"

"Not the weest peep at all," Miss Annersley said firmly. "So don't waste your time coming over. Neither is in San., by the way. When we saw the awful extent of it, Matey expelled everyone from the dormitories nearest San. and turned them into wards. So don't try any creeping in when our backs are turned, please. I may as well add that she's almost always on the spot, so you'll have *her* to deal with if you do anything like that."

"Oh lord!" Jo said dismally. Then her voice became anxious again. "You're *sure* Len's better, Hilda? You're not just saying it to keep me away? It's so unlike her to be really ill. She's always been the sturdiest of the three. Con's given us one or two nasty shocks with her sleep-walking propensities; and I don't need to remind you of all the worry we've had with Margot—"

"No; but do I need to remind *you* that she's been a different child since her two years in Canada?"

"Oh, I know. When I think of the miserable, white-faced shrimp I saw off to Toronto with Madge that awful April day and then remember the Bouncing Bet who did her best to strangle me when *we* went out the next year, I can still hardly believe it. She's never been really ill since. And you say she's had this lightly?"

"As lightly as possible. Oh, she was wretched the first two days with fever and aching. But that soon passed off. It's Len who's frightened us this time. That soaring temp. that nothing seemed to reduce and the severe pain! To quote Rosalie, 'The poor brat's had a doing' this time. But she really is better this morning. I shouldn't say so if it weren't true. You ought to know me better than that! And now, I *must* ring off, seeing that my staff is reduced to Nancy Wilmot, Peggy Burnett and myself. Jack or one of the other doctors will be in shortly and I'll see he's told to report direct to you before he goes on. Good-bye!"

Miss Annersley cut short what Jo might have been going to say by hanging up firmly and turned to her secretary. "That's Jo settled, thank goodness! And thank goodness she still holds Matey in wholesome awe!"

"Don't we all?" Rosalie asked, laughing.

"Even myself," the Head agreed, joining in the laughter. "At least, so far as Jo is concerned, it will keep her from haring over here in an effort to see her daughters. Well, now to work! The Sixths can manage by themselves. It won't hurt them for a day or two and Jeanne de Lachennais is really better and should be back into school by the end of the week. The same applies to Ruth Derwent and Joan Bertram. Once we have those three, we shall be all right."

"Unless any of us starts it," Rosalie suggested wickedly.

"Don't suggest such a thing! And don't waste time! You'll have to go in ten minutes' time if you're to catch the nine-ten train to Interlaken. Now, what I propose to do is to give all the Fourths tests in Hall and invigilate myself. Peggy has a certain amount of remedials, still, and won't be available until half-past eleven or thereabouts. She can take over from me at noon, and this afternoon they can go out and practise their ski-ing with her. You might get out some test papers for them before you go, Rosalie."

"How long are you doing tests?" Rosalie asked, hunting in a drawer for the stock-room keys.

"The first part. After Break, I'll give them a stand-up class in Hall and take General Knowledge."

"That's a real brainwave. You *will* be popular. I suppose the weather will hold for this afternoon? I hadn't time to listen in myself this morning."

"The radio promises us fine weather for the next twenty-four hours, so that should be all right. Get me those papers before you go, please. Leave them on the desk here. I must go and see Karen about Mittagessen. I think we'll have it early to give them a good long afternoon out-of-doors."

Miss Annersley departed on that and Rosalie Dene, having sorted out question papers from a pile kept in the stock-room for just such emergencies, hurried away to catch her train and do what she could with Mr. and Mrs. Allen who had written to say they had two daughters to send to the school if they liked it.

The first the girls knew about the latest calamity was when the Head sent for Pat Collins and Veronica Worsley, both Catholics, and told them that they must take Prayers for the Catholic girls as Miss o'Ryan, who had been attending to that duty, had fallen victim.

"Pat can take Prayers and Veronica, you can play for the hymn," she said.

The two prefects looked startled, but they agreed rather limply and went off to choose the hymn.

After Prayers had ended, and when the Catholics had joined the remnant in Hall, the Head explained to them what was going to happen during the first part of the morning. She kept the "stand-up" class in reserve.

Most people pulled very long faces at the thought of tests—especially when she blandly told them that the first, lasting from nine till nine-forty-five, would be arithmetic. From nine-fifty till ten-forty, they would have literature.

"Break will be at ten-forty," she said, "and will last till eleven. After that, you will be told what happens next. Sixths—both of you—you may work by yourselves. The only embargo is on science. You may prepare notes if you like, but there must be no lab. work until Miss Armitage is able to be with you again. Lower V will take their writing materials into Upper Fifth and do tests there with Miss Wilmot. All the Fourths will bring folding desks here. I will invigilate for you as Miss Burnett has remedial work all the first part of the morning. Now that is all for the present. Seniors, stand! March out to your form-rooms!" She nodded at Veronica who was at the piano and the elder girls went out to the tune of 'Sir Roger de Coverley,' that being the first thing that entered Veronica's head. Then the Middles were sent off to get their folding desks and chairs and, by five past nine, they were all seated, scanning their test papers sadly.

Once they were settled, Miss Annersley turned to the correspondence Rosalie had left and began sorting it out. A goodly pile she set to one side to be distributed among the girls and staff at Break. The rest she tackled herself, rapidly skimming letters and accounts and placing them in two heaps—one to be attended to at once and the rest to await her secretary. Then she got down to work.

The first part of the morning passed off quite peacefully. The girls worked steadily and the Head got through a number of important letters. Once, glancing up from a sentence she was finding hard to frame to her liking, Miss Annersley noticed that Con Maynard seemed to have finished and was scribbling as hard as she could go at her own concerns. She smiled to herself, but took no further notice. The sooner Con got the present great work of literature out of her system, the better for all concerned! Judging by the rate at which she was going, genius was burning brightly.

At twenty to eleven, she collected the papers and then sent them to have their milk and biscuits before taking a run in the garden. When the bell rang at eleven, she had informed Peggy

Burnett that she herself would keep the Middles until the end of morning school as she was giving them "stand-up" class. Peggy Burnett, who had wanted to write up her case-book in any event, was only too glad to be let off ordinary teaching. When the school came in, fresh and rosy from their run in the keen air, they found that their first job was to clear away the desks and chairs. When that had been done, the Head called them one by one to stand in line and every face was beaming at once. They guessed what this meant and "stand-up" class was a treat they seldom got.

The line began with the Lower IVB folk and went on until it ended with Mary-Lou at the foot of the class. The method was always the same. If you could not answer your question, it was passed on down the line until someone did answer it. Then you changed places with her. The girls looked on it as something of a game, for the most unexpected results sometimes happened.

The questions began—simple ones for the youngest girls, harder and harder as they went down the long line. History, geography, mental arithmetic and literature, they all had their turn. By this time, a good many people had changed their places and Upper IV girls were at the top while Lower IVB seemed to be clustering at the bottom. Con Maynard, still looking dreamy, though she had managed so far to answer correctly all the questions addressed to her, was somewhere near the middle.

It seemed good to Miss Annersley at this point to switch over to Old Testament. Both Upper Fourths had read *Joshua* and *Judges* during the previous year. The Lower Fourths, who had all been Third Formers then, had done stories from the Old Testament with special emphasis on the later books as *Ruth*, *Esther*, *Daniel* and *Ezekiel*.

Hilary Bennet was at the head by this time. The Head looked at her and asked, "What were the names of the two chief spies sent by Moses to view the Promised Land?"

With a complacent smirk, Hilary replied, "Joshua the son of Nun and Caleb, the son of Jephunneh." She knew that one all right.

Miss Annersley nodded and passed to Christine Vincent. "What proof of all they said did they bring back with them?"

Christine was eager to tell her. "A bunch of grapes so huge it took two men to carry it," she replied.

Miss Annersley left this and went direct to *Joshua*. "What do you know of Rahab, Maeve?"

Now Maeve had fallen down badly on her last two questions after reaching the top of the class. She knew the story of Rahab and the Israelitish spies and she poured it forth at length. The sympathetic Miss Annersley allowed her to finish before she passed on to Mary-Lou and asked, "What do you know of the Gibeonites?"

Again, Mary-Lou knew the story nearly by heart and she gave it in full. Con, standing about nine lower down, let her attention wander. She forgot Hall and the Head and "stand-up" class. She was away down the centuries, with the beautiful Lady Alys who was left alone in her castle while her Knight, Sir Godefroi, went on a Crusade. The Lady Alys was not only beautiful, she was immensely wealthy and she had a neighbour, one Sir Hubertus, who coveted her rich possessions. He caused word to be sent to her that her knight was dead, slain by the infidels. Then he rode over to her castle and asked her to wed him—Con's heroes never did anything so modern as ask their ladyloves to *marry* them—but she refused and said her heart was in her knight's grave in the burning desert sands of the East. Sir Hubertus then gave her her choice. She could either marry him or she would be besieged and when her castle was captured, she would be forced to be his bride and all her wealth would be his. It will be seen that Con's latest masterpiece bore a striking family resemblance to several hundred others of the same kind.

The difficulty was, what was Lady Alys to do? Con became absorbed in this problem and failed to notice that Mary-Lou had ended at last and Miss Annersley, sympathetic or not, had asked questions of Josette Russell and Clare Kennedy that demanded quite brief replies. She further never noticed that the Head, having reached a little bunch of Lower IVA, had left *Joshua* and gone to *Daniel* and the story of the three Holy Children. When the Head said with a quick look at her dreamy face, "Now, Con!" she never heard but looked straight ahead with eyes that saw nothing of her surroundings.

Miss Annersley knew what had happened and her voice sharpened. "Con! Wake up!"

"Wake up, idiot!" muttered Emerence Hope standing next her. Emerence emphasized her remark with a dig of a sharp elbow into Con's ribs and that young woman came to the surface in a hurry. She was still not properly awake, but her eyes showed some recognition of her surroundings. The Head hoped for the best and gave her an easy question.

"When Daniel was thrown into the lions' den, what happened?"

For a moment, Con still gazed dreamily ahead. Then she replied. "Er—Daniel bit the lions."

There was a deathly silence. Then someone spluttered and that did it! The class literally howled with laughter. The two Fifths, labouring faithfully at a French test, heard the shrieks and exchanged envious glances. The Head bit her lips till her teeth nearly broke the skin in her efforts to keep grave. Con started and looked round. The Lady Alys and her problems fled back to the past and she was standing in Hall and—what on earth *had* she said? The soft pink of her round cheeks deepened to crimson which flooded her face and neck and even her ears. Her dark head sank and she stood there looking and feeling supremely silly.

When she could trust her voice, the Head spoke. "I—I think

we had better end the lesson. Mittagessen will be half-an-hour earlier to-day," she said shakily. "Hilary, will you go and ring the bell for the end of morning school? The rest of you—turn! Forward—march!"

They filed out, still giggling helplessly and Miss Annersley followed them as far as the end of the corridor down which they turned. There, she left them and fled across the entrance hall to her own sitting-room where she contrived to shut the door before she fell into the nearest chair and laughed till the tears poured down her cheeks and she was sore with laughter. But Con had created a sensation all right and had also added one more to the many legends of the Chalet School!

Chapter VI

WINTER SPORTING

BY the end of February, the epidemic had run its course. It had spared no one from the Head, who had been the final victim and was still not quite herself, down to Margot Maynard, the youngest girl in the school by a scant hour and a half. Len had been the only one to be seriously ill with it and once she was able to be up and about, she was packed off home for a week or two of home care and petting to give the final touch to her convalescence. She came back on 1st March to be greeted by her sisters with shrieks of dismay. The high fever had stimulated her growth as it often does and here she was, a good half-head taller than they were!

"Well, after all, I'm the oldest," she said in reply to their reproaches. "It isn't *my* fault, anyhow. Papa says that when people have fever they often grow huge."

"Well, it didn't make *me* grow," Margot returned. "Just *look* at your legs! They're miles below your tunic!"

Len glanced down at her length of leg with a broad grin. "Mamma says I've got to make this do for the rest of the term. She's let it down as far as it'll go, anyhow. But she says I can wait till September for a new one. We'll be wearing summer frocks next term, and they'll all have to be new, we've all grown so much since last summer. I'm away past her shoulder now," she added with a smirk of satisfaction.

Margot looked at Con. "We'll have to *do* something about this!" she said darkly.

"You can't—the Bible says so!" Len retorted. "Never mind that now. You tell me what's happened about the Welsen panto. I know it hasn't come off yet."

"It's put off till the end of term. They all had 'flu as badly as we did, so it's been decided that they'll give it the night of the Sale and that'll help the funds a bit," Con said, hopping about on one leg. "I heard Julie telling Veronica and Clem that she was afraid we'd have an awful let-down from last year 'cos there weren't anything like the number of people here and, of course, we shan't have anything like the stuff to sell, even *with* the Welsen stall."

"Beth's knitting a marvellous twin set for it," Len remarked. "Blue—and the jumper's got a lacey yoke. They'll have to make it a draw and I'm going to take two tickets for it. It 'ud be a lovely Easter gift for Mamma if I got it."

Matron came along at this point. Hearing voices, she went into the little boot-room where the three had elected to hold their re-union, seeing that it was the only place where they were likely to be private at that hour. She promptly ordered them out.

"Yes; I know it's a month since either of you saw Len, but you aren't supposed to be here at any time," she reminded them. "Let me look at you, Len. Yes; you look like yourself again. But remember; you are not to go rushing about and over-heating yourself. I don't want you on my hands again this term. I've had more than enough of you as it is. Margot and Con, why are you not with your walking parties? Run along at once, or there'll be trouble for you. Len, you'd better come upstairs and unpack that case and put your things away. We'll excuse you from the walk this morning. Mind you do it tidily. I'll be up presently and come along to see how you are getting along."

The triplets parted reluctantly. They still had any amount to say to each other, but they knew better than to disobey Matron or try to coax her. Once her foot was down, it was *down*. The younger pair went off to join their respective walks and Len picked up her case and trailed away upstairs to unpack it and put her possessions away. That done, and everything approved by Matron, she wandered off downstairs rather disconsolately. She had reported to the office when she first came, so there was nothing she *must* do until schooltime. She finally fetched up in Hall where she amused herself by reading the Honours board on the walls. Then the sound of voices told her that the school was returning and she made tracks for her own form-room where she plumped down at her desk, tucking her legs under her chair. There, the rest found her when they swarmed in, rosy and fresh from the brisk walk in the keen air.

Emerence Hope led the rush. When she saw who was in the room, she stopped short. "Len Maynard! When did you come? You never said anything, Con. Did you know she was here?"

Con nodded. "Of course I did. But Margot and I said we'd say nothing in case we had a shortish walk and could get hold of her again before school."

"Well, you had it this time," Emerence told her. She turned again to Len. "When exactly did you come?"

"Just before you went for the walk," Len responded. "You didn't see me 'cos I came in by the front door with Mamma. The prees. did, though."

"Are you all right, now?" Isabel Drew demanded. "We've missed you a lot."

"They wouldn't have let me come back if I hadn't been O.K.," Len retorted. "You know that as well as I do." Then she stood up and grinned at them.

They shrieked as they saw her length.

"Len Maynard! You've *grown*!"

"Hasn't she just! Goodness, you're taller than Charlotte!"

"Stand back to back with her, Charlotte! Let's see which really is tallest!"

Charlotte chuckled and stepped forward, but their form-mistress, Miss Bertram, arrived before they could measure the pair. Her eyes widened as she looked at Len and she laughed. "Why, Len, what a height you are now! Nice to see you back, dear. We've missed you. Now then, girls, seats, please! Time for register!"

They went to their seats and Miss Bertram called over their names rapidly. When she had finished, she closed the register and handed it to Isabel. "Take it to Miss Dene, dear. The rest of you get out your books for the first lesson and be quick."

Isabel scurried away to the office and the rest proceeded to take arithmetics, scribblers and history-books out of their desks. That done, and pens, pencils and rubbers laid out, they sat back and began to give Miss Bertram the latest news.

"Miss Bertram, Len's taller than Charlotte," Connie Winter announced.

Miss Bertram laughed. "It often happens to people of your age when you've been ill—and this is French day," she reminded her pupils in French. "Repeat that remark, please, Connie."

Connie went very red and stumbled through her sentence, in French this time. She had to be prompted by the mistress as the word "inch" was not in her vocabulary, and received a battery of glares from her peers who knew all too well what would follow. They had made no mistake. Miss Bertram, having helped Connie out, turned to them and said, "Hands up, any girl who did not know that 'la pouce' means 'the inch'."

A forest of hands responded, not even Len and Con having known it. They were set to repeating it ten times, by which time, everyone had it and their time for any gossip was up. They did not even have a few minutes after Prayers, for Miss Wilmot was pleased to accompany them from Hall and set them to work at once. But when Break came and they had finished their milk and biscuits and were out in the garden which was still snow-covered, their tongues wagged hard and fast to make up for lost time. Back in school, they were kept too busy to bother about anyone's growth and Len, finding with deep dismay how much she had missed, worked like a nigger and would have nothing to do with anyone so long as it was a question of lessons.

Len herself had outside worries. So far, she had not even seen Prunella since her return, except in the distance during Mittagessen. She had an unpleasant duty to perform by her and she wanted it over and done with. Two nights before, when her mother had come to her at bedtime, she had confessed all that had happened on that memorable Saturday. Jo had been hard put to it not to giggle over the affair. She kept a straight face with an effort and talked very seriously to her erring daughter.

"However anyone else talked about Papa and me, you had no right to lose your temper and be so rude," she had told Len.

"But she said such horrid things about you," Len pleaded. "I couldn't help it." There was a pause. Then she acknowledged, "But I did set out to be as rude as I knew how. I really was mad at her!"

"Prunella's rudeness didn't make any better of yours. Now you know what this means."

Len did. She also knew that there was no getting out of it. "Very well. I'll say I'm sorry," she agreed dismally.

Being Len, she was anxious to get it over. From baby-hood, she had always gone straight at anything unpleasant and this was no exception. She got her chance after Mittagessen when they were collecting their deck-chairs for the half-hour's rest in Hall. Prunella and she were alone at one pile and the younger girl, going darkly red, spoke.

"Er—could I speak to you, Prunella?" she asked.

Prunella likewise went red. She had had plenty of time to think things over and she had come to the conclusion that she had been very much in the wrong. Like Len she had reached a certain decision, so she said, "I wanted to speak to *you*. Come over to that corner, will you?" At this point, she took in the leggy object beside her and gave an exclamation. "Goodness! How you've *grown*!"

"I know," Len said in a resigned voice. She was getting very tired of being told this. She followed Prunella to the comparatively isolated corner. Then she blurted out, "Look here, Prunella, I was awfully rude to you that Saturday and—and I'm sorry."

Prunella flushed again. "I was just as rude to you. Please accept my apologies," she said.

There was a moment's silence, then Len held out her hand. "Let's shake on it," she said.

The two shook hands and then stood in embarrassed silence for a moment. Len broke it. "Well I—that is, il faut aller au Hall," she said.

"Oui vraiment," was all Prunella could find to say.

They went off then, but that was the beginning of a friendship for both though neither knew it just then. Prunella hurried to pick up her chair and go to join Barbara Chester with whom she was as friendly as she was with anyone at that period of her existence. Len scuttled off to join her sisters, though talk was forbidden during the rest hour. Still, they were together and after being parted for a full month, that meant something to them. The Maynard triplets had their spats, but they were devoted to each other for all that.

The bitter weather had held through February and to-day was just as cold though it was bright. But the radio weather reports had hinted at a coming change and the Head sent word to the staff-room that lessons for that afternoon were to be foregone and the girls to go out until half-past fifteen.

Miss Dene arrived in Hall just as the half-hour ended. She

mounted the daïs and rang the bell on the reading-desk. "Attention, everyone!" she said in her fluent French. "When the bell rings, you are to go and put on your outdoor clothes. Collect your skis and sticks and meet outside. Seniors, in the drive; Senior-Middles, on the lawn; Junior Middles, on the path at the back. That is all." She glanced at her watch and added, "It is time now. Julie, ring the bell, please. Go quickly, all of you, and *quietly*, if you please." Then she stepped down from the daïs and left Hall by the top door as Julie Lucy hurried out of the bottom one to ring the bell.

Her last injunction had been highly necessary, for an extra afternoon's ski-ing was sheer delight to them all and the Junior-Middles, at any rate, were aching to set up a cheer at the thought that they would be excused needlework for once.

Chairs were packed away in short order and books were taken to the common-rooms and shoved into the bookshelves as fast as possible. Then everyone fled to the Splasheries where only the fact that this was French day and there were too many prefects about for them to risk English kept the tongues of the younger girls in check. But once they were safely outside, the polyglot speech that babbled out was enough to make any Frenchman shriek with dismay.

"Venez avec moi, Margot! Je veux que nous—er—skier together—I mean, tous les deux," Emerence ordered Margot Maynard who was passing.

Len had joined Con already and Margot, after a wistful glance after them, went with her friend. She was very fond of Emerence, but she did think that the elder girl might have realized that she would want to be with her sisters for once. But Emerence was a demanding young person and the idea never entered her head. She slipped a hand through Margot's arm and drew her to the tail of the long procession.

There was a good slope towards the back of the Görnetz Platz.

It ran down to a narrow meadow which lay behind the chalet where Sue Meadow's aunt was living. Here the girls practised their ski-ing. It was quite safe and isolated enough for them to make a reasonable amount of noise without raising the rest of the Platz. Besides, the Head had learned that Sue's small cousin Leila loved to watch the fun.

Leila was there for treatment for tubercular hip trouble. The child suffered greatly at times and Miss Annersley was only too glad to be able to bring some fun and gaiety into her life. When Easter came, the doctors at the Sanatorium insisted that she must go there for treatment she could not be given at home. It should have been done before, but Leila was outrageously spoilt, poor child, and had fretted so at the bare suggestion when they first came to Switzerland, that it had been decided to let it wait for a few months until she could bring herself to leave her mother and home. As Dr. Jack Maynard had said, if they forced her, it would do more harm than good. He had told Miss Annersley that it was doubtful if they could do much to help the poor child in any case.

In the meantime, the school all took an interest in her. Little parcels arrived nearly every day for her. Mere trifles, mostly; but it kept Leila amused and happy. She had letters and cards from total strangers. She went home for the week-ends whenever the weather permitted. Very slowly, they had managed to build up her frail strength to something that would enable her to bear the specialized treatment that might help her. This afternoon's ski-ing would bring her an hour or so of amusement, for her bed was drawn close to the window and she was propped up with pillows and could see out.

Arrived at their chosen spot, the girls fastened on their skis. Then, sticks in hand they glided away over the smooth surface. At least, that was the idea. It quite frequently didn't come off!

Most of the Seniors, who were becoming experts by this time, set off up the slope at once. Mdlle went with them. She was an experienced alpiniste and the whole school watched her easy, flying movements with envy. Most of them still didn't believe her when she told them that by another year they would be moving quite as easily.

Some of the others, less daring, preferred to remain on the level ground. None of the new girls had ever attempted the sport before coming from England and they floundered about, laughing and shrieking when their skis, with the malevolence of their kind, insisted on rushing across each other, flinging the wearers down.

Prunella was as bad as everyone else. She could *not* seem to manage them at all. When, for the sixth time she went sprawling, Len Maynard, who had been enjoying herself hugely with the rest, saw her. She left her crowd with a word or two and came flying across just as Prunella began to struggle to her feet. All the triplets were experts, having learned in Canada.

"Look here," she said, stopping short by the elder girl, "what about me giving you a bit of a hand for a minute or two? I mean, I've done quite a lot and I might be able to help you. The staff are full up with the rest. Come on! I'll tell you how to manage, shall I?"

Prunella stared at her. Len poured all this out in a flood of prettily spoken French—another relic of her Canadian days when she and her sisters had attended a French convent school.

"How *do* you manage it?" she asked enviously.

"We learned in Canada—us three," Len explained. "Here's your sticks. Are you ready? Now then, slide that foot forward a little—it's never any use trying to *lift* your feet when you're ski-ing! Keep your ski pointing out, whatever you do. That's it! Now the other—keep the points *outwards*! Use your sticks to give you balance. Oh, and don't try to make the slides too long," she added with a giggle.

"Why not?" Prunella asked as she did as she was told.

"Push the other foot forward—keep the points *out*! You'll be over if you don't!" Len shrieked. Then, as Prunella obeyed, watching her feet anxiously, "If you'd been here last term, you wouldn't ask *that*! Emerence tried to do it and—and—she did the—the *splits*!" She wound up with a peal of laughter as she remembered that very funny incident.

Prunella looked startled and stood still. "What happened to her?" she asked.

"Oh, nothing—at least, nothing much! She was awfully stiff next day, though. She said," Len continued between gurgles of laughter, "that she felt as if she'd been racked in the Tower of London! But she didn't hurt herself at all—not really. Try again, Prunella. Only do be careful to keep the skis pointing outwards. It'll come soon. It's only a question of practising."

"I hope so. I am so sore with falling," Prunella replied ruefully.

"It'll come—honest, it will!" Len repeated. She stood watching her pupil as she slowly slid first one foot and then the other forward. Suddenly, "Use your sticks—use your sticks!" she shouted in English as Prunella's skis began the fatal approach to each other.

She was too late. The points crossed and Prunella outdid everything she had done before. With a wild yell, she went over in a complete somersault from which she ended up the opposite way round and sat gazing before her with a stunned face.

"However did I get this way round?" she asked dazedly.

With an effort, Len stifled her screams of laughter. "You threw a *lovely* somersault. I wish Burnie had seen you! You aren't hurt, are you?"

"No; but it was rather—surprising," Prunella replied, struggling up again.

"Never mind. You took quite a lot of slides before you did it.

It's coming now," Len said consolingly. "Try again."

Thus urged, Prunella set off once more and this time she managed to go quite a distance before the inevitable happened and over she went. However, whatever else she might be, she was stubborn as they all knew by this time. Her chin went out and her lips set. She was not going to be beaten by some strips of cane—not if she knew it! She moved off once more, Len watching her, looking comically like an anxious little mother hen watching over an extra large duckling.

"Len, you are not to stand about," said the Head Girl's voice behind them at that moment. "Off you go and warm up with a good skim! I'll give Prunella a hand. Go on, Prunella. You're doing quite well. Len, did you hear me tell you to go?"

Len dared not argue the point. On the whole, the younger members of the school would rather have got across a mistress than a prefect any day of the week. She was no exception. She turned now and skimmed off with a motion so easy and graceful that Prunella, watching her, sighed deeply.

"I shall never do it like that—not if I try till Domesday!" she said.

Julie gave her an inquisitive glance, but she only said, "Oh yes, you will. I was as bad as you when I began. Come along; try again! It's too cold to stand about."

As it turned out, they had only another quarter-of-an-hour left. Then the whistle Miss o'Ryan carried rang out and they had to finish and tramp back to school, waving to Leila at her window as they went. Everyone was glowing with exercise and most of them were beginning to feel tired with their strenuous work.

The weather had held, though the weatherwise kept casting glances at the sky. The sun had disappeared behind the western mountains by this time, so though greyness was descending on the Görnetz Platz, that could be accounted for by the onset of night.

"I don't believe the weather's going to change at all," Mary-Lou observed as she changed into house-shoes in the Senior-Middles' Splashery. "However, we've had a glorious afternoon out of it, so who are we to complain?"

"Sez you!" retorted Vi Lucy—and was at once and very properly caught by her sister Julie who happened to be passing and overheard her.

"I thought," Julie said, pulling up and speaking in chilly French, "that you had been told *not* to use that disgusting expression? And why are you speaking in English at all? This is French day, let me remind you."

Vi went scarlet, but she said nothing. Julie looked at her. Then she added, "Pay your fines into the Sanatorium box and don't do that again, please."

Vi waited until her sister's back was turned before she relieved her feelings by making a fearful grimace after her. "Julie's always there when you least want her!" she complained to her cousin Barbara Chester who was standing near her.

"If you make faces like that, your face'll turn inside out and you'll stay that way," Barbara said calmly. "You asked for it, Vi."

Prunella had seen the grimace and was staring at Vi with fascinated eyes.

"Qu'as-tu, donc?" Vi demanded in no very amiable tones.

"I had no idea," Prunella replied in her slow and still very British French, "that anyone as pretty as you are, Viola, could look so ugly!"

Vi was left breathless and not very sure whether to feel pleased at the compliment—though Prunella had merely stated a fact and had had no idea of complimenting her—or insulted by its finale. While she was trying to decide, Prunella left the Splashery to go upstairs and change for the evening, so Vi had to leave it for the time being. She raced off upstairs herself, still undecided.

Kaffee und Kuchen followed at sixteen o'clock and then came preparation which would last till eighteen. After that, they were free for half-an-hour when they would have Prayers and Abendessen would come immediately after. Prayers over, they would have Hobbies Club. The Junior-Middles would go to bed at half-past twenty and the rest at nine.

"I hope you will all work hard at Hobbies," Miss Annersley finished—she had come into the Speisesaal to tell the girls the arrangements for the evening. "This is the first of March and we have our Sale on the first Saturday in April, so you haven't much time left. I'll hold an inspection on Saturday evening, so get as much finished to-night and any other times you have as you can."

Then she left them and they promptly fell into discussions—rather restrained by the fact that they must still speak French—over what was near enough to being finished to be ready for Saturday and what would need strenuous work if it was to be done. They tried to reckon how much they would have for each stall, and finally Mary-Lou brought up a most important question.

"What sort of a Sale is it to *be*?" she demanded of her table at large as she made a long arm for the plate of cakes.

Lesley Malcolm pushed it nearer. "I haven't heard a word," she said. "You had better ask the prefects if you really want to know."

Lesley spoke with a certain amount of sarcasm, but it was never well to do that with Mary-Lou. "So I jolly well will after this," she said, forgetting to speak French in her earnestness.

"French, you idiot!" Vi warned her in a hiss. "D'you *want* to set someone on top of you for speaking English?"

"Well, I like that!" was Mary-Lou's instant retort. "That is, j'aime celà! Tu parles en anglais toi-même!"

Vi had no answer to that one, so she only grinned. However,

Mary-Lou was a canny creature. She fully intended to find out the answer to her question and it was no good having a scrap with the prefects beforehand.

"These cakes are very good, are they not?" she inquired in her best French. Then she suddenly relapsed into a giggle. "I say! Did you all see young Len helping Prunella with her ski-ing? I was so surprised I nearly fainted!"

"I was surprised myself," Barbara Chester agreed as she ate her cake thoughtfully. "The last we heard of those two they were having a violent quarrel."

"Well, they seem to have made it up," Vi put in, taking the jam dish to scrape the remnants on to her bread-twist. She set the dish back and took a bite. When she had swallowed it, she added, "I saw them myself, and I was as startled as you."

"Perhaps it's the effect of 'flu?" Lesley suggested.

"Much more likely to be the effect of Auntie Jo," Mary-Lou said with decision. "If she got to hear of it, she'd talk to Len."

Catriona Watson, who sat at their table and was opposite them, had overheard all this. Now she leaned forward. "If you ask me, I should say that Len was feeling bad then and that's why she lost her temper as she did. I mean, it isn't *like* her, is it? And goodness knows Prunella can be maddening enough for anything when she tries!"

"I expect that's really the top and bottom of it," Mary-Lou agreed with distinctly muffled utterance since her mouth was full of cake. She swallowed it and then stood up and, to the horror of her friends, called across the room to the prefects' table, "Oh, Julie, is it decided yet what the Sale is to be?"

Julie looked up from a heated discussion on that very point with her peers. "Oh, Mary-Lou!" she said resignedly. "No; we have not yet decided. We hope to do so this evening and you shall all know as soon as possible after that."

“Thank you very much,” Mary-Lou responded politely as she sat down perforce, since Vi and Lesley, who were on either side of her, had pulled her down.

“Comme tu as un *nerve*!” the latter muttered.

“Mais pourquoi?” Mary-Lou demanded. “Je n’étais pas impolie. J’ai demandais à Julie avec toute la politesse du monde, et elle m’a répondu—er—en plaisanterie.”

“If you mean ‘Pleasantly’, I’d say so!” Vi grinned. “I know Julie was as polite as you, but she certainly didn’t joke about it—and that’s what ‘plaisanterie’ means, let me tell you!”

There was no time for more, for the prefects had risen and were pushing in their chairs to the table. Mary-Lou drained her last half-cup of milky coffee so hurriedly, that she choked on it and had to be patted on the back. Julie waited patiently until the table was standing properly behind its chairs and then said Grace. When that was over and the crockery cleared away, they had to fly to wash and from then until eighteen o’clock, it was hard work for everyone. Preparation hours at the Chalet School were definitely limited, but you were expected to make the most of them. As the general attitude was that the sooner your work was done properly the better for you, it was rarely that any bad conduct had to be complained of during prep. To-night was no exception. For the hour-and-a-half of work, there was a deep hush over the school. But when it had ended, the prefects went off to their own quarters, to talk over the Sale and the rest, congregating in common-rooms and Hall, chattered like magpies. It was just as well for them that neither mistress nor prefect came near them during that half-hour, or several people would have had to spend the time repeating the proper French of their remarks and trying to acquire a better accent in doing so.

Chapter VII

"THE WILLOW PATTERN"

IT'S no use! We can't possibly come to any decision just now," Julie Lucy said definitely. "We'll have to have a proper Prefects' Meeting after Abendessen. Then we can go into it thoroughly. I can get on with my tea-cloth at the same time, so it won't be wasted. Most of us can do our work while we talk, I think?" She looked round questioningly.

The prefects agreed. They were to take charge of the Needlework stall this year and those of them who were not sewing were either knitting or crocheting. Zoé Wylie was the one exception. During the previous summer, a young aunt on the verge of marrying and leaving England, had bestowed on her sole niece her small handloom and all her bundles of silks and wools. She had even paid for Zoé to take lessons in weaving and Zoé, neat-fingered and artistically inclined, had made rapid headway. The loom really was a small one, only capable of producing scarves and narrow strips of weaving and Zoé, in a rash moment, had promised her peers that she would make at least a dozen scarves for the Sale. She had finished ten of them, by dint of hard work in every spare moment, and was busy on the eleventh; but she found warping-up a tedious process, even for so small a loom and she still had one to make completely. The Head had allowed her to bring the little loom and set it up in a corner of the Prefects' room; but she had warned the girl that schoolwork must not be neglected for weaving, fascinating though the hobby was.

When Julie spoke, she was hard at work and Clem looked across at her with a grin.

"I'll bet Zoé can't," she said. "Hi, Zoé! Come to the surface a moment! How much have you heard of our conversation above the clackety racket of that affair?"

"Everything," Zoé replied, completely unruffled. "It doesn't make as much noise as all that."

Clem heaved herself out of her chair and went across the room, knitting in hand, to admire the work. "I can't think how you keep it so smooth and even. Much more to do?"

"Twelve more rows of the plain weaving and then the border. That won't take long. But you needn't worry about the meeting," Zoé added as she threw her shuttle through the warp with a sure movement. "I'll give this a miss then and go on with that bedjacket I'm knitting. I couldn't follow a pattern and join in your nattering at one and the same time. I'm not expert enough for that."

"Oh, that's all right, then," Clem replied, watching her deft movements with fascinated eyes.

Zoé laughed. "Could you do your stocking-tops and talk at once?" she demanded.

"*These*, I could." Clem finished her row and began on the next needle of the Greek key pattern she was knitting into a boy's stocking-top. "I've done so much of this pattern, I believe I could almost do it in my sleep."

Rosalie Way changed the topic. "What exactly did we bring from the dressing-up cupboards?" she asked.

"I couldn't tell you offhand," Julie answered, pausing to choose a fresh strand of silk for the rose she was shading on an afternoon tea-cloth. She threaded her needle and continued, "The Abbess and Matey decided all that and I haven't given it much thought since the Christmas play. We had all we wanted for that, I know. But there again, Miss Dene gave it out."

"What about getting the list from Matey?" Madge Herbert suggested.

"You'd better," Clem agreed as she returned to her seat at the table. "I don't see how we're to decide anything until we know what's available."

"You and that devastating common sense of yours!" Julie laughed.

"Well, my child, *someone* in this place has to show a little sense now and then. Don't blame *me* if I'm the only one that does it," Clem said blandly.

The rest protested at this statement with some vigour, but Julie hushed them. "We haven't time for barneying at present. I'll go to Matey after Abendessen and ask her if we may have the list. Clem's right when she says we can't fix anything until we've seen it. There goes the gong!" She ran her needle into the work which she folded neatly. "Come on, folks!"

The prefects left the room in a body and strolled down the front stairs as was their privilege. They reached the Speisesaal by the corridor from the front hall and entered it in time to hear Prunella addressing a remark to her next door neighbour which made them grin.

"Er—voulez-vous donnez-moi—er—un petit plus de la chambre, s'il vous plaît?"

"And *that*," Julie muttered with a suppressed chuckle to Clem, "is supposed to be French! It's to be hoped Mdlle's nowhere about!" She glanced round in search of that lady, but none of the staff had arrived as yet, so she said gently to Prunella, "Mais, Prunella, ça n'est pas le propre français pour, 'Please give me a little more room.' Attendez, s'il vous plaît!" And she repeated with her charming accent, "Voulez-vous me permettre un peu plus de l'espace, s'il vous plaît?"

Prunella thanked her and repeated the phrase. She was correct in French, this time, but her accent was appalling. However, the tables were filling up and Julie, who took charge of one where some of the rowdiest Junior-Middles sat, left it at that. Prunella would pick it up in time, she supposed.

The chatter during the meal centred on the Sale. The new girls were told its history and also some of the legends attached to it. It is true that phrases quite as peculiar as Prunella's were used; but when the meal was ended and they all stood for Grace, Miss Annersley, in mercy for their excitement, announced that for the rest of the evening they would be excused from French and might use their own languages, once Prayers were over. Then she said Grace and they marched out to Prayers.

When they were finally dismissed to their own rooms to go on with their work, Julie left her own gang to go up to the prefects' room and ran after Matron to beg the list from the "dressing-up" cupboard. She caught the little lady just outside her own room.

"Well?" Matron said, looking at her sharply. "What do you want with me, Julie?"

"Oh, Matron, could I have the list from the dressing-up cupboard, please?"

"Why do you want it now?" Matron demanded.

"We want to see what sets of dresses are available before we decide the form the Sale is to take," Julie explained. "You know we left part of the things for the English branch and so far we haven't seen what came with us. Let me have it, Matron—please, do!"

Matron laughed and went into her room. "Come along in then, and I'll give it to you." She fished for it in her desk and found the two or three sheets of typing and handed them over. "Here you are! Mind you don't lose any of it and let me have it back as soon as you've finished with it."

Julie took it with a joyous, "Oh, thank you, Matron!" She

turned to the door and was about to join the rest of the grandees of the school, when Matron checked her.

"One moment! You've been all right this term? No aches or pains anywhere?"

Julie laughed. "Not so much as a little finger ache!" Then she sobered. "It was just about this time last year when I felt so ghastly, wasn't it? A week or two earlier, perhaps. But I really am all right now. We met the Russells when we were in London for a few days during the holidays and Sir Jem gave me a good overhaul. He said he'd pass me fit as a fiddle now."

"Good! I don't want another experience like last year's!" Matron said brusquely.

"Oh, neither do I!" Julie assured her. "I promise you, Matey, if I have the faintest touch of tummy-ache again I'll come straight to you. I—I learnt my lesson last Easter term," she added, flushing. "Dad gave me a ticking-off about it when I was all right again. He said there need never have been all that fuss and bother and Mother and everyone needn't have been so upset if I'd had any sense and come to you when I had that first bout of pain."

Matron nodded. "I'm glad to hear it! You certainly gave us all a bad time." She turned back to her desk. "You can run along now."

Julie made no delay. She scurried off with her list and Matron was left to recall those terrible ten days when Julie was taken from St. Briavel's to the cottage hospital at Carnbach on the mainland for a difficult and dangerous operation for acute peritonitis. The girl had nearly slipped through their fingers that time, and no one in authority was ever likely to forget the experience. However, she looked well and strong after a year and, as she said, she had had a stiff lesson. Matron put the affair behind her and sat down to write a letter.

Meanwhile, Julie ran along to the Prefects' room, waving her list as she entered. "Here we are! Come to the table, Zoé, and let's try to get something settled. We haven't any too much time left, you know."

They gathered round the table, work in hand, and she spread out the sheets and scanned them eagerly.

"Remember," Clem said over her knitting, "that it's no use having just the dresses. We've got to have the sets as well."

"I know that as well as you. Let's see." Julie looked down the sheet. "There are all the fairy-tale dresses—"

"No use at all," Madge interrupted. "The Welsen crowd are safe to want those for their panto. Come again!"

"I'd forgotten that for the moment," Julie owned. "Well there are all the Greek dresses we had for those scenes we did from *A Midsummer Night's Dream*."

"We used those three or four years ago," Veronica said as she tempted Providence and the dentist by biting off her thread. "And it's awfully difficult to make Greek sets with the stalls. What else is there?"

"Well, what about the Chinese dresses then? The whole of *The Willow Pattern* dresses are here and we have the cottages as well. We could do something about the balcony, I suppose. We could make it awfully pretty, you know. There are all the wreaths of imitation flowers and we've even got that huge cardboard Willow Pattern plate Herr Laubach painted for one end of Hall so that people would know what we were after." Julie looked at her lists again. "We've got the pagoda roofs, too. What do you all think?"

"It sounds rather good," Madge Herbert said thoughtfully. "Didn't you have that Sale before we four came to the school? I don't remember it, anyhow."

"We did. Our crowd were—let's see—oh my goodness! We must have been Fourth Form then! Heavens! How time does fly!" Julie exclaimed in elderly tones. "Well, what about it? Shall we put it to the vote? Someone propose, please."

"I will," Annis Lovel, Head of the games, said quickly. "I think it sounds awfully jolly. How many stalls do we have, by the way, and how do we arrange them, Julie?"

Julie considered. "Well, there's the Mandarin's house for one, and the Gardener's cottage for another. Then there's the balcony where *Li-chi* sat—"

"Who on earth is *Li-chi*?" Rosalind Wynyard, who had also come to the school after that particular Sale, demanded. "I've never heard of her before."

"Don't you know the story?" Madge asked incredulously. "*Li-chi* was the lovely daughter of a rich Mandarin. She and *Chang*, the Gardener's son, fell in love with each other. Of course, her father nearly had a fit at the idea, and he told *Li-chi* that he had arranged for her to marry a wealthy friend of his. *Li-chi* was broken-hearted over this. She told *Chang*—he used to row down the river every evening and stop under her balcony and they used to make love—and he promised that he would do something about it. He had a little cottage of his own on an island in the river which flowed past the Mandarin's and on past another great estate. This island was part of that and if only they could get there, her father couldn't touch them."

Madge paused, out of breath, and Veronica took up the story. "*Li-chi* was delighted at the idea. She promised to elope with him as soon as it could be managed. *Chang* said he would go to the nearby temple and ask the gods to help them and he promised to come for her before the wedding day. *Li-chi* said she would beg her father to put it off until the old willow tree outside the house had flowered. It was just beginning to bud then and they both felt that ought to give them time enough."

"And then," Julie went on as Veronica stopped for a moment, "*Chang* went away to see what he could do. The days went by and *Li-chi*, sitting on her balcony every evening, watched the willow growing green as the spring advanced. There was no sign from *Chang* and as the time passed, she grew sad. She was afraid her father might have captured him and sold him as a slave and her wedding-day was drawing nearer and nearer. The day before the wedding, her maids brought her piles of most beautiful dresses that she might choose which she would wear on the morrow. They wanted her to have one of peach-blossom silk, but she refused, for she had always worn peach-blossom colour when she was expecting *Chang* and she couldn't wear that if they married her to another man. At last, to get rid of them, she chose one of blue, embroidered in gold thread with flowers and butterflies. It was very lovely and the maids went away at last, satisfied."

"And then," Clem butted in, "just when she had given up all hope, a servant came to say that a man wanted to see her. She didn't care much what happened, so she said he could come in. When the servant had gone, the stranger swept off the enormous hat he was wearing and it was *Chang*!"

"How thrilling!" Rosalind exclaimed. "Go on! What happened? Did they get away with it?"

Madge took it up. "He told her that he had had a dreadful time, keeping away from her father but he had managed it. He had gone to the temple and the gods had promised that if they were caught, they would turn the lovers into two turtle-doves or else twin stars. Then they would be together for always. *Li-chi* gave *Chang* the casket of jewels her dead mother had left her and carried her distaff and they slipped out of the house. But the Mandarin saw them and he snatched up his whip and rushed after them. They tore to the bridge which crossed the river to the island where the Gardener's cottage stood. *Chang* had left his boat there and if they could only get to it in time, the Mandarin could do nothing, for they could get away down the river before he could summon help. But *Chang* was burdened by the heavy casket of jewels and he wouldn't leave *Li-chi* and she couldn't run fast because her feet had been bound as all Chinese girls' were in those days. The Mandarin gained on them. He stretched out his hand and touched *Chang's* shoulder. But at that moment, the gods kept their word. The man and the girl vanished. The casket of jewels and the distaff fell into the river and above the heads of the furious Mandarin floated two turtle-doves. And, so the story goes, every year the doves nested in the trees on *Chang's* little island and the gods let them live for ever."

"And so they all lived happy ever after," Clem said with a toss of her red-brown pigtail. "It doesn't say what the disappointed bridegroom had to say about it. However, that was her father's headache, I suppose. It would make a lovely Sale up here, Julie. Annis proposed it. I'll second that."

"Very well," Julie said. "We'll vote on it please. Everyone who likes the idea? Anyone who doesn't? No one? Then that's settled, thank goodness!" She picked up her work.

"Now," said tall Pat Collins, one of the sub-prefects, "let's get down to the number of stalls. Lend me some scissors, please, someone. I've left mine in the dormy."

Veronica passed hers over. "You mentioned three—the Mandarin's house and the Gardener's cottage and the balcony. Go on from there, Julie."

"Well, we had *Chang's* cottage and the willow tree. We made that out of crinkled, green paper with branches from trees in the garden. I suppose we could manage it again. It was a weeping willow, you know."

"We used the bridge, too," Zoé said thoughtfully. "D'you remember? We made it the flower-stall. Griffiths manufactured it out of some trellising he had and it was set across the middle of the Hall. It looked awfully well, I remember."

"Griffiths bagged his trellising back after the Sale and he isn't here now. I doubt if we can manage it this time," Clem remarked. "However, we can see if we can possibly fix up anything. And couldn't we use *Chang's* boat for the lucky dip?"

Julie nodded. "That's a good idea! I haven't the vaguest notion what a Chinese rowing-boat looks like, but there's sure to be a picture of one somewhere and we can use cardboard. After all, it only has to lie still somewhere and hold the parcels. Shall we settle that, too?"

They all agreed and she turned back to her list. "There's plenty of dresses. And we can decorate Hall with the flower-wreaths. We have half the stalls and we can fix the pagoda roof on them. I should think we could make Hall look really Chinesey if we tried."

This, too, was agreed. Then Veronica proposed that they should decide which stall should go to each place.

"The kids had better have the Mandarin's house," Julie said thoughtfully. "They're doing toys this time, and they're to have Tom Gay's model chalet as well, so they'll need plenty of room. The two Fifths are doing the produce stall. They'd better have the Gardener's cottage."

"What are Welsen doing? Don't forget them, for goodness' sake!" Rosalie put in.

"They're doing arts and crafts—all but things like Zoé's scarves. Those come to us. But they are having hand-painted pottery and wood-carvings and fretwork and things like that. They'll need—"

A tap at the door broke in on her remarks and she turned to call, "Come in!"

The prefects all looked up as the door slowly opened to reveal a tall, slender woman, her delicate, mobile face framed in a black fringe and "ear-phones", ablaze with laughter as the fifteen big girls assembled first stared and then leapt to their feet with cries of joy.

"Auntie Jo!—Mrs. Maynard!—Aunt Joey!—when did you come?—Why haven't you been to see us before?—Come along in and sit down!"

Joey Maynard came in briskly and shut the door behind her with emphasis. "Are you prefects or Lower Fourth? If you make a row like that, you'll have someone on your track, prefects or no prefects! That's better!" as they cooled down a little. "Thanks, Clem! Yes, I'll sit down for a minute." She dropped into the chair Clem was offering and looked round them with a friendly smile. "Sit down and don't overpower me like that, you—you young giantesses! Now tell me all the hanes!"

She planted her elbows on the table, leaned her chin on her hands and looked round them with another grin. "You all look fit enough, despite your 'flu efforts. How Matey must have loved you all!"

"She didn't act like it," Julie assured her. "Oh, Auntie Jo, how lovely to see you again! We haven't set eyes on you this term. How are the family?"

"I suppose you mean the boys and the twins. They're all well now. But I've had a time, what with the twins cutting double teeth and letting the whole world know about it, and Charles and Mike indulging in your 'flu. I haven't had time to go anywhere, not even here. And then Len came as a wind-up. I must say I think you might have tried to celebrate your first Easter term in the Oberland with something a little less trying than 'flu!"

Her dancing eyes went round the group and they all laughed.

"We didn't go for to do it," Clem said. "It just happened."

"Very careless of you to allow it! That's all I've got to say! Oh, well, it's over now. We'll shove it all behind us as Kipling so beautifully says and get down to business. What were you all discussing when I arrived? You seemed to be up to your ears in it, whatever it was."

"We're discussing the Sale," Julie explained. "We're going to make it a Willow Pattern Sale this year. We've got all the dresses and the pagoda roofs. Sit in and give us the benefit of your advice and—er—experience."

"Advice and experience? You've come to the right shop for that! I was in on all the early Sales, remember. In fact, apart from the year we were in Canada, I don't think I've missed one since the school started them. By the way," she suddenly fumbled in the pockets of the coat she was wearing, "I've brought a small contribution for your stall. Here you are!" She tossed two small parcels on to the table.

Clem made a dive and snapped up one. Julie grabbed the other. They opened them eagerly and displayed a dozen "daisy" necklets which they passed round with loud approval.

"Rather natty, I think," Jo said modestly. "When we were turning out to come here, I found a priceless book that must date from Madame's extreme youth, entitled *Arts and Crafts for Girls*. I thought it might be useful, so I brought it along. One day, when Beth Chester and I were fed to the teeth with keeping the boys out of draughts and chasing round after a pair of howling babies with teeth coming—poor lambs!—I fished it out and we refreshed ourselves by going through it. Lots of it is no use now—things like how to make barbola pottery, for instance—but they did tell you how to manufacture these necklets. I've boxes and boxes of small beads so I turned them out and we tried our hands at one each. They were so successful, that I decided I'd make some for the Sale and Beth said she would, too. I sent off my first to my sister. Now I'm waiting to hear what she thinks. Anyhow, we were so pleased with ourselves, we just turned to and made that lot for you."

"Aren't they *dainty*!" Rosalie Way said, holding up one made of blue glass beads to let the light twinkle on it. "I simply must buy this one. It would look lovely with that blue cotton I had last summer."

"I thought they were rather decorative," Jo agreed. "Anyway, I knew the kids would like them and they cost so little to make, you can sell them quite cheaply. If you like them and want any more, we can do a few. They're easy enough, once you get into the way of it."

"Oh, we'll have as many as you can make," Julie said. "Everyone will go for them. But—our stall? I don't know." And she shook her black head till the thick curls danced madly.

"Why not?" Pat demanded. "Oh, Julie, we simply *must* have them! What d'you want to do with them?"

"Well—what about Welsen? They're having the Arts and Crafts."

A groan arose. In their excitement, the girls had forgotten the rules that governed the Sales. A needlework stall claimed all needlework. Craft objects went to the Arts and Crafts. Sweets belonged to produce; and so on.

"No mixing allowed!" Clem moaned. "What rotten luck!"

Jo laughed. "I'm sorry. I didn't know you were doing Needlework this year. Julie's right, though. Hand those back, Rosalie. They must go to Welsen, I'm afraid. But anyhow, Beth's knitted you what Len describes as a *wizard* twin set. You'll have to raffle it if you want to get its full value. And I brought all the odds and ends of knitting-wool out and Anna has knitted them into squares and crocheted the squares together with black wool. It makes a simply gorgeous bed-cover, and so warm and light. I don't know if you want another raffle, but if you do, you could use that."

"Sounds good," Clem remarked. "I say, Aunt Joey, what about donating that book of yours to the school library? It sounds rather the sort of thing we could do with. What about it, Madge?"

Librarian Madge laughed. "Oh, absolutely! May we have it, Mrs. Maynard?"

"Well, it's my sister's, but I don't suppose she remembers the first thing about it. Anyhow, we'll risk that. I'll bring it along the next time I come. It's rather dilapidated, I'm afraid. You'll have to do a spot of repair-work on it."

"That'll be O.K., and thanks a lot," Madge said fervently.

"Well, who's doing which stall? You might let me have some idea of what I'm in for."

"The two Lower Fourths are doing toys," Julie said, pulling a list out of her blazer pocket. "Upper Fourth are having books, pictures and all that sort of thing. The Fifths have the produce stall and we do needlework as you've already heard. Welsen are doing arts and crafts. Oh, and some of them are taking over the refreshments. I say, Auntie Jo, you've lived in the Alps before. What sort of weather are we to expect in early April?"

"Depends largely on the Föhn, I imagine," Jo said, leaning back in her chair. "The warm wind that blows from the south around then, you know. If it comes early, look out for a thaw—oh, and avalanches, just to make everything pleasant."

"*Avalanches!*" It was a chorus of dismay.

She explained, her black eyes dancing with mischief. "The warm winds melt the snows and great hunks break off and come down, bringing boulders and tree-trunks with them. Not," she added as she saw the horror in the young faces and relented, "that you need worry too much up here. For one thing, the whole of the lower slopes—and that includes our shelf—are well wooded which helps to break up the avalanches. For another, it's on the really high mountains with summits well above the snow-line that you can expect the worst. Our mountain is bare of all snow in summer. You've very little need to worry. In fact," she added, "none at all. Anything that comes this way will be a minor affair and the stretches of pines will break it up and disperse it before it can do any harm."

"Thank goodness for that!" Julie said fervently. "I've no wish to be buried alive, I can tell you!"

"Don't worry! The school wouldn't be up here if there were any risk of that. Well, if you get the Föhn about then, you can look for rain. If not, there'll still be snow lying, though in what condition, I couldn't say. At the Tiernsee, we generally reckoned to be more or less clear of it by April; but we're a good deal higher up here than we were there. Why do you want to know?"

"Well, you know we've always had clock-golf outside and I was wondering if we could manage it here."

"I doubt it. You'd better give it a miss and have the Sale at the end of the summer term in future. What other entertainments do you propose having?"

"Miss Burnett thought we might give a display of morris dancing," Annis said.

"Yes—that ought to go down well. And here's an idea. Have a couple of sword dances as well. You could do 'Flamborough', couldn't you? And finish up with one of the Northumbrian 'Rapper' dances. That would bring the house down."

"Oh, good idea!" Pat said enthusiastically.

Jo stood up and bowed to her. "Thanks for the flowers! Now what else?"

"Welsen and we are trying to make up an orchestra to—to discourse sweet strains of music," Madge replied with a gurgle. She paused. Then she gave an exclamation. "*Eureka! I've* got an idea now—they must be catching!"

"What is it?" half-a-dozen voices demanded.

"Speak now, or forever hold your peace!" Jo added, grinning.

Her grin vanished when Madge said simply, "You to sing."

The rest took it up at once and made as much clamour as if

they were Junior-Middles instead of serious-minded Seniors and prefects at that.

"It's a real brainwave!" Julie cried. "You can't refuse, Auntie Jo! It's all for the good of the cause *and* the school!"

"But, my good child, I haven't practised once since we came here!" Jo protested.

Clem gave her a twinkling look. "We've given you a month's notice. That ought to be quite enough. Anyhow, with your voice, you don't need much."

"A lot you know about it! I tell you, I haven't practised since we left Canada."

"Still, I suppose you can manage not to sing flat," Clem said sweetly.

Jo gave her a glare. Then she laughed. "All right! Have it your own way! But I warn you, it's only this once!"

"It won't be in our hands next year," Julie reminded her. "*We* shall all have gone on to Welsen or other things. This is our last year at the Chalet School proper. It'll be in the hands of my young sister Betsy and her little pals." She took up her work. "That's as much as we can settle now. The Abbess has to okay it before we break it to the school at large. Anyhow, we've talked enough about it for one night. Instead, Auntie Jo, you can tell us about the twins and the boys while we get on with our jobs and give our brains a rest!"

Chapter VIII

Jo is Called into Council

MISS ANNERSLEY proved to be as complaisant as anyone could ask when the prefects put their ideas before her next day. Julie had seen her before Prayers and begged for time for discussion and she had told them to come to her at Break.

"Yes; I think a Willow Pattern Sale would be very effective," she said when she had heard all they had to say. "I remember the one we held at Plas Howell was as charming as any we have had. Up here, it will be something quite new, too. I really don't think you could do better, girls."

"The only snag is that we haven't got a bridge and we haven't any Griffiths, either, to make us one," Julie remarked. "He grabbed his precious trellising back at the very first moment. And he only let us have it on condition that we took care of it. I remember hearing Jacynth Hardy—she was Head Girl that term—grumbling about it to Gay Lambert. I wonder where those two are now," she added. "They were a jolly decent couple. In fact, all that set of prees. were decent."

Miss Annersley chose to ignore this. Instead, she gave the girls a gently pitying smile at which they gaped. They could think of nothing Julie had said to provoke it.

Miss Annersley, having reduced them to a sense of their own witlessness, proceeded to explain. "My dear girls, have you forgotten that we are in the land of wood-carvers and wood-workers? What *are* you thinking about? Of course you can have your bridge. I'll make inquiries and let you know what I can arrange as soon as possible. I suppose you'll be content with the arrangement we had last time—a zigzag of double trellising across the centre of Hall? I'm afraid we can hardly manage a raised bridge like the one on the plates."

"I remembered the zigzags," Julie said. "Miss Linton told us that Chinese bridges used to be built like that to keep off evil spirits as they—the spirits, I mean—were supposed not to be able to turn round corners."

"That is quite true," the Head agreed. "All the same, if you look at that Willow Pattern plate over my secrétaire, you'll see that the bridge there had three sets of piers and two arches. We can't rise to that. It would mean heavy carpenter's work if it was to hold some of you, all the objects for sale *and* purchasers. But the zigzags are an easy matter."

The girls had all rushed to cluster round the secrétaire and look up at the old Caughley ware plate hanging above it. Now they turned and went back to their seats.

"That's awfully good of you, Miss Annersley," Julie said earnestly.

"Nonsense! I'm as anxious as you are for the Sale to be a really good one. Now what about the sampan—which is the proper name for the boat. Who will take charge of it?"

They looked at each other. So far, they hadn't thought of that. Hitherto, it had always been given to the Juniors; but there were no Juniors at the Görnetz Platz. Quiet Edris Young, the Magazines prefect, had the first idea.

"Why not let the new girls in the Lower Fourth do it?" she proposed. "There are eight or ten of them, aren't there? And couldn't that queer, new girl in Upper IVB, Prunella Davidson, be in charge?"

"A very good idea!" Miss Annersley said with approval, for Edris was so quiet and reserved, that it was the policy of the staff to encourage her on every occasion. "That would solve the problem nicely. But here is something else. Have you arranged for the lucky dip parcels?"

There was another silence. To tell the truth, they had forgotten all about the lucky dip until the night before. The Juniors' own mistresses had always been responsible for that side of it and so they had overlooked the fact that they must provide objects for it. Madge broke it at last.

"We'll have to go through everything we've got so far and give the trifles," she said. "And Miss Annersley, couldn't some of us spend an afternoon or two with the sewing-machines, making bags of muslin and silk? We could fill them with sweets and—and beads and so on. After all, it's the younger ones who mostly go for the dip and that's the sort of thing they like."

The Head nodded. "You could certainly do that. I'll send out an appeal for scraps of silk and muslin for the bags and you can choose some afternoon you're all free for their manufacture. But Madge, I doubt if you'll find very much among your trifles that small folk would like. They will probably be needlebooks, pincushions and articles of that kind. I don't see people like Margot Maynard, for instance, being very pleased with that."

"Would Mrs. Maynard cut us a few tiny jigsaws do you think?" Annis asked. "She always did before they went to Canada."

"Did she bring her treadle fretsaw to Switzerland?" Polly Winterton, a red-haired, gangling member of Lower VI and a sub-prefect, queried.

Miss Annersley laughed. "You know, Polly, I haven't the faintest idea. I do know she hasn't used it since she came back if she did bring it. I tell you what. You run along to the office and ask Miss Dene to ring up Freudesheim and see if she can come and join us."

Polly was up and off on the word. She returned in short order to say that Miss Dene was on the phone to Mrs. Maynard when she arrived at the office and had given her the message and Mrs. Maynard had said she would be over in five minutes.

"Then we'll leave that question until she comes," the Head said. "And now, how do you propose to entertain your visitors?"

"Well, there's the Welsen pantomime in the evening," Clem said thoughtfully.

The Head nodded. She knew all about that, having had a deputation of the Welsen girls the previous Saturday. They had come to ask if the school had brought the fairy-tale dresses and sets and, on hearing that they had, had promptly staked a claim to the lot.

"That will be in the evening," she reminded the prefects. "What are you doing in the afternoon?"

"Our usual display of dancing," Pat replied. "Miss Burnett advised morris when we discussed it with her. And when Mrs. Maynard was in last night, she said we ought to open with a sword dance and close with one—a 'Rapper' dance if we could. I saw Miss Burnett again before Frühstück and she agreed that it would made a sm—er—splendid opening and closing to the show."

"And we and Welsen are getting up an orchestra," Rosalind Wynyard put in eagerly. "We wanted to ask you if it would be possible to arrange for some rehearsals. Our idea was to play at intervals during the afternoon."

"And," Julie remarked, "Mrs. Maynard will sing for us."—This being a formal occasion, she managed to remember not to say "Auntie Jo".

Miss Annersley's eyebrows went up at this intelligence. "How in the world did you manage to get her to agree to that?" she exclaimed.

"It was Madge who thought of it," Julie responded. Then she added demurely, "You see, we all pointed out to Auntie Jo what a help she could be both to the San. *and* school if she only would. She dithered about it at first, but she gave in finally. But she did say that it was only because this is our first Sale up here and she wanted to do what she could to start us off. She won't make a practice of it, though."

"Well, I congratulate you all on pulling it off. Now is that all?"

"All we've thought of so far," Annis returned. "We did think of clock-golf, but Mrs. Maynard seems to think the garden won't be fit for use by that time."

"She's quite right there. Even if the snow has gone, which is most unlikely, the garden will be a sea of mud. No; I'm afraid you'll have to miss that."

"Mrs. Maynard said we ought to move the Sale to the end of the Summer term," Rosalie put in. "Then we could use the garden for everything, of course."

"We'll think of that for another year," the Head promised.

"And then *we* shan't be here!" Clem groaned. "There are times when I wish I was a good two years younger. I've had such fun here!"

"But you're going on to Welsen for a year, aren't you?" the Head asked. "At least, that was the last I heard. If you're there, you'll be coming up with the rest and you'll be on the Welsen stall no doubt. Don't be so gloomy, Clem!"

There was no time for Clem to repudiate this, for the door opened and Joey Maynard entered. She tossed down the huge shawl in which she had muffled herself for the run across from Freudesheim and came over to sit by the Head.

"Well, here I am. Why d'you want me?" she demanded. "I was in the middle of the new chapter of *Ruth goes Camping*—my new juvenile, you know. I've got *Ruth* and her chum, *Shirley* into a very sticky patch and I don't see how to get them out, so I thought I might as well come over here and see what's going on. If it hadn't been for that, I may tell you, you wouldn't have seen me much before this afternoon."

Miss Annersley glanced at the clock, "Almost eleven," she said. "Girls, what are you doing after Break?"

"History essay for us," Julie said promptly. "And we have gym at eleven-thirty. Our history essay is unsupervized—" she broke off and looked at the Head hopefully.

"And you Lower Sixth people?" Miss Annersley queried.

"Art—and we ought to be going over now," Nora Penley informed her.

"Then I won't keep you. Yes; you must go. You have only one art lesson in the week unless you are taking extra art and you mustn't miss any of it. You can get all the news from the others afterwards. Off you go!"

There was no arguing with the Head when she spoke in that tone. Off the disgruntled Lower VI went, leaving their seniors to enjoy a cup of hot chocolate which Miss Annersley rang for when they had gone. Their only comfort was that the Head scribbled a note for them to take to Herr Laubach, the irritable art master, explaining why they were late.

When they had gone, Miss Annersley laid all the latest plans before Jo who instantly agreed to cut some tiny jigsaws for their bags. She had brought her fret-saw machine with her, but owned that she had never touched it for the last two or three years. Still, as she pointed out, cutting jigsaw puzzles is something that doesn't need continual practice.

"I've heaps of small pieces of wood and a pile of pretty pictures," she said. "It's quick work, once you get started, and I can easily do you a couple of dozen. The worst part of the job is sticking the pictures on to the wood. What about some of you coming over this afternoon for Kaffee und Kuchen and helping me? Then I could begin cutting to-morrow."

"It would be wizard," Julie replied, "but what about your book, Auntie Jo?"

"That won't hurt for a few days' rest. In fact, it might be quite a good thing. I've been going hard ever since Christmas and a short break will freshen me up. And I've got two lovely *big* pictures and I think I've got wood the right size for them. If so, I'll cut you a couple of monsters and you can either sell or raffle them, whichever you please. And *they* can go to the toy-stall, whoever has it."

"It's the two Lower Fourths this year." Madge said. "They'll be thrilled to bits, Mrs. Maynard. They're to have Tom Gay's toy chalet for a raffle, but I know they haven't anything else. Your jigsaw will just fill the bill."

"It's only if I have large enough sheets of wood," Jo warned her. "Better say nothing about it to them until I know that. I'll have a good rootle round this afternoon and you can tell them to-morrow. Now how many of you can come to me?"

The girls looked eagerly at Miss Annersley who laughed as she said, "What about time-tables? I know Lower VI have science, so they must be counted out. What about you people?"

Afternoons at the Chalet School were largely given up to specialist work for Upper VI. For example Julie, who hoped to read Law at Oxford when schooldays ended, had work in logic and Roman Law with Miss Armitage three afternoons in the week. Madge Herbert, who meant to teach modern languages later on, had extra work in French and German and also an Italian lesson with Miss Denny. Rosalind was musical and took extra lessons in harmony, counterpoint and thoroughbass. The same sort of thing happened to most of the others. Only lovely Rosalie Way and the quiet Edris Young took no extras. Rosalie was destined to appear in society with a capital S when her schooldays were over and Edris was looking forward to giving help in her father's big, slum parish in a north country city. Time-tables, therefore, were of paramount importance in Upper VI.

After ten minutes or so, Miss Annersley discovered that only Edris, Rosalie and Veronica would be free at sixteen o'clock. Julie had a coaching in logic at seventeen and the rest would be working until then.

"O.K.," Jo said cheerfully. "You three come along at sixteen this afternoon. I'll give you Kaffee und Kuchen—cream-cakes, my loves!—and then we'll all turn to and glue pictures to wood until eighteen. That O.K.?" she turned to Miss Annersley who nodded assent. Then she added, "I'll send a cream-cake each for the rest of you when those three come home."

"And very nice, too," the Head said, anticipating the excitement this would rouse. "You can change for the evening before you go over and take overalls with you. Now you had better go to your form-room. The bell will ring in a minute or two and you should be ready to go to gym. Jo, I want a word with you, please."

Jo had stood up and reached for her shawl. Now she sat down again as the prefects left the room and when the door had closed on Veronica, she turned to the Head.

"Well, what's all this in aid of?"

Miss Annersley went to the point at once. "You've heard about our new girl, Prunella Davidson?"

Jo nodded with a chuckle. "*And* how! She seems to have accomplished what I should always have said was the impossible where Len is concerned."

"What do you mean?" Miss Annersley demanded, sitting bolt upright at this.

"From Len's own confession, Prunella sent her into a real,

tearing rage. I got the whole yarn from her last Friday when I went up to her after she was in bed. I nearly collapsed with shock! I must say they both seem to have gone out of their way to be as rude to each other as they possibly could!"

"This is news to me. When did it all happen?"

"The day Len came down with 'flu. No doubt that had something to do with it. She's far and away the sweetest-tempered of the whole eight. If she were feeling off-colour, though, she might lose her temper as badly as she seems to have done. Still, that's all in the past now. What *about* Prunella?"

Miss Annersley gave up the question of Len's temper and leaned forward. "It isn't often that I'm puzzled by a girl, Jo, as I think you'll own; but I must confess Prunella has me guessing—and not me only. It's *all* the staff."

"In what way?" Jo demanded, wide-eyed. "I should have said there wasn't a girl in the world you couldn't see through sooner or later. I know you saw through *me* soon enough!" she added with a rueful chuckle.

"It's rather a long story. To begin at the beginning, when Mrs. Davidson wrote to me, she told me that they were sending her to us because she really was impossibly naughty. Professor Davidson had been offered an appointment to a group of scientists who were going out to the Congo regions to investigate insect bearers of disease. It was a very good appointment, so he accepted. Mrs. Davidson went with him. Her mother was delighted to take Prunella who was not quite ten then and who was at a quite good preparatory school in the town where they all lived."

"Why didn't she stay and look after Prunella?" Jo asked.

"Because, it seems, he is rather a delicate man and she wanted to be able to keep an eye on him."

"Oh, I see. Well, go on—though I can guess what happened."

"Old Mrs. Purdy spoilt Prunella outrageously. I should explain that she is the only grandchild, though she has three uncles. None of them happen to be married so Prunella is the one child of her generation in *that* family."

"What a mistake!" Jo, the proud mother of eight, had no use for single children or very small families. She always declared that the more you had the easier it was and the better for the children themselves.

Miss Annersley smiled at her before she went on. "Six months ago, old Mrs. Purdy died. The work of the commission was more or less finished by that time, so Professor Davidson resigned his post and he and Mrs. Davidson came home. They were looking forward to having the child with them again, but unfortunately, she made life hardly worth living after the first day or two. She was rude, noisy, either sulked or flared up into downright impudence when she was called to order, and her language—well, Mrs. Davidson said she'd had no idea so much slang existed."

"And—but look here, Hilda! From all my three and Barbara Chester have said when they've come home, Prunella is the exact opposite of all that. They've all four complained to me that she talks like her own great-grandmother and I gather that the Great Row took place because she would insist on giving Len her full name. Len hates it—silly little ass!—and ticked Prunella off. Then Prunella made remarks about people using foolish abbreviations and applied them to Jack and me. That made Len see red, of course. Hence, the row!"

"I have been privileged to hear that Prunella insists on calling everyone by her full name," the Head said drily. "I must say that, so far as I've met her in form, she isn't too unlike the rest—a little quieter and distinctly more formal in her language and certainly entirely free from all slang. But that is all."

"Then what are you worrying about?"

"Well, I have the feeling that much of her demureness and prim speech isn't natural to her. It's put on, in fact. No; I can't tell you *why* I feel that way; but I do. And in view of all her mother wrote to me, I simply can't understand it. By the way, she doesn't use any really startling language in lessons."

"I see." Jo ruminated for a minute or two. Then she spoke. "It's rather a problem, I admit. You say that you feel all this primness isn't like her. In fact, unless her mother was pulling your leg—and I must say that strikes me as a most outrageous thing for a prospective parent to do!—it *is* unlike her."

"It's no more outrageous than your suggestion!" the Head said heatedly. "Do try to be serious for once, Jo! I'd better tell you that she came up at Staff meeting—her name, I mean. Don't be so absurd!—and everyone says the same thing."

Jo grinned before she relapsed again into deep thought. "Well," she said finally, "I should say that, for one thing, she had a bad shock over her grandmother's death. Do you know if the old lady was ill long?"

"Only a few days. It was bronchitis and turned to pneumonia. She was very old—well over eighty, I believe—and she couldn't stand up to it."

"I see. Well, so far as I can judge, this is what's happened. Grannie spoiled her precious grandchild to the top of her bent. Then she died suddenly and a girl of fourteen was left to face parents she hadn't seen for four years or more, so they were more or less strangers to her. They come home and instead of finding the dear little daughter they've been fondly picturing, come up against a queer, half-grown creature who has been allowed to get badly out of hand—she *must*, or her mother would never have written to you like that!—and, as you might expect, they try to reform her. Now I don't for a moment suppose that Prunella realized it. She's too young, for one thing. But sub-consciously she probably felt that when they tried to bring her to heel a bit, they were criticizing her grandmother. That put her back up and probably made her a great deal worse than she would have been."

The Head nodded as Jo stopped for breath. "I'd got that far myself. But how do you account for her complete change of attitude since she came to school?"

Jo chuckled. "If you ask me, her mother told her she had written to you and the kid made up her mind she'd show everyone. I don't know her from Adam as yet, but I know what I'd have done if it had been me!"

"But Mrs. Davidson told me in her letter that she was saying nothing to Prunella and I thought that was wise of her. I quite see that the child would be furious if *that* had happened."

"Then she found out somehow! I'm certain of it! And the result is that she's come over all prunes and prisms—at any rate with the other girls. Just what I'd have done myself! I'd have tried my level best to keep everyone guessing. But I doubt," she added thoughtfully, "if I could have kept it up all this time. I'd have broken down much sooner than this."

"I—wonder! It would explain a good deal."

"It would explain everything. I expect Prunella came here feeling completely out of gear and at odds with the whole world. From being Granny's darling who can't do anything wrong, she has suddenly become a naughty, tiresome child who can't do anything *right* and is pulled up for things that everyone ignored or laughed at until her parents came home and took it on."

"There's a good deal in that. But in that case, there's nothing we can do about it."

"Not a single thing," Jo agreed. "*But* if Prunella can once make friends—*real* friends—with any one girl, she'll probably begin to slip and then the true Prunella will come to the surface."

Miss Annersley gave her a queer look. "I'm rather inclined to think that that very thing has begun to happen."

"Not really?" Jo spoke eagerly. "Who is it? Someone like our one and only Mary-Lou? Or—or Vi Lucy? Either of those two would do her a world of good."

"Not so far as I know. No, my dear. You must prepare yourself for a shock. During the past day or two the girl with whom she has seemed most friendly is your own Len."

"*What!*" Jo gasped aloud and sat silent for a full minute. Then she burst out, "But that's mad! Len's only eleven! Prunella must be at least three years older!"

"I know. But I've seen them together three or four times and I must say they seemed to be getting on amazingly well together."

"But—but—the last I heard, they'd had this row I told you about and Len wasn't at all anxious to apologize for her rudeness—and she *was* abominably rude from what she told me!" Jo cried.

"I can quite believe it. Sweet-tempered people are always the worst when they do let themselves go. I can imagine that once she was really roused Len would be worse than ever Margot is—or *could* be might be better. I also think that the training your girls have had has taught them that one doesn't let everything go, even when one is in a righteous rage. And I don't doubt Len felt she was right."

Jo was silent again. Then she said more quietly, "I can't see why those wretched girls of mine seem to fall for people older than themselves. Look at Margot and Emerence Hope!"

"I know. But don't forget, Jo, that their time in Canada made them very much more independent than the average English girl of their age. Their years may be only eleven, but in most other things, they are a good two years older than that."

"Yes; I suppose there's something in that."

"And so far as Emerence is concerned, she has behaved much better these last two terms. I really begin to think we shall make something of her. And Margot has improved enormously, too. And this isn't the first friendship we've had between girls of those ages. Think of Mary-Lou and Clem Barrass. They have other chums of their own ages, but those two are still heart and soul with each other, though Clem is almost eighteen and Mary-Lou isn't fifteen till July."

Jo nodded. "I see. But there again, Mary-Lou is older than her age. I'm glad to hear about Emerence. She was little short of a young criminal when she first came, from all you told me. As for Margot, she's a long way from being a little pink angel, my dear, so don't deceive yourself! But she has learnt to control her temper in the main, poor lamb, and that's something for which we may all be deeply thankful. But she's still chockfull of mischief, bless her!"

"I know," the Head said calmly. "She wouldn't be your girl if she wasn't! When I look back and remember all the times you did the maddest things, I wonder my hair isn't as white as Nell Wilson's!"

Jo grinned broadly. "Yes; I did stand you up on your ears at times, didn't I? But *look* what a nice creature I've grown into since!"

"Well, for sheer bounce and conceit, commend me to that!" the Head cried.

Jo stood up. "I must be off! Duty calls! I can see my way through that wretched chapter now. As for Prunella, my advice is leave her alone. She'll come out of this fit sooner or later and it looks like being sooner, from what you say. She's a little wretch, all the same. But I do sympathize with her if I'm right, and I'll bet my bottom dollar that I am!"

"It wouldn't surprise me. You have an uncanny knack of getting into other people's skins, Jo. You always did have. Very well; I'll take your advice and leave her to the girls. But I'm glad to have things ironed out. I was really worried about the whole thing. Prunella didn't seem normal, especially in view of her mother's letter. Now you run along to your chapter. I'm due for Upper IVA's general literature as soon as the bell goes."

"And there it goes." Jo muffled herself in her shawl. "Ta-ta! See you later!" With which she went racing off while the Head picked up an anthology of poetry and made her stately way along to Upper IVA for their lesson.

Chapter IX

Trip to Lucerne

THANKS to the influenza and the weather, the school had had no expeditions worthy the name, to quote Julie Lucy. Neither, for that matter, had they had what might be called a proper half-term holiday. The Head, after consulting the staff and Miss Wilson from Welsen, had decided against it. So much time had been lost in other ways that in a short term like the Easter term, work had suffered badly.

"Sickening!" Vi Lucy grumbled one evening after Abendessen when they were all in their common-rooms, working hard at objects for the Sale.

"Sickening all right," Mary-Lou agreed. "Just the same, you can't really blame anyone, Vi."

"Can't you? *I* jolly well can. I can blame the Head—and Auntie Madge—and—and everyone who says what about our hols."

"O.K. You go and do it to their faces, then!" her friend retorted.

Vi grinned. "I'd like to live a *little* longer," she said simply.

This event took place during the third week in March. They had had a few days of warm sun, followed by a rain-storm that helped to wash away quite a good deal of snow. The sudden warmth had also affected the snow on the great mountains and, more than once, the girls heard a distant sound like thunder and knew it for an avalanche. They even had the excitement of a minor one themselves. But luckily, the thickly wooded slopes dispersed the snow, though some trees went down beneath the impact of boulders carried along with the snow and ice. However, no harm was done to the village. In the meantime, they had their thrills free.

Another thrill was coming for them that week—quite a different kind of thrill. On the Friday morning, the Head, instead of dismissing them after Prayers, desired them to sit down. When they were all seated and looking eagerly at her, she made an announcement that set the whole school agog with excitement.

"You haven't been able to have any proper expeditions so far this term," she began in her fluent, easy German. "You all know why. However, the weather forecast is good for the weekend and the 'flu seems to have cleared up, so to-morrow we are going down to spend the day at Lucerne. Frühstück will be at half-past seven and we go down to Interlaken by the half-past eight train. From there, we go by motor-coach to the end of Lake Brienz to Brienz itself where we take another train to Lucerne. Now listen to me!" as the buzz of excitement rose high. "I have a warning to give you."

The school hushed at once and looked at her anxiously.

"This is it," she went on slowly. "Any girl who is reported to me to-day for any kind of bad behaviour *will not go*. Is that understood?"

They were silent before this awful idea. Then Julie, as Head Girl, stood up and said very properly, "Yes, Miss Annersley. But I'm sure," she added, "that everyone will be able to go. And thank you very much for arranging it for us."

The Head hid a smile. Julie's German was by no means as fluent as her French and she expressed herself very stiltedly and correctly. When the Head Girl had sat down after this effort, Miss Annersley concluded her remarks with a glance at her watch.

"You will all go to bed early as to-morrow you must be up

a good half-hour sooner than usual and it will be a long day for you. You will be called at half-past six and when you are dressed, you may finish your cubicle work for once. School uniform and your big coats and berets, please. One last thing. Miss o'Ryan will take Bank immediately after the rest period this afternoon. Lower IVB go to her first and so on, up the school. Don't try to draw too much. It will only mean a refusal and you'll want just enough to buy a souvenir or two of your visit."

At this point, the faces of one or two people fell considerably, notably Emerence Hope's. That young woman was always far too plentifully supplied to please the school authorities and unless a check were put on her, would have squandered her money lavishly. However, they knew better than to protest, so they said nothing. The Head, watching from her vantage point on the daïs, chuckled to herself. She knew what they were thinking.

She spoke a final sentence or two. "That is all for the moment. You will hear about the other arrangements later on." She nodded to Miss Lawrence who was seated at the piano and at once swung round, struck up *The Teddybears' Picnic*, and the school turned and marched out, form by form, only prevented from giving way to its excitement by that horrid warning of the Head's.

As a result of that, however, they behaved as much like angels as any normal schoolgirl could be expected to behave. No one merited the punishment and when half-past eight came next morning, they were drawn up in serried ranks on the tiny station platform and marched smartly into the little coaches when the mountain train drew up for them. They all knew what they had to do and who would be their escort mistresses and they had also been reminded that they would be in uniform and must behave decently or they might bring disgrace on the school.

No one wanted to do such a thing, and everyone had made up her mind to be good. But the best of human kind is only mortal and before they returned to the Görnetz Platz that night, they were to be involved in behaviour that was anything but good—some of them, at least—and one girl was to establish herself with them for the remainder of her school career.

They had been divided into eight groups of seventeen girls each. Each group had two mistresses and two prefects in charge and, as far as possible, friends had been allowed to be together. This was why Emerence Hope and Margot Maynard, two thoroughly naughty girls, were paired off. In the rest of that particular set was what was known as "The Gang", eleven girls, led by Mary-Lou. To it had been added the two sinners, Len and Con Maynard, and Prunella Davidson. In charge of them were Miss o'Ryan and Miss Wilmot, two old friends, and Julie and Clem as prefects.

"And surely, with those four *and* Mary-Lou and Co., even Emerence and Margot can't get into any mischief," Miss Annersley had said to Mdlle when she was arranging it two evenings before. Much, much later, she was to own that it would take a flock of archangels to guarantee *that* and fully agreed with Miss Lawrence's dictum that even so the guardian angels of the pair must work overtime, anyhow!

When they were turned out of the train at Lucerne, the girls instantly formed up into their proper groups, accompanied by mistresses and prefects and were all marched out, looking very trim and proper and all that girls ought to be.

Miss o'Ryan sent Julie and Clem to the tail of her little procession, asked Miss Wilmot to head it with the two leaders, Vi Lucy and Barbara Chester, and herself walked in line with Mary-Lou and her "sister by marriage", Verity-Anne Carey, who were about the middle.

"And with luck, no one can possibly make a show of herself in *that* order," she had remarked to Nancy Wilmot when they were settling it. “Sure, Mary-Lou can keep order nearly as well as Julie or Clem or Annis, any day of the week, and *I’ll* be there as well to back them up.”

“Joey Maynard says that Mary-Lou is slated for Head Girl when the time comes,” Miss Wilmot had replied. “She certainly looks like achieving it. All the same, Biddy, Margot and Emerence are a lovely handful for anyone, so we’ll just keep an extra eye handy for them.”

Biddy o’Ryan fully agreed with this.

Some of the groups were marched straight across the Seebrucke which crosses the Reuss very nearly at the point where it emerges from Lake Lucerne. The group in charge of the Head and Mdlle turned left as they left the station and made for the Jesuitenkirche. Miss o’Ryan and Miss Wilmot turned right and Miss Wilmot, with Vi and Barbara swung off down the Fronburgstrasse, making for the Inseli Park.

“What is there to see there, I wonder?” Len observed to Prunella with whom she had paired off.

Miss o’Ryan overheard the question and replied to it. “A good view of the lake for one thing,” she told the pair. “However, I’m really taking you this way to let the rest get off. Then we’ll go back and cross the Seebrucke to get into the old town which is much the most interesting part.”

“Isn’t that where the Dying Lion Monument is?” Julie asked. Miss o’Ryan’s clear voice had carried on the air to her and she had wondered about this, having seen and admired the wonderful memorial to the Swiss Guard.

“It is so. We’ll go and see it presently. Meanwhile, just be turning across this little bridge.”

“Is the park on an island?” Verity-Anne asked in her silvery voice.

But Miss o’Ryan was busy explaining something to Len

Maynard and did not hear her. No one else knew, so the question had to remain unanswered.

Miss Wilmot knew her way and she led the girls across the comparatively narrow Park to the far side where she lined them up and flung out her hand. "Look!" she said dramatically.

They pressed forward eagerly and a chorus of, "Ooh!" of admiration broke from them as they saw the two great peaks of the Rigi and Pilatus. The Rigi, with its gentle slopes clad in pasture and woodland with drifts of snow still lying here and there on the upper slopes, enchanted them. When they turned to Pilatus with its terrible precipices and scarred flanks and the great, craggy spires of rock, they gave another, "Ooh!" this time, of awe.

"The Rigi—and Pilatus," Miss o'Ryan said, pointing to each in turn.

"Pilatus? Is that after Pontius Pilate?" Mary-Lou asked after a long, thoughtful look at the great, sinister-looking mountain.

"It is!" Miss o'Ryan told her. "There's a legend that when Pontius Pilate died, his body was flung into the Tiber—you know he got into trouble with the Roman authorities after the Crucifixion? And he was sent to Spain, I believe it was, which was practically exile. Claudia Procula, his wife, went with him. She seems to have been a most devoted wife!—and the Tiber wouldn't keep it. It was cast up somewhere along the banks. Then they tried a lake in the Appenines and that rejected him, too.

"So at last they brought his body to the lake near the summit of Mount Pilatus and cast it in there and there it is until the Judgment Day."

"How ghastly!" Mary-Lou turned to look again at the cleft and river mountain. Then she said with the severe common sense which characterized most of her statements, "I suppose all those precipices and so on were caused by an earthquake? D'you think it could be an extinct volcano?"

Miss o'Ryan shook her head. "Now that's asking something, Mary-Lou! I'm afraid I can't tell you. You must ask Miss Moore when we get back to school."

"Oh, I just wondered," Mary-Lou replied in her nonchalant way.

"Goodness!" Len cried at that moment. "There's a train on it! Look!"

They all turned and stared in the direction in which she was pointing and there, sure enough, was a train creeping up the steep slope to the summit.

"Gosh!" Lesley Malcolm said in awed tones. "A train going up to where poor old Pilate was buried!"

Miss o'Ryan laughed. "I don't suppose it worries him. Well, the rest should be clear now. Suppose we go back and cross over to the Old Town?"

She formed them into line again and marched them along the Inseli Quai, down the Bahnhof Platz and across the Seebrucke. In the middle of the bridge, she stopped them and bade them look down the lake. They swung to the side and gazed eagerly. One or two exclaimed with disappointment.

"Why, I thought Lucerne was quite a large lake!" Barbara cried. "But it looks quite small from here."

The two mistresses looked at each other and laughed. Miss o'Ryan took pity on them and explained. "Sure, 'tis a most deceiving lake it is. If we went on a steamer, though, you'd see that where it seems to close up under the shoulder of the Rigi, there is a passage, and beyond that the lake fans out in another stretch of water, running away to Brunner which is the second largest town on its shores."

"Are we going to do that?" Clem asked eagerly.

"Not to-day. There wouldn't be time. But I shan't be surprised if we manage it later on—say next term. Now turn to the other side of the bridge and look at the river—Hi, Margot! I didn't tell you to climb up! Come down at once!"

When Miss o'Ryan spoke like that, she meant to be obeyed and Margot slid to the ground again, murmuring something about, "I only wanted to have a good look at it."

"Behave yourself, you little ass!" Julie told her in an undertone. "Do you want to miss the next expedition?"

Margot definitely did not. She pressed up to the side of the bridge in silence and they saw, to their delight, the Kapellebrucke with the Wasserthurm built on to it. Miss o'Ryan pointed out how the bridge is thrown diagonally across the Reuss and the elder girls listened. But Con Maynard, peering down at the green waters of the Reuss below, gave a violent shiver.

"What a rate it goes at! Look, Mary-Lou! Isn't it *swift*?"

Mary-Lou looked. "You're right," she said. "It does go at a lick. I wouldn't like to fall in. It strikes me it would take something to get you out again."

The mistresses heard her and Miss Wilmot promptly retorted, "Well, you're getting no chances of falling in to-day I can assure you. Come along, all of you. You've stood and stared long enough and we've quite a good deal to see before Mittagessen."

They moved on, but Mary-Lou murmured to those near enough to hear,

> "'What is this life if, full of care,
> We have no time to stand and stare?'"

"You've had all the time you need," Miss o'Ryan swiftly interposed. "Get *on*, Mary-Lou, and don't be quoting poetry at your elders and betters like that."

Mary-Lou went scarlet. "I forgot she had ears like a hare," she said *sotto voce* to Verity-Anne as the girls finally left the bridge to cross the Schwannen Platz, walk along the Schweizerhof Quai, and finally turn down the Alpenstrasse in quest of the Lion of Lucerne.

When they reached the famous monument to the Swiss Guard, they stood silent as they gazed at Thorwaldsen's masterpiece, the huge lion, lying dying with the shaft of a broken spear protruding from his flank, one enormous paw flung protectingly over a shield, bearing the arms of Royal France, while at his head stands the red cross on the shield of Switzerland.

"How simply marvellous!" Barbara Chester breathed. "Fancy cutting it like that in the limestone of the cliff."

"And the clear pool below adds to it," Prunella remarked, pointing to the still water in which the Monument is reflected clearly. "What does it mean, please, Miss o'Ryan?"

"You've all heard of the Swiss Guard which stood against the Revolutionaries when they were trying to break into the royal apartments in search of Louis XVI and Marie-Antoinette? As you know, the Guard died almost to a man. Thorwaldsen, the famous Danish sculptor, designed this in their honour, though it was cut by a Swiss sculptor whose name I forget for the moment. Yes; it is a wonderful statue."

"Mother told me that it was a man from Constance, called Ahorn," Len Maynard put in. "She told me that when she was telling us about the French Revolution."

"Trust her to know!" Miss Wilmot laughed. "She always did have a memory like a fly-paper!"

"She seems to have passed it on," Miss o'Ryan said thoughtfully. "Now, girls, look at that little chapel over there. A solemn Mass is said for the repose of the souls of the Swiss Guard every tenth of August when the event took place. Some other time we'll go and look at it and see if we can see the altar-cloth embroidered by the Duchesse d'Angoulême, the eldest daughter of Louis and Marie-Antoinette, after she had escaped into Switzerland. Just at present, we'll go and visit the Glacier Gardens which are next door, so to speak."

They moved away to the Gardens where they were regaled by the sight of glacier mills, great holes worn by the ice of the prehistoric glacier that covered all this part of Europe at one time, skulls and bones of prehistoric animals, and great boulders which were the remnants of moraines of that same glacier and were now connected by a series of steps and bridges.

What really thrilled the younger girls, though, was the reconstruction of a prehistoric village, and they shrieked with excitement when Miss o'Ryan pointed out that there had been careless cooks long before the days of Alfred the Great for, still stuck to one side of the remains of the pot in which it had been cooked, were the remains of some well-scorched food!

"Where next?" Julie asked as they finally turned away.

Miss o'Ryan consulted her watch. "Goodness! It's nearly thirteen o'clock! We've been ages over this. We must cross to the New Town and hunt up our restaurant at once or we'll be throwing out all their arrangements!"

"Oh, *could* we go by the crooked bridge?" Margot pleaded.

"We can. Come along, all of you, and step out, too. We'll have to hurry!"

Hurry they did, and reached the opening to the red-tiled bridge in short order.

"Keep your eyes open as you go across, girls!" Miss Wilmot called.

"Why?" Emerence asked suspiciously.

"Oh, I'm telling you nothing. You'll see for yourself!" Miss Wilmot glanced at her colleague and the pair went off into fits of laughter, greatly to the mystification of the girls who saw nothing to laugh at.

They entered the bridge and then cries of delight broke from everyone. It had been odd enough to see a roofed-in bridge. But underneath the roof were triangular pictures of different events in the history of the Swiss Confederation. They were all enchanted and would have lingered a good hour if it had been allowed.

"No; you can't loiter," Miss Wilmot told them firmly. "Besides, we'll be coming again one day and you can take time for it then."

However, once they were across, she relented enough to bid them turn and look back and fresh cries broke from them, for now they saw pictures of the lives of the two great local saints—St. Maurice and St. Leodgar, better known as St. Leger nowadays.

"What a *wizard* idea!" Catriona Watson exclaimed. "Oh I do like that! I hope we do come again—and jolly soon, too! I want a good look at *all* the pictures!"

"So do I!" cried her chum, Christine Vincent.

"I'll bring it up at the next Staff meeting," Miss o'Ryan promised them solemnly.

They both went red and said no more and Miss Wilmot hurried them on.

Mittagessen was at the Restaurant Schwannen, a garden restaurant and, as they found when they reached it and had settled round their table, a glorious view was to be had of the lake and the two great mountains which were still snow-covered on the upper slopes, though further down, the fresh, young green of spring was appearing.

"I'm glad spring is coming!" Len remarked to Prunella as they disposed of their Kaassuppe, a cheese soup for which Lucerne is famous. "It's been fun to have ski-ing and tobogganing and all that, but I'm getting tired of it now."

Prunella, who seemed, for some reason, to have forgotten that she was the school's "Miss Prim", nodded. "I'd like to see flowers and grass myself for a change. Not that winter-sporting isn't fun. But it's gone on so *long*!"

Miss Wilmot overheard them. "You'll get accustomed to it in time," she said, eyeing Prunella with interest. "Anyhow, spring and summer out here should be wonderful. I remember when the school was in Tirol how we used to revel in the flowers." She raised her voice. "Miss o'Ryan, do you remember the Valley of Flowers, up above the Tiernsee?"

Miss o'Ryan nodded. "I should just think so! You could smell it long before you ever got to it. And the flowers! The most marvellous flowers you ever saw!"

"It sounds wizard," Mary-Lou said pensively. A familiar voice struck on her ear and she looked up to see another group filing in to join them at the long table which had been half-empty up to this. "Hello, Betsy! Aren't you *late*?"

Miss o'Ryan, at the head of the table, was making more or less the same remark to Miss Dene who headed the party.

"What on earth have you been doing, Rosalie? Haven't your crowd behaved themselves like little ladies?"

"They might have been worse," Miss Dene said cautiously. "What about yours?"

"Apart from young Margot trying to climb to the parapet of the Seebrucke, they have been a credit to the school, the creatures."

"Ah! But I have Heather Unwin, Nora Fitzgerald, Connie Winter and Nancy Wadham," Miss Dene said with meaning.

"Ye poor creature! Still, I *have* got Margot, and Emerence into the bargain."

"If all the archangels took charge of my four demons, I believe they'd *still* find some way of distinguishing themselves!" Miss Dene retorted as she left them and went to take her seat at the other end of the table, leaving everyone near enough to have overheard this colloquy agog with curiosity to know what the wicked quartette had been doing. However, for that they had to wait until they were back at school when they learned that the young sinners had contrived to lose themselves well and truly in the wooded grounds of the Château Gutsch where they had been taken for coffee as a special treat, and it had been a good twenty-five minutes before they were found.

However, no one had much time to worry about their doings, for the waiter was removing the empty soup bowls and replacing them with plates of Kugelipastete, a vol-au-vent or meat-patty for which Lucerne is renowned. In the season, it is served with a salad of vegetables and mushrooms. To-day, the mushrooms were missing, but that made no difference to hungry schoolgirls who revelled in it. As Vi Lucy said afterwards, there really is a *something* about foreign cookery! Julie and Clem were rude enough to laugh at this dictum, but Vi remained unperturbed, for her own clan fully agreed with her.

The meal was crowned by something they all enjoyed—large, high, bun-like cakes hollowed out and filled with stiffly-whipped cream. These luscious things are known as Kugelhopfen and it was as well they had not to be eaten in the fingers!

"Aren't they *wizard*!" sighed Barbara as she scraped the last remains of cream off her plate.

Miss o'Ryan gave her a twinkling look from the end of the table. "Like another, Barbara?"

Barbara grinned. "I *couldn't*," she said truthfully. "They're simply gorgeous, but—"

"Rather sick-making if you ate more than one, I should think," Emerence calmly finished for her.

Miss Wilmot, sitting opposite the young lady, looked at her with a peculiar thoughtfulness which made Emerence blush furiously and drop her eyes. All the mistress said, however, was, "Now you be careful, Emerence."

As Margot chose that moment to kick her bosom friend under the table as a gentle reminder that you didn't say that sort of thing in front of the staff—not if you knew what was good for you—the stormy petrel of the school—one of them, at any rate—thought it advisable to hold her tongue and the meal ended in amity.

"Finished, everyone?" Miss o'Ryan demanded. "Then come along, all of you. Some of the others are due now and we mustn't keep them waiting. Line up and lead off, Julie and Clem. Turn through that doorway and you can all wash your hands before we go on to see what else we can."

Twenty minutes later, they crossed the Reuss again, this time by the Spreurbrucke which crosses the river below the Kapellebrucke and has a roof like the Kapellebrucke only the pictures inside are rather fearsome representations of the Dance of Death. As it is a good mile down the river, they went by motor-bus to the bridge and when they had crossed, took another up to the National Quai where the mistresses proposed they should work off the effects of their substantial meal by strolling along the lake-side under the chestnut trees which were just beginning to show buds.

"You may break lines," Miss o'Ryan said. "Only remember that you must not make exhibitions of yourselves. When you've had enough, we'll find a bus and go to see the cathedral; but I know the Head and Mdlle meant to take their party there after Mittagessen, so we'll give them a chance to finish before we go."

It *should* have been safe enough. The Quais are all railed off and the girls had been well reminded about the need for good behaviour. But, as Miss Annersley said resignedly when discussing the affair with the staff later on, you can never back on schoolgirls.

It began with Lesley Malcolm tripping over something and landing on all fours on the ground with a resounding *cr-rack!* that made those near at hand rush to help her up. Miss Wilmot came flying to see what she had done. The damage was grazed hands, a nasty cut on one knee and a huge bruise beginning on the other and, of course, the knees of both stockings cut out.

Luckily, Matron allowed no one to go off on expeditions without a small first-aid case. Even more luckily, there was an empty seat close at hand. Helped by Miss Wilmot and Julie, Lesley was assisted to the seat and, while the mistress set to work to dab her injuries with iodine and then bandage them, Miss o'Ryan looked round to call the others together. There could be no more walking for poor Lesley, who was biting her lips and trying not to cry out as the iodine stung her up. They had better all board a bus and make a circular tour of the city, after which they would have time only for Kaffee und Kuchen before they went to the station, homeward bound.

Some of the girls were fairly close at hand. Some were quite a little way off. Margot and Emerence were the furthest, with Prunella and Len not far away. Even as the mistress set off at her best walking pace to fetch them, Margot suddenly dabbed at Emerence and then turned and fled along the Quai, laughing as she went. Emerence followed in full chase. Just as she reached her partner in crime, Margot swung herself up on to the top railing and sat there. Emerence, going full tilt, was unable to stop herself at once. She stumbled and floundered up against Margot who overbalanced and fell into the lake with a wild shriek which brought everyone within earshot to the spot. At the same moment, Prunella, who had seen the whole thing, wrenched off her coat, tossed aside her beret, kicked off her shoes and, before anyone could prevent her, had climbed the railings and dived with a perfect dive, straight for the spot where Margot's golden head had just appeared above the steely blue waters of the lake.

Chapter X

Prunella to the Rescue

THE first thing Miss o'Ryan had to do was to catch hold of Len and forcibly restrain her from going in after her sister. Mercifully for everyone, Con was with the group round Lesley, hemmed in by some of the bigger girls, and Miss Wilmot, who had glimpsed what had happened, kept the young woman very busy, holding plaster and scissors and bandages while she gave the others a look that warned them to hold their tongues about what had happened. Con had heard the scream, but seeing the mistress continuing to first-aid Lesley in the calmest way, she took it for granted that her sister was, as she said later, just fooling as usual and gave her full attention to her present chore.

Miss Wilmot enforced the command she had looked by saying rather fiercely, "Stand round, girls, and be a screen. We don't want passers-by to imagine that Lesley is half-killed!" Which kept them there, though those at the back were unable to refrain from turning their heads to see what was happening.

As for the others, they all rushed to the rails, as well as such other folk as happened to be taking a stroll that sunny afternoon. In any case, help was speedily forth-coming for the two in the water. A man who had been rowing lazily towards the nearest landing saw all that happened and bent to his oars in a way that literally drove his boat through the water to the spot where Prunella had already reached Margot and was holding her up. But the snow-fed lake was icy cold and even as she trod water as vigorously as she could, she was wondering how long it would be before the numbing chill would paralyse her completely.

Even faster than the boatman, however, came help from the land. A doctor from nearby had been taking a turn with his huge Newfoundland dog. The latter had already leapt into the water, swum to the struggling pair and, with the instincts of his fine breed, had gripped the collar of Margot's coat in his teeth, thus relieving the tiring Prunella of some of the weight.

The boatman arrived and, using all his skill, contrived to get first Margot and then Prunella into his boat without upsetting the lot of them into the lake again. There was no room for the dog, but when the man took up his oars and made for the landing-stage, he swam after them with undiminished vigour. In fact, he was first to land and, by the time the boat had reached the slipway where Miss o'Ryan, white with fear, was standing waiting, he was shaking himself violently and bespraying the young mistress lavishly.

Further up on the Quai, Clem was clutching Len who was struggling furiously. The rest, apart from Julie who had come to help, were standing there, too, prevented from coming further by Miss o'Ryan's vehement, "Stay where you are, all of you!" flung at them as she thrust Len into Clem's arms and ran. The passers-by were not, of course, to be stayed, but they proved of assistance in helping to lift the girls from the boat. Prunella, by that time, was so frozen that she moved with difficulty and Margot was unconscious. Biddy o'Ryan caught her in her arms where she lay, white and still, her long dark lashes sweeping her cheeks in terrifying immobility. Remembering that she had always been the frailest of Joey Maynard's flock, the mistress was shaking with fear internally, though to all appearances, she was self-possessed enough, except for her tell-tale pallor.

The dog's owner was foremost of the helpers. Now he stooped and took Margot from Miss o'Ryan who could scarcely hold her, seeing that she was small and slight and Margot a well-grown eleven-year-old. His fingers went to the child's wrist and he nodded. "Bitte, mein Fräulein," he began, "permit that I help. I am a doctor."

Miss o'Ryan gave Margot up to him in silence and he carried her up on to the Quai, leaving Prunella to be helped by a kindly lady and an elderly gentleman while he put the younger girl down on a nearby seat and swiftly examined her. It was so quick, that it almost seemed as if one moment the girls had been in the water, the next they were all up on the Quai and he was saying, "Nothing to be anxious about, Gott sei dankt! It is the shock which has caused her to faint. See, mein Fräulein. Already she rouses."

It was true. The long lashes quivered and lifted. The blue eyes looked up into his kindly face bent over her. The white lips moved.

"H-hello!" Margot whispered.

"Good!" he said, standing up and lifting her in one movement. "The first thing now is to get her and the other somewhere where they can be warmed and dried—"

"Bitte, Herr Doktor," said the lady who had helped Prunella and was standing near, "bring them to my flat."

He gave her a smile. "Frau Helder! Danke sehr! But I think—yes; the Burgerspital will be best." He turned to Biddy o'Ryan. "My car is over there. Will you come with me, mein Fräulein? And bring the other girl, also."

He set off with long strides only to pause as the group round the seat moved and he saw Lesley, bandaged and with her eyes swimming, for the iodine had stung badly.

"Another casualty!" he exclaimed. "No matter! Bring her also. We must make haste, you understand. We have more to fear from cold than anything else."

Emerence, who had been standing horrorstruck at this ending to their play, suddenly burst into howls and tears. "Oh, is Margot dead? Is she drowned?" she sobbed.

"Of course not, little ass!" Clem said, still clutching Len, while Mary-Lou performed the same office for Con who had suddenly wakened up to the fact that Margot was in trouble again. "She'll have to go into a boiling bath and probably spend a few days in bed, but that'll be all, unless you kids make such a hullabaloo that you hold everyone up and give both her and Prunella a fighting chance of pneumonia."

That settled everyone. They drew back a little and Len and Con stood still, though tears were rolling down their cheeks. The doctor had paid no heed to all this. Accompanied by Miss o'Ryan who had tossed an urgent, "Take charge, Nancy!" to Miss Wilmot as they passed, he made for his car and a minute later they were all packed in, Margot wrapped in a huge rug and Prunella tucked up in another. The dog bounded in after them and if his wet coat did nothing to add to their comfort, at least he provided some more warmth as he crushed himself against Lesley and Prunella in the back while Miss o'Ryan, with Margot in her arms, sat in front with the doctor who drove off at as fast a speed as he dared.

They had paused only to give Miss Wilmot the name of the hospital and for Biddy to tell her friend to march the girls to the cathedral and try to find Miss Annersley and tell her what had happened. Then they had gone.

Once the car was away, Miss Wilmot ordered the girls into line and walked them off at their best pace after she had rewarded and thanked the boatman and the would-be helpers. Frau Helder, indeed, insisted on going with them to show them the short cuts. She cheered them all up by saying that the Herr Doktor Courvoisier was a very clever doctor and the Burgerspital a fine hospital where the half-drowned pair would soon be all right again. She gave Nancy Wilmot her own name and address and telephone number, saying that she would be delighted to do anything she could to help. Then she brought them to the Hofkirchen where, much to Miss Wilmot's relief, they saw a blue string emerging from the west door, and said good-bye.

Miss Wilmot gave Clem and Julie a swift command to take charge and sped across to claim the Head and give her a brief and succinct account of the afternoon's doings.

"Which hospital, did you say?" the Head asked when the mistress had finished.

"The Burgerspital," Miss Wilmot replied.

Miss Annersley thought swiftly. "Mdlle," she said in rapid Italian which, naturally, the girls could not follow, "will you join forces with Miss Wilmot. Take the girls to see the Rathaus and anything else you like. Give them Kaffee und Kuchen at the time we arranged and meet me at the station ten minutes before train-time. If I cannot leave the hospital myself, I'll send Biddy o'Ryan to meet you and tell you the latest news and any further plans. Now I must go. Girls!" she turned to the silent girls. "No more trouble, if you please. No, Len and Con, I can't take you with me. But I know you needn't fret. Margot will be all right. Stop crying, Emerence. What's done is done and, in any case, I can't attend to you now. I'll see you later and we can talk all this over then. In the meantime, you can show that you are really sorry for your share of the business by pulling yourself together and being good."

With this, she was off with Clem who went to find a taxi for her, and Mdlle, after a few words with her young colleague, assumed command of the suddenly increased band and when Clem returned, ordered them to line up properly and set them off in the direction of the Rathaus, bent on filling their minds as far as she could with fresh sights.

Meanwhile, Miss Annersley was whirling through the streets of Lucerne to the great Burgerspital in the New Town. As she sat there, she was experiencing some of the worst moments of her life, though that had rarely lacked excitements of one kind or another. She knew, almost better than anyone else there, what anxiety the Maynards had had to go through on account of their Margot. It was true that two years in the dry, Canadian climate had made an enormous difference, but there had been nothing, so far, to test how deeply the improvement had gone. The Head could well imagine that the sudden plunge into the icy waters of the lake might try her stamina up to the hilt. And then she had Prunella to consider. So far as she knew, the elder girl was a sturdy young thing, but even the sturdiest specimen can hardly go diving into the waters of a snow-fed lake in her clothes without feeling some effects from it. She was a thankful woman indeed when at last the taxi slowed down and she was set down at the great doors of the city hospital.

Biddy o'Ryan met her inside. She was white, but the worst fear had left her face and she was able to smile at her Head.

"How are they, Biddy?" Miss Annersley demanded. "Be quick and tell me!"

"All's well, so far as anyone can tell as soon as this," Miss o'Ryan said. Her glorious, blue eyes suddenly brimmed over and the tears trickled down her cheeks. "I'm *not* crying!" she gulped fiercely as she brushed them away with the back of her hand. "I'm *not*! But oh, it's such a relief to have you here!"

The Head's mind was partly relieved about her pupils. Now she put an arm round Miss o'Ryan's shoulders and drew her to a nearby seat. "Sit down, Biddy. You've had as nasty a shock as anyone. Let go now. I'm here to take responsibility!"

Biddy bit her lips and leaned against the Head's comforting shoulder while she made an effort to pull herself together. At last, "One of the nurses came down to me just before you came," she jerked out. "She said that they'd both had hot baths and hot drinks and were safely tucked into hot beds. Margot had fallen asleep at once and Prunella wasn't far off it. They *think* it should be all right. They may have sniffley colds after this, but everything was done so quickly, they don't expect anything worse and just possibly not even that. I—I told them you'd be coming at once and want to see them and they said that would be all right. Thank goodness my German didn't go back on me! Oh, by the way, they've taken Lesley to have some stitches put in her knee. It's a nasty cut, though Nancy Wilmot nearly *washed* it in iodine. They were going to give her a light anæsthetic, so she'll have to stay here for the night, at any rate, as well. But that seems to be the worst of it."

At this point, Dr. Courvoisier appeared. He took the pair in at a glance and came over to them at once with outstretched hand, saying, "Fräulein Annersley? I am glad to see you and to be able to report that we hope that no real harm will come of this afternoon's events."

Miss Annersley gently put Biddy to one side and rose. "Herr Doktor Courvoisier? I hear I owe you a big debt for your care of my bad pupils," she said in her excellent German. "And your dog, as well. My other mistress told me how he went to the rescue."

He smiled, looking relieved. "You speak my language? That makes all easy. I speak English, but not too well. Come with me and I will tell you exactly what we think."

He took them to a sunny, little room, half office, half sitting-room, where he rang for coffee after he had settled them in comfortable chairs. Then, while they waited for the coffee, he told them all he could. Some hours must elapse before they could say definitely whether their unexpected bath had affected the girls badly or not. He thought not. So far, now they were dry and warm, both had settled down comfortably and were both sound asleep. If, as he hoped, neither produced a temperature or a cough, they might quite well go back to school on the Monday or Tuesday. The same applied to Lesley who would be drowsy from the ether when she left the operating theatre. But he had every hope that there would be no need to worry about any of them. Sleep was the best thing for the youngest girl after the shock she had sustained by falling into the lake, and sleep was exactly what she was getting.

"And now, mein Fräulein," he added, "here comes our coffee. Drink it, for I am sure you both need it. Then we will go up to the ward and you shall see your pupils for yourselves and make sure that little ails them."

Miss Annersley laughed shakily as she took her cup. "That is very good of you. You will understand that I feel anxious, since I am responsible for them—especially for little Margot Maynard. As a little child, she was terribly delicate and her parents have had a difficult time with her health."

He looked amazed. "You surprise me! I should have said she was a splendid specimen of girlhood. In short, I have little fear for her."

The Head explained about the years in Canada and he nodded. "No doubt that has proved the turning-point for her. I should say they need have no future worries about her. Indeed, all of them are fine examples. But did I hear you say her name is Maynard? That has a familiar sound to me."

"I expect you have heard of her father, Dr. John Maynard. He is head of the Sanatorium just opened up at the Görnetz Platz."

"But of course! I know him—we have met several times. I have already sent him two patients and a third will go next week. But are you the Chalet School he told me would be coming to the Platz? You are? Then I shall have two new pupils for you next term. This patient I hope to send next week has two daughters—Anneli who is fourteen and a little one, Odette, who is not yet twelve. She will be glad to have her children near her. She is a widow and the only aunt who could take charge of them lives in Zurich and that is too far away, when one is ill. Frau Bertoni will be rejoiced to hear that you have opened your school."

Miss Annersley laughed again. "Do you really feel you can recommend us after what has happened this afternoon?"

He smiled broadly. "You have a saying, 'Boys will be boys' and I have no doubt that girls will be girls, also. I shall visit Frau Bertoni to-morrow and tell her she may send her daughters to you with a light heart. Now, I see you have finished your coffee, so I will go and see if you may visit our patients. Excuse me."

He got up and left the room. The moment he was gone, Miss o'Ryan demanded, "And what about 'the little one'? I thought we were to have no Juniors for a year at least."

"Oh, well, I always knew that we must start them sooner or later and we have the Maynards who aren't twelve until November. Little Odette must certainly come if it will keep her near her mother, poor soul! I have had several applications for girls of ten and eleven, so I suppose we must just begin at once."

There was no time to say more, for the doctor returned to summon them to the little, semi-private ward where the three were lying, fast asleep. Lesley was still white from the effects of the anæsthetic, but Margot's cheeks were healthily pink again and Prunella had lost the blue, pinched look which had rather frightened Miss o'Ryan in the car. Unless they produced any fever within the next few hours, the Head felt that Dr. Courvoisier was right and she had no need to worry. She drew a long breath of relief as they left the ward and relaxed at last.

"Thank you, Herr Doktor. I feel much happier about them," she said as they went down in the lift. "In fact," she added, "Lesley looks the worst of the three. However, I suppose when the ether or whatever she has had has worn off, her colour will return, so I don't worry about that."

"Oh, without doubt. All are doing as well as possible. And now, mein Fräulein, what else can I do for you?"

The Head thought. "We must catch our train back—or, rather, the rest of the school must. If I might, I should like to wait till the next, just in case I am needed."

"But of course! If you wish, I can find you a friend who has already offered her flat. I am sure she would be glad to receive you for the night if you would like to stay till the morning. Or, if you prefer it, there are plenty of hotels, you know."

In the end, he went to telephone Frau Helder who insisted that Miss Annersley must go and spend the night at her flat and the Head finally agreed. She decided to go to the station and give messages to Mdlle for the school and the Maynards. In the morning, after she had visited the trio, she would ring up the Platz and tell them what she proposed to do, for Frau Helder asked her to stay till the Sunday evening, at least. Her husband was abroad on business and her three boys were all at school in Basle, so she was lonely and would welcome a visitor. The Head was grateful for the invitation, but she felt that if she could get back to school next day, she ought to go, so she would not promise. It all depended on the patients.

"I'd like to wait for the next train," Miss o'Ryan said. "Then I can take back the latest news."

Miss Annersley shook her head. "I'd rather you didn't. You'd have the long walk from the train alone and it would be dark by that time."

"But if Margot should produce a temperature? After all, the first responsibility was mine," Biddy urged.

"I know that. But in view of all we said to them, there was no reason why you should expect any of them to behave so badly.

Margot and Emerence will have an interview with me presently," the Head said firmly. "They have both been very naughty girls and so I shall impress on them."

At this speech, the last of the heavy burden which had been on Miss o'Ryan's mind slipped away. She knew very well that the Head would never have spoken like that if she had been really anxious about either Margot or Prunella. She accepted Miss Annersley's proposal that they should go and look at the shops, since they had no idea where the girls were likely to be. After shopping, they had Kaffee und Kuchen and then it was time to go to the station.

"I'll come with you," Miss Annersley said, "and give Mdlle a message for Matron. Don't bother about Joey. I'll ring her up as soon as I've paid my second visit to the hospital and tell her the latest news of her bad daughter. By the way, you might warn Matron to keep an eye on Con. She still seems to walk in her sleep when she has any extra excitement and she might just do it to-night."

Miss o'Ryan nodded. "Very well. I'll see to it. I expect Matey will push Con and Len into San. for the night so that they can be together. She's nippy," she added thoughtfully, "but she's awfully understanding when you get under that."

"Yes," the Head assented. "All the same, the one I really expect there may be a fuss with is Jo. Or she may take it all in her stride. You never can tell."

"Not with Jo, you can't," Biddy agreed.

At the station, they were met by anxious girls and mistresses, all wanting to know how the bathers were. Miss Annersley soothed them and then bore Mdlle off for a brief confab. After that, they had to hurry into the train which slid away from the platform, leaving her waving to them. She was not due at the hospital until nineteen o'clock, so she spent the time in buying herself a nightdress and toilet articles and a small case in which to bestow them for the homeward journey next day. For she felt fairly sure that she would have no reason for remaining in Lucerne after the morrow. Then she strolled down to the Reuss and watched the headlong river pouring down to join the Emme until she had to go to the hospital.

It was good news as she had expected. All three had wakened about an hour before and Prunella and Margot had enjoyed a light meal and promptly fallen asleep again. Lesley was still awake. Her knee was stiff and sore, but the nurse told the Head that she would have something to help her to sleep later on. In the meantime, she greeted Miss Annersley with a delighted smile, said that she was sorry she had been so clumsy and then asked anxiously about Margot and Prunella.

"Both sleeping themselves back to normal," the Head said at once. "I want you to do the same. Yes; I know your knee hurts, but that will soon be at an end and Miss Burnett will give you massage later on to prevent any stiffness. So you needn't worry about your games, Lesley. Anyhow, you'll all be coming back to school on Monday. I expect Dr. Jack will come with the car for you. So you must get all the rest you can in case we have to leave you behind because you aren't well enough."

She rose from her chair and bent to kiss the girl. Lesley sat up cautiously and put her arms round her neck. "I'll do my best," she promised. "But I can't stay here alone. They're awfully decent, but they all speak German and my German isn't too brilliant. So I really will try to sleep to-night."

The Head laughed, kissed her again and left the room after a final look at the other two who never stirred. Then Dr. Courvoisier appeared to take her to Frau Helder's flat where, after she had had a good meal, she was left with the telephone to break the news to Joey.

Joey took the story calmly on the whole. "Just like those two!" she commented. "You're sure they're all right, Hilda? No temps. or anything like that?"

"Both quite normal," her friend assured her.

"Good! Well, I don't see that we can do anything about it at the moment. I'll break the glad news to Jack and he'll probably run us both down to Lucerne to-morrow just to see for ourselves. So if you want to come back then, we'll pick you up at the hospital. Give me your telephone number and I'll ring you in the morning."

Miss Annersley repeated it and then Jo said, "Well, that's that. Thanks a lot for staying. If you hadn't, Jack would have had to bring me down to-night and I don't suppose he'd have been at all pleased. Well, I must go. I can hear Felix murmuring and I don't want Felicity roused up at this hour. What I've done to be blessed with such imps is more than I can say!"

She chuckled deeply and rang off and Miss Annersley went to join her hostess and spend the first peaceful hour or two she had known that day.

Chapter XI

Joey Straightens Things Out

TRUE to her word, Joey Maynard arrived in Lucerne shortly before noon next day, complete with husband. Jack drove up to the big block of flats not far from the National Quai which Miss Annersley had given as her temporary address. That lady was waiting for her, having visited the hospital earlier in the morning and returned with the heartening news that neither Margot nor Prunella seemed much the worse for their icy dip on the previous day.

"In fact, poor Lesley is mainly the one to be pitied at present," the Head said when she had relieved the Maynards' minds about their daughter. "Her knee is really very stiff and sore and she certainly won't be able to walk for the next few days."

"I was on to Courvoisier before we came off this morning," Jack said. "I'll take a dekko at it when we get there—which is almost at once, if Jo is to be kept quiet. Where's our proper hostess, Hilda? She's very trusting, isn't she?"

"She went to eleven o'clock Mass," Miss Annersley explained. "And just *what* do you mean by 'trusting', may I ask?"

"Well, don't you call it trusting to leave a comparative stranger alone with all her treasured possessions?" he asked teasingly. "Of course," meditatively, "you *have* an honest face."

"I should hope so!" The Head spoke shortly.

"Oh, never mind his nonsense, Hilda!" Jo interrupted eagerly. "Finish that coffee, my lad, and take us to this hospital we've heard so much about and let me see my young sinner for myself."

"The calm, impersonal mother!" he murmured. "Over the 'phone, I know she sounded the most modern of parents. But away from it, she's just an old-fashioned mamma. She lay awake half the night worrying."

"How do you know?" Jo asked swiftly. "You were asleep most of the time."

"That's what *you* thought. Come off it, Jo! If I don't know you after nearly thirteen years of married life, I never will!"

"Oh—*you*!" Jo gave him an indescribable look. She drained her cup, set it down and stood up. "I'm ready now. Are you coming with us, Hilda?"

"No, my dear. I've paid my visit already. You and Jack go off and I'll pack my belongings and be ready to go up with you. Mittagessen will be ready about half past thirteen. Frau Helder thought you'd probably want to see the three for yourselves and we knew you couldn't get here much before noon unless you started off at some unearthly hour. Besides, I want you to meet her. You'll like her. She's charming. I shall never forget how quick she was with offers of help when it all happened."

"Someone else is trusting, as well as Frau Helder," Jack remarked to his wife as they drove off to the hospital.

"What *are* you talking about? You said you knew Dr. Courvoisier, and this Frau Helder is an old friend of his. Besides, if Hilda weren't used to sizing up folks at a glance by this time, she wouldn't be much good as Head of a biggish girls' school."

"No; I suppose not. Now stop talking for a minute or two like a good girl while I try to fathom this maze of streets. This is new terrain for me, remember. I don't want to lose us. Time is limited at the moment. Round here, I think—yes; there's the lake and there is the bridge. Now we shan't be long!"

They reached the hospital safely and were welcomed by Matron who assured Jo that the girls were all right before she had a few words with Jack about Lesley's knee. Then she summoned someone to take them up to the ward where they found the three patients still in bed and all reading.

Margot tossed her book aside and held out her arms when she saw her parents. "Mamma!" she cried. "Oh, Mamma! I have so wanted you!"

In a flash Jo was at the bedside and holding her closely. "My bad, precious girl! I might have lost you! Oh, thank God I didn't!"

Margot snuggled to her like a baby. "It—it was my own fault, Mamma. But oh, I'll never do such a thing again! You don't know how awful it was when I went down and down and *down* into that awful icy water!" She shuddered at the memory and Jo was quick to try to take her mind off it.

"That's all you know, my child! I've a very good notion, thank you. I went through ice on the Tiernsee when I was only three years or so older than you. Another girl went in with me. She fainted and I had to hang on to her *and* the edge of the ice as well until they fished us out. You can't tell *me* anything about going down into freezing water, my lamb! I know all about it. Now have a chat with Papa while I go and speak to the others."*

She kissed Margot and released her and stood up. Jack took her place at once and she went over to Lesley, who was an old friend, and said a few cheering words to her before she finally sat down beside Prunella, who had been looking at her with hungry eyes.

"Prunella," she began. Then she stopped short. She slipped an arm round the girl's shoulders, drew her close and kissed her. "Oh, my dear, I can never repay you for what you've done! Thank you more than I can ever say for going to the rescue as you did."

Prunella stared at her in silence. Then she wrenched herself free, her lips quivering uncontrollably, and dived under the bedclothes. Jo glanced round. Margot was fully occupied with

* *Rivals of the Chalet School.*

her father who seemed to be teasing her unmercifully, judging by her exclamations and giggles. Lesley, after a startled look, had turned her back to Prunella and was, to all appearances, deep in the grown-up adventures of *Heidi*.

There were two or three screens standing at one side of the ward. Jo got up, lugged them round the bed and when it was screened off, sat down again. Under the clothes, she could see that Prunella's shoulders were shaking and she was sobbing bitterly though quietly.

Jo acted at once. She pulled back the clothes, hauled the girl up on the pillows, then produced a freshly unfolded handkerchief scented with eau-de-verveine and tucked it into a hand. "Now then, mop up with that!" Her tone was cheerfully matter-of-fact. "And stop crying like that, too. It won't help you at all. What *will* help will be to tell me what's wrong and see if we can work it out together. Come on, Prunella!"

Prunella took the handkerchief. Despite herself, its freshness and the faint, sweet perfume soothed her. All the same, it was a minute or two before she could get a grip on herself, for the tears had had a good start. Then she gulped and said, "Th-thank you!"

"That's right; dry your eyes," Jo urged. "You've had a nice little cry which should have done you all the good in the world. Now you're going to tell me all about it and that will be another step forward."

Much to her own surprise, Prunella gave a shaky laugh. She had never been treated in this way before. Her grandmother had fussed and, once she had realized that her parents were horrified at her behaviour and meant to pull her up, willy-nilly, she had stiffened her upper lip and refused to cry before them. Jo's placid treatment did her as much good as those sudden tears, as that wily young woman had known it would. The tears were dried, though she still shook with an occasional sob. When she had reached this stage, Jo took all her courage in her hands, breathed an inward prayer for wisdom and began to talk.

"I think I know what's wrong with you," she said in carefully casual tones.

"D-do you?" Prunella jerked.

"Yes; I think so. I'll tell you and you can stop me if I go wrong. Your grandmother petted and spoilt you and that was quite natural because you seem to be the only grandchild in the family. Then you were away from your parents so she was trying to make up to you for that. It was all right and shouldn't have done you much harm but the pity was that you'd got into a silly, slangy set at school. Between the two, you began to forget what your own folk had taught you. Then your grannie died and that was a dreadful shock to you."

"It—it was," Prunella assented with a gulp. "She—she was all right one day. The next, she had one of her chesty colds, but sh-she'd had them b-before and I—I d-didn't think anything of i-it. And then—and then—"

"And then she died," Jo said gently as the girl stopped, unable to go on.

A smothered sound gave assent. The tears filled Prunella's eyes again.

Jo closed a warm hand over hers. "Dry your eyes and don't cry about her. I'm going to try to show you something that may help to heal *that* hurt, anyhow. Tell me, Prunella, do you know how old she was?"

Prunella swallowed hard. Then she said shakily, "*Ancient!* She was eighty-seven!"

"Yes. Well, you know, I expect she was beginning to grow very tired. I think she missed your grandfather—"

"I know she did. She talked of him every single day." Prunella paused and Jo waited. Presently the girl went on, "I've just remembered. One day she said she wondered so what he was doing and if he would see much change in her when she went to join him and she hoped not, though she was twenty years older now, of course."

Joey nodded. "Just what I thought. My own idea is that she'd tried to go on without him and being happy, too. She *was* happy in one way. But it must have been a strain. God saw that it was all getting too much for her, so He took her from this world. You have your parents, you see, and He knew that they would come to you at once. But it was time that *she* had a rest."

Prunella looked at her, wide-eyed. No one had ever put it to her like this and she had not thought of it herself. She said slowly, "Yes; I see what you mean."

"Then you won't fret any more over her going, will you? I mean, it would be selfish. Besides, I'm sure it would be the last thing she wanted. She'd be so grieved and distressed if she thought you were making yourself wretched. The thing for you to do, Prunella, is to look forward. We all have to do that. You'll meet her again some day. Until then, you've got to live your life and make it something fine and beautiful. You won't do that while you're tied up in yourself, being unhappy."

Prunella said nothing, but she knew very well that if Grannie had known about her recent broodings, she certainly *would* have been both grieved and distressed. Jo guessed what she was thinking and waited a moment or two before she went on. "Now about your parents. You've been thinking about *your* side of the business; but what about theirs?"

Again Prunella gave her a startled look. Jo was making her think hard and along quite new lines. "What about them?" she asked wonderingly.

"When they went away," Jo said thoughtfully, "they left a little daughter who was, I suppose, just what they wanted. They've been counting all this time on having her again—oh, older, of course, and therefore much more of a companion. And what did they find when they arrived?"

"But—but you change—and you grow older and see things differently," Prunella said defensively.

"Of course! But the trouble was that you hadn't changed in the way they wanted. From all I've heard, I don't suppose I'd have liked it any too well myself. I had to part with Margot for a whole year two years ago, and I rather think I'd have had a horrid shock if I'd found her slangy and all the rest when we met again. In fact, I'd have had a good deal to say about it, I can tell you."

Silence! But Prunella had gone very red at this plain speaking.

"You see," Jo went on, choosing her words carefully, "there *is* something to be said on your parents' side as well as on yours. *They* may have been a shock to you when they started pulling you up for doing and saying things no one had bothered about before. But *you* were a shock to them. Then, you went off at half-cock, didn't you? Your idea was, 'O.K. If they're going to tick me off for every little thing, I'll give them something to tick me off for!' And so, my lamb, you did!"

As this was exactly how Prunella had felt, she was struck dumb by Mrs. Maynard's prescience. Jo took instant advantage. "Things got so bad that they sent you to school. After all, it must have been plain to them that you were hating them pretty badly. No one wants its child to hate it," she went on, with a lovely mixing of her pronouns, "so they decided to put a stop to that and let the school come in for the hate. Unfortunately, your mother seems to have an out-size in consciences. She couldn't leave the school to find out for itself what you were like, so she wrote and told Miss Annersley what to expect. Now this is where I may be wrong; but did she warn you what she was doing?"

"N-no," Prunella stammered. "I—I heard her t-telling one of my uncles. I—I was reading in the alcove and the—the c-curtains were drawn. But I w-was sort of s-sure she knew I was there or I'd have c-come out at once."

"Yes; I don't really think you're the kind of girl to go in for eavesdropping," Jo said blandly; whereat Prunella went even more darkly red.

"I—I didn't—even think of it—that way," she said unevenly.

"That's just what I'm saying. Anyhow, you got on your high horse and my goodness, you seem to have ridden him true and plenty! You made up your mind to give us all a shock and I don't mind telling you you've succeeded up to the hilt! Mary-Lou says your language would grace the pages of any Fanny Burney novel!"

This piece of information brought a faint giggle from Prunella. "It—it was most awfully hard to remember to keep it up," she confessed.

"So I imagine! I can see myself doing exactly what you did—for about three days. After that, I'd have given the show away. I just couldn't help it," Jo said with a chuckle. "You *are* a young ass, Prunella! You might have made every girl in the school loathe you. You'd have had good reason to think yourself miserable in *that* case, let me tell you. As it was, the nice girl that is really you couldn't help showing through in spots so they don't. My young Len is beginning to think you quite a decent sort."

"I like Len. She's a jolly decent kid." The walls were down at last and Prunella spoke like any schoolgirl of her age.

"I'm rather that way of thinking myself." Jo was quite matter-of-fact about it. "I'm glad she and you are by way of being pals, though I hope you'll also find some friends of your own age. Len is nearly three years younger, you know. When's your birthday?"

"27th January," Prunella replied.

"There you are, then. Len's not twelve till 5th November.

Nearly three years between you. Make a pal of fourteen or fifteen and keep Len as a standby as Clem Barrass and Mary-Lou do. By the way, while I think of it, I hope you won't teach Len any more slang than she knows already!"

"Oh, I won't—I honestly won't!" Prunella promised fervently.

"Then that's all right. Incidentally, I shall be rather surprised if you find yourself lapsing into that again after the way you've managed to discipline yourself this past three months or so. I should think *that* treatment will have written 'finis' to anything of that kind!"

Prunella thought this over. "Why—I—I believe you're right," she said with surprise. "Though that wasn't what I meant when I began it," she added honestly.

"All right. I *know* I'm right," Jo told her complacently. "Now I've one more thing to say to you. I suppose you know that the girls will make a young heroine of you when you get back to school?"

"*What?* Oh, they couldn't! How simply *awful*!" Prunella gasped, once more nearly stunned. Really, Mrs. Maynard had administered one shock after another to her that morning! "Oh, Mrs. Maynard, don't say you think they'll be such—such *chuckleheads*!"

"After all, you did risk your life for Margot and they'll think a lot of that. But you drop all your silly nonsense and just be the real Prunella Davidson and the chances are they'll get such a shock they'll forget about the heroine business more or less. What's more, when you go home again, you'll also find your people are liking you much better than they did. I don't mean they haven't *loved* you all along. For pity's sake, don't get any mad ideas of that kind into your head! But loving and liking are two very different things. They *love* you all right. If they didn't your mother wouldn't have taken the trouble to write to the Head as she did. When you go home, the old nice Prunella, the liking will start up at once. And here's an idea for you. Why don't you let them know that you realize what a young pest you were making of yourself and that you've taken a turn?"

"I—I—" was all Prunella could find to say.

Jo explained. "If I were you, I'd write to them and let them get over the shock before holidays begin. You needn't go talking about it and I don't suppose they will once they've heard from you. They'll be only too anxious to forget it all as soon as possible. Now I've said all I'm going to say on the subject. In fact I'm off now to find out if we've got to leave you three here for a day or two or if we can take you back with us. We've got the big car here, so we can manage it, even if it is rather a squash. It would certainly be a saving of time and trouble if we could do it. I'll leave the screens up and Nurse can move them when she comes. Good-bye, Prunella, until we meet again." Jo bent and kissed the girl tenderly. Then she slid out between the screens to find that Dr. Courvoisier had arrived and was examining Lesley's knee with Jack, so she had to wait. She went over to Margot and began to chatter with her. She meant to say nothing about her daughter's sinful behaviour. That was a matter for the school and she never interfered in school discipline. Margot had known this would happen; she knew her mother's views. However, she was bubbling over with all she had seen the day before and she and Jo entertained each other very well until Jack brought the young Swiss doctor to be introduced to his wife.

"May we take them back with us to-day?" Jo asked eagerly when she had said all the polite and proper things.

"Your daughter and her rescuer may certainly go. Both are very well. But for the other, she must keep her leg up for the next few days. We do not want the stitches to break away."

"Then that settles it so far as Lesley is concerned," Jack said. "Don't forget we shall have Hilda as well as ourselves and the kids, Jo. It wouldn't be possible to arrange for Lesley to keep her leg up at that rate."

"You don't know what I can do with a car," Jo told him; but he only grinned and requested her to pipe down.

"We're not going to risk any trouble." He turned to Lesley. "Lesley, old lady, can you bear to stay on by yourself till the day after to-morrow? Dr. Peters is coming down then and he can pick you up and bring you back. Can do?"

"Of course, Dr. Jack," Lesley said. "I'd *like* to come back with you all to-day; but I'm not risking anything that'll dish my tennis next term."

"Excellent wench!" he commented. "Then we'll leave it like that, Courvoisier. If Prunella and our own young monkey can be ready by fifteen o'clock, we'll call for them then. I expect you'll be glad to have the beds and they seem all right. Peters will call for Lesley some time on Tuesday. I'll give you a ring when I've talked it over with him."

So it was settled and, after a final kiss all round, Joey and Jack left the ward with Dr. Courvoisier, who discussed the case of his patient, Frau Bertoni, with Jack all the way downstairs.

"Bring her along yourself when she comes," was Jack's parting word. "I'd like to discuss this new treatment with you. Can you get a night or so off duty? Good! We'll put you up. You can take time off to go and have a look at your present patients while you're with us," he added with a broad grin.

"And see the school as well," the doctor added. "I should like that."

"Then give me a ring when you're coming. Here's our number. All set, Jo? We're going to be fearfully late for that meal Hilda talked about."

But when they were off, he said to his wife, "Get that, my girl?"

"Get what?" Jo demanded, staring.

He chuckled. "Courvoisier wants to see the *school*. Not, mark you, the *San.* which you might expect from a doctor; but the *school*."

"Well, what about it?"

He did not answer her directly. Instead he said, "Our Bridget is a pretty lass."

Jo went off into peals of laughter. "Jack Maynard! What a sentimental ass you can be! The man's seen her *once* and, if I know anything of Biddy, she was looking ready to go up in smoke the whole time."

"All the more reason for a kind-hearted and gallant young man to fall a victim. Oh, you may turn up your nose, but you wait and see. I'll bet you a new typewriter to a box of cigarettes that I'm right!"

"I never bet on certainties," Joey told him. "If you *must* know, Frau Bertoni has two girls and she wants to send them to the school. Hilda told me so while you were washing your hands before we went to the hospital." She paused a moment to let this sink in. Then she added triumphantly: "So put *that* on your needles and knit it!"

Chapter XII

A *QUIET* EVENING

"AND now," said Jack Maynard, as he backed the car preparatory to turning it, having deposited Miss Annersley and Prunella safely at the school, "we're going home to have a *quiet* evening, finished off by early bed. I know *you* had practically no sleep last night, and I didn't have much to speak of myself. We're making up for it to-night."

"Just as you say," Jo agreed with a yawn. "I could do with a spot of early bed quite well, now you speak of it."

Margot, seated in the back of the car, where she had been very silent and subdued throughout the eighty-mile run from Lucerne, looked up at this and seemed about to speak. However, she thought better of it, and closed her lips firmly. Her father got the car safely manœuvred and they rolled down the drive, along the road round the curve, and through their own gates.

At Freudesheim, the family, reinforced for the day by Len and Con at Jo's request, were waiting for them. The twins and Michael were in bed and it was nearly time for Charles to go. He was listening as hard as anyone, and hoping against hope that Anna would not appear with her invariable, "Nun, mein Kind!" before Papa and Mamma came.

He was unlucky. Anna arrived and bore him off just as the laden car had reached the school gates and by the time it arrived home, he was tucked into his bed and Anna was lighting the nightlight.

"Bitte, Anna," he begged in German as she bent over to kiss and bless him, "if they come, I may get up, mayn't I?"

"If you are awake," Anna said smiling, for his grey eyes were heavy with sleep. "Now lie down, Jungling. May the good God bless thee and thy guardian angel watch over thee all night."

"Danke sehr," he said sleepily. The next moment, he was sitting up, wide awake.

"I can hear the car! Let me get up, Anna! You promised!"

Anna lifted him out of bed and wrapped him in his dressing-gown. "Now the slippers," she said, sitting down to pull them on. Charles could have stamped. However, he stuck out first one foot and then another quite meekly and she pulled them on. Then she released him. "Only to the top of the stairs," she warned him. "And be quiet and do not wake the others."

"O.K.!" Charles was out of the room, and pattering along to the head of the stairs where he crouched down, peering through the railings to the hall below.

Meanwhile, in the salon, other people had heard the car. Len and Con curled up together in the biggest arm-chair, tossed their books down anywhere and shot out of the room, along the hall and across the doorstep with such vim that Len tripped and nearly went headlong down the steps. Con squealed and clutched at her. Thus, when the car drew up, the first thing Jo saw was her two eldest daughters, apparently indulging in a free fight on the top step.

"Girls!" she exclaimed as she sprang out.

"It's O.K.! I nearly fell down the steps but Con grabbed me!" Len yelled as she plunged down them, closely followed by Con. "How's Margot?"

"Is she all right?" Con added a screech to the greeting.

The next moment both were shrieking again, this time, with delight as Margot herself wrenched open the hinder door and literally fell out on to the path. She was up in a moment and the triplets made a wild dive for each other and became an inextricable mass of arms, legs and curly heads as they hugged each other all at once.

"Quietly—quietly!" Jo hushed them. "You'll wake the little ones if you howl like that!"

"Into the house with you all!" their father ordered, pulling them apart. "You'll wake the entire neighbourhood if you go on like that!"

He clapped his hands and they raced up the steps and into the house where Con and Len fell on their third and hugged her all over again. Jo broke into laughter. "Not much to worry about there," she said to Jack who had shut the car-doors and was following her into the house. "Should we pack them straight back to school *now*, do you think?"

"Have a heart!" he said with a grin. "Let them have it out among themselves, poor kids—and I *don't* mean Margot! Anyhow, after asking Hilda so urgently if we could keep them for the night, I shouldn't think you'd have the face to return them now."

"No; I suppose I'd better not. Just listen to them! They'll have the babies yelling their heads off if this goes on much longer!" She swept forward into the hall, took Len with one hand, Margot with the other, and pushing Con in front of the three of them, got them into the Speisesaal where she warned them again about making a noise and then shut them in to get over their first raptures alone.

"Margot's got to face Hilda in the morning," she said to Jack as she tossed off her cap and coat.

"You'd think that would slow her up, wouldn't you? She's forgotten about it for the moment, though."

"It won't be really bad. Hilda always tempers justice with mercy. But young Margot's got to be impressed with the fact that you can't go haywire on an expedition and hope to get away with it. However, it's nothing to do with us, thank goodness!"

At this point, she heard a small voice saying anxiously, "Mamma—Mamma!"

She looked up and saw her second son's anxious, small face pressed between the landing railings. "Charles!" she exclaimed. "All right! I'm coming!"

She ran upstairs to be clutched round the waist and told in agitated tones, "Mamma—I've had an accident!"

"Well, come in here and tell me about it," she said, swinging him up in her arms and carrying him into her own room. "Quietly, though. We don't want to wake the twins or Mike. What sort of accident have you had?"

"I broked your Little Flower. I—I was kissing her—she *is* so sweet!—and—and—I dropped her and she was all broked up."

She turned and looked where a stumpy finger was pointing. It was too true. The statue she had had since her schooldays was lying in a dozen pieces on the table at the window. Jo was decidedly vexed, for Charles had been forbidden to touch it unless she herself was there. She turned back and looked into the wide, grey eyes which were swimming with tears.

"Didn't I tell you not to touch her?" she asked gently.

"Ye-es; but you wasn't here to be with me and I wanted to kiss her good-morning."

"And now you've broken her. She won't be pleased, you know. Oh, not because it's *her* statue, but because you disobeyed me. She was a good little girl and very obedient and I don't suppose she likes disobedient children."

"Oh, Mamma-a-a!"

"Hush! Don't cry! It's done and can't be undone. I'm sorry, sonny. I thought I could trust you. Now I see I can't."

"Oh, Mamma, I'm so *awfully* sorry!" Charles had to bite his lips to keep from crying at this dreadful statement.

"You must tell Papa about it, of course. But that will do to-morrow. Have you told God when you said your prayers?"

"No; Anna heard them and I thought I'd rather be *private* when I did it," Charles said with such immense dignity that his mother nearly collapsed on the spot.

"Very well. Go and do it now and then I'll tuck you up for the night."

Charles went and when his mother came to him after washing her hands and tidying her hair, he was in bed, his face tear-stained, but at peace again. "He'll forgive me, Mamma, and will you, please? I won't do it again."

"I'll forgive you and I hope you *won't* do it again." Jo bent to kiss him and tuck the bedclothes round him. His arms went round her neck and she hugged him at once. "Go to sleep now, sonny. You must tell Papa in the morning, but after that we'll say no more."

She left the room and went to the night-nursery for a peep at the three babies. All was well there, so she left them and went downstairs, thinking, "A quiet evening, indeed! I can't say I think it's begun awfully well! Thank goodness I needn't do anything about Margot. It's Hilda's job!"

However, when it came to bedtime for the triplets, she found that she was to have quite a lot to do with it. When they said goodnight, Margot asked, "Will you come up to us presently?"

Jo cast a regretful look at the new book she had meant to begin, but she said, "Very well. I'll be up in twenty minutes' time."

She timed them and when the twenty minutes were up, she stood up, laying her book aside. "I'm going up to say good-night to the girls," she said as she left the room.

"Mother, I want to confess," Margot announced before she was well into the room.

While they had been little girls, Jo had trained them to talk over the day's doings with her at bedtime and own up to their small sins. Latterly, she had left it to themselves to decide whether they would or not, though she still did it with Charles and Michael and meant to start the twins as soon as they were old enough to understand. Stephen, her eldest son, had felt himself too old for it when he came home at the Christmas holidays; but Len and Con frequently confided in her. Margot, since her time in Canada, had got out of the way of it altogether. So Jo realized that her third girl must be feeling the need of her help pretty badly when she asked for it.

With a swift, inward prayer for wisdom, she sat down in an armchair and waited while they settled themselves round her on stools. Margot crowded close to one side and the other two sat in front. All three looked very serious.

"I'm ready," she said, stroking the red-gold head at her elbow.

Margot swallowed hard. Then she said, "Mother, I didn't *really* mean to be naughty yesterday afternoon. It was just my devil inside me."

Jo had to suppress a giggle. Margot was apt to blame a good many of her evil-doings on the devil inside her and the matter-of-fact way in which she spoke of him had its comic side.

"Why did you listen to him?" she asked.

"Well, I didn't mean to, but I was getting bored with just plain walking and I thought I'd wake Emmy up a bit. So I gave her a smack and ran. Then I climbed on the railings and she dunched into me and so I fell in. And that's how it was."

"I see. And so you gave us all a nasty fright and, I'm pretty certain, have caused poor Emerence to have a very miserable time of it just because you *wouldn't* listen to your guardian angel, but preferred to hear what your devil had to say. I call that abominably selfish," Jo said judicially.

"I didn't mean to," the culprit muttered.

"My lamb, that's always your excuse. You never 'mean to', whatever you've been up to. Are you going to go on using it all through your life? For you're going to land yourself into some nasty messes if you do."

"Oh, but, when I'm older, I'll *want* to listen more to my guardian angel," Margot argued.

"Don't you believe it! You see, every time you give in to the devil, you're making it easier and easier for him to talk to you and coax you into doing things even when you know them to be wrong. It's like practising your tennis. When you first began, you couldn't get a ball over the net unless you stood quite close to it. But you worked at it and now you can get it over quite well, even from the back-line. Do you see?"

"Do you mean that when we listen to him we're *practising* letting him boss us?" Len struck in, horror in her face. "But—but that's an *awful* thing to do!"

"Well, what else can it be? And when you turn away from him and listen to your guardian angel instead, you're practising *that*." Then Jo added earnestly, "Listen, you three. What you do in that way now is going to make it easier for you to grow up either good women or bad ones. Whichever you practise hardest now, you'll go on doing when you're older. Don't think that there comes a time when you can turn round and say, 'I'm not going to listen to the devil any longer,' and be able to stop it at once. It just doesn't happen that way. You've got to fight *all* the time or make it ten times harder for yourself when you do decide it isn't worth the game."

There was a silence. Then Margot broke into a wail. "Oh dear, oh dear! What can I *do* about it? It's such a lot easier to do as he says!"

"Of course it is! All the same, you've got to do your best to stop it. You can, you know. You've done it before. Remember the awful rages you used to fly into when you were little and things didn't please you? It very rarely happens now. But that is only because you've practised so hard at trying to keep hold of your temper."

Margot brushed the back of her hand across her eyes. "But I still often *do* feel rageous, even if I don't show it," she owned.

The new word nearly finished Jo. She had to bite her lips hard before she could trust herself to say, "I dare say you do. But you don't *show* it, and that's what matters. And you come out of it very quickly. I've seen you and I've often thought what a tough fight you've put up."

"Well, as you've done that, you can jolly well stop listening to your devil when he tells you to do mad things!" Len said. "You used to be *awful* when you were a kid, Margot. Just let yourself go and be as mad as you could. Now you sit on it. I know! I've seen, just as Mother has."

Margot looked rather less dismal. "It'll be frightfully hard," she said with a gusty sigh that nearly blew her sister away.

"It will," Jo agreed. "I know all about that, for I used to do the sort of things you do when I was a kid. But by the time I'd given people some ghastly shocks and landed myself into various sticky messes, I realized that it didn't pay and I'd *got* to get hold of myself. So I did—though it doesn't *always* come off," she added with complete truth.

"There you are!" said Con, speaking for the first time. "If Mamma can, so can you. And you can't possibly let her down when she's owned up to us like that."

"No; I s'pose I can't." Margot heaved another deep sigh. "All right; I'll have a go at it. But life's going to be awfully dull, it seems to me."

"Think my life's awfully dull?" her mother asked with dancing eyes.

"Of course not! But then you've got Father and all of us. I've heard you say often that no one could be dull with a family like ours in the house."

"How right you are! But you've got the family as well, you know. And you've got school and don't you dare to tell me that you find life dull there, for I shan't believe you. So now you know what you've got to do about it and I'm saying no more. You've got to face Auntie Hilda to-morrow and I don't imagine you'll find that too pleasant. But *you* chose to call the tune so you've got to pay the piper and all you can do about it is to take your medicine as well as you can and try to remember to keep the promise you've just given me. That will pay for all the worry we've had over you this last two days."

She might have said something more, but at that moment, there came a yell from the night nursery and she was on to her feet in a moment.

"Out of my way, you three! Mike'll wake the babies if he howls like that!"

Then she was gone and the triplets were left alone. Margot tossed off her dressing-gown, kicked her slippers under the bed and scrambled in with the firm announcement that she wasn't talking any more.

"But your prayers!" Len exclaimed.

"I can say them in bed for once. I'm not *talking*, I tell you!" And she disappeared under the clothes, leaving her sisters looking at each other.

"We must say them ourselves," Con said, going over to the prie-Dieu meant for three, which stood before the little shrine in a corner of their room. "Come on, Len. I'm awfully sleepy."

They said their prayers, kissed each other good night and, after a final look at the hump in the middle of the far bed which was all they could see of Margot, retired to their own. When Jo looked in an hour later, having had to console Mike for a bad dream and hush the babies who had been well awakened by his howls, she found her daughters fast asleep. She tucked in the clothes more closely round Len, turned Con on to her side and rearranged Margot's bed, leaving the red-gold head to view. Then she departed to toss herself into the most comfortable chair in the salon and announce that she was worn out with uttering preachments.

"If you've been saying anything that will make that young demon of a daughter of yours think a little, it's work well done. That's all I've got to say!" Jack told her as he refilled his pipe.

"She's as much your daughter as mine!" his wife retorted indignantly.

"I know that; but she gets her wickedness chiefly from *you*!" was the soothing reply. "I haven't forgotten the hair-raising antics you got up to in your salad days!"

Jo glared at him. Then she began to giggle. "I wish you hadn't such an indecently long memory! Well, she may get her monkey tricks from me, but her temper comes from *your* side of the family. She told me just now that she still had times of feeling 'rageous'. There's a lovely word for you!"

"Did she really say that?" His deep laughter pealed out and his wife hushed him at once.

"For goodness' sake remember the twins! Mike woke them just now with his yells—a bad dream, poor little man! Beth, what did he have for supper?"

Beth, who had been sitting getting on with her knitting, laid it down and thought. "Only milk and a lightly-boiled egg broken over bread-crumbs. But he did insist on having *the* most gory yarn read aloud to him and Charles this afternoon," she owned.

"That's what's done it, then. I must issue a ukase against such things until he can read them for himself," Jo decided.

Beth laughed. "That won't be for a jolly long time. It isn't that he isn't as bright as they come, but he's horribly lazy over lessons. Still, perhaps his passion for horrors may gee him up a little."

"Not it!" Jo said comfortably. "Mike has no use for anything that means sitting still. He likes to be stirring around. Even Margot wasn't as bad that way as he is. I'll be thankful when the holidays come and Stephen returns to take a hand with him. Steve's like Len—quite responsible. There's peace where the boys are concerned when he's at home. Oh, dear! Why do children have to grow up?"

"Because that's the normal procedure," her husband said severely. "Any coffee going, Jo? I could do with a good cup of coffee."

"Anna would leave the perk. ready. I'll go and see to it," Jo said.

Beth was before her. "Don't you move! You said you were worn out, so you can just stay where you are and rest. What am *I* here for, anyhow?"

"Have it your own way. I shan't argue," Jo assured her, sinking back again. "Oh, I do feel all in, what with all the worry and excitement and having to tick two silly girls off for the good of their souls!"

"And having next to no sleep last night on top of it all," Jack said. "We'll have our coffee and then you can go to bed and make a long night of it for once."

"I couldn't ask for anything better—" Jo began. Then a wild shriek of terror came from the kitchen and Jo was out of her chair and heading for that spot, her weariness forgotten. He followed to do battle with whatever might have scared Beth when his steps were hastened, for a second yell came from his wife. When he burst into the kitchen, he beheld a tableau that he never allowed either of them to forget. Beth was standing in the middle of the kitchen table, her skirts held tightly round her and Jo had mounted Anna's special chair which stood near the door. In the middle of the floor, looking round with mild interest, was a large, white rat with pink-lined ears and phenomenal whiskers.

Jack stared at the vision speechlessly. Then he made a great stride forward and swept up the creature which snuggled into his hand as if accustomed to such treatment.

"Jack! It's a *rat*! Take it away—take it away!" Jo shrieked. "It'll bite you! Put it down! You'll—"

"*You'll* wake the kids again, if you yell like that," he said calmly. "Come down, you two, and stop making idiots of yourselves. It's only a tame, white rat. Rather a decent little chap, too. Must have escaped from somewhere, I suppose. I'm ashamed of you both! Come on down and see to my coffee and don't be so silly."

Jo came down in a hurry and fled upstairs once more, for her quick ears had caught warning sounds. Granted that all the Maynard children learned early in life to sleep through normal noises. Between her own and Beth's yells, they had managed to break through custom and well she knew that she might expect the twins to be thoroughly cross to-morrow unless she got them off to sleep at once.

Beth, very red and sheepish, also descended from her perch while Jack, carrying his confiding captive carefully, went to find a temporary home for it. He suspected that it belonged to the small son of a chalet near at hand. How the thing had escaped remained to be explained, but he was glad that it had succeeded in finding warm night-quarters. The nights were still frosty and the poor little beast would probably have died if it had been out all night.

All the same, as they went to bed a little later, Jo looked at him with mischief dancing in her black eyes. "Did I say I wanted a nice, quiet evening?" she asked, tossing back the heavy masses of hair she had just released from its plaits and hunting for her hairbrush. "I was never more mistaken. If *this* has been a quiet evening, Heaven defend me from a noisy one!"

Chapter XIII

Preparations

JO sent her daughters back to school next morning.

Margot looked very sober as she kissed her mother before following her sisters who had scampered down the drive and were waiting impatiently for her at the gate.

"Is—is Auntie Hilda *furious* with me?" she asked anxiously.

Jo gave her another kiss. "She's not pleased, my lamb. You couldn't expect her to be. I told you last night you'd have to take your medicine. I'm sorry, but that always follows when we've made idiots of ourselves—as you certainly did. Off you go! The sooner it's over, the sooner you'll be at peace again."

All the same, her eyes were soft as she watched the sinner's lagging footsteps. "Poor little soul!" she thought. "Well, let's hope that this means the turning for her. If it does, I shan't regret that involuntary cold bath of hers!"

As soon as they reached school Emerence, who had been lying in wait for them, grabbed Margot with an eager, "Are you all right—I mean," with a belated remembrance of the fact that this was Monday and French day, "Comment allez-vous?"

"I'm all right," Margot said, also in French and in very melancholy tones.

Emerence gave her a sharp look. Then she said carefully, "Il faut aller à Mdlle Annersley à neuf heures moins vingt minutes."

"Well, it's twenty-five to now," observed Len who was still outside and felt she might risk English until she had entered.

"That's only five minutes to wait, Margot, and it'll soon be over. Aunt—I mean the Head—never *nags*, anyhow!"

"No-o," Margot agreed, still in those melancholy tones as she trailed off to her own Splashery.

Emerence went with her while the other two sought their own to change and hang up coats and berets. Once they were safely there, Margot looked at Emerence.

"Has she said anything to you yet?" she asked.

Emerence shook her head. "Not a word. I wish she had. I had a ghastly day yesterday!"

"Well, I don't see why she wants you at all," Margot said as she sat down to change her shoes. "It was my fault from beginning to end as you jolly well know."

"Phooey! I didn't *need* to chase you, did I?" her chum retorted.

"No; but I jolly well knew you would, all the same," Margot returned. Then, "I say, we must remember to talk French! We'll have another row with someone if we're caught and I've got enough on my plate as it is."

Emerence looked conscience-stricken. "I forgot—I always do. I'll try to remember, though. Everyone is disliking us just now and they'll dislike us *more* if they catch us speaking English on a French day," she said in careful French.

Len and Con had vanished in search of their own gang when the two left the Splashery. Margot had looked round anxiously.

"What do you want?" Emerence asked.

"I thought Len and Con might have waited for us." Margot's lips drooped. She could sin freely enough, but she was always miserable when consequences came and a last word with her sisters would have buoyed her up just then.

However, they were nowhere in sight. Con had run on to the form-room and Len had stopped to have a word with Prunella who was hurrying to the Splashery to get ready for the morning walk.

"Are you all right?" she asked in the pretty French that was second nature to all the triplets after their time at the La Sagesse convent school in Canada.

Prunella nodded. "Oui, merci bien," she returned with a good British accent. "Comme est Margot?"

"Oh, elle se porte bien, merci beaucoup." The sound of a footstep cut short whatever else Len might have had to say. She turned and fled with a wave of her hand and Prunella went on to the cloakroom, chuckling to herself.

She had found that, among the lower half of the school, at any rate, she was regarded as something of a heroine. They were full of admiration for the way she had dived straight in after Margot and insisted on considering that she had saved that young woman's life practically unaided.

In vain had she pointed out that the man in the boat *and* the dog had had quite as much to do with it as she had and that, in any case, she was a good swimmer and had thought nothing of that little distance. They refused to accept this, pointing out that it was one thing to go swimming in summer when the water was warm and quite another to plunge into a freezing, cold lake at the end of March.

"Why," Nancy Wadham had cried, "the cold might have *paralysed* you! You might have got cramp or—or *anything*! I think it was a marvellous thing to do!"

"Oh, do talk sense!" Prunella had cried, goaded to fury by this. "There were plenty of people about to haul us *both* out, weren't there? And a boatman did do it and there was the dog as well! For heaven's sake, *be* your age, Nancy! You don't seem to have the sense you were born with!"

She had escaped after that; but she had created a fresh sensation. They had stood goggling after her in silence until Isabel Drew put it into words.

"Christopher Columbus! Notice that, anyone? Prunella's taken to talking like a *Christian*!"

"It must have been the shock of the cold water," Connie Winter said, awestruck.

To-day being a French day, no one had much time or any chance to notice how Prunella talked, which was just as well for her temper. And whatever you might say for her English, her French had altered very little, apart from a marked increase in her vocabulary.

She went off with the rest of Lower IVA for her walk. Meanwhile, Lower IVB who had to use this time on every other Monday to cram in extra practice, remedial exercises with Miss Burnett, any mending left undone and various other chores, greeted their restored member with enthusiasm before they fled to their duties under the eagle eye of Miss Derwent who was duty mistress for the day.

At twenty to nine promptly, the two sinners were standing outside the study door, already shaking in their shoes. It was rarely that Miss Annersley administered rebuke. When she did, she did it in a way that you didn't forget and that ensured your doing your level best not to have to meet it again in a hurry. Besides, with the Sale coming off in less than ten days' time, the pair had good reason to fear that their punishment might be connected with it and neither wanted to be out of the fun. So when Emerence, as the elder of the two, applied her knuckles to the door, it was in very gingerly fashion and if the Head had not been expecting them, she might have been excused for not hearing the very gentle tap.

But she was and she called, "Entrez!" in a voice that left them no chance to do anything else. She gave them very short shrift and by the time she had finished what she had to say, Margot was weeping copiously and Emerence only just escaped it by biting her lips and making the most incredible faces.

Miss Annersley spoke only a few trenchant sentences—as Len had said, she never nagged—but they were quite enough. Then she spoke their sentence. As they had shown themselves so untrustworthy in public, for the rest of the term they were never to leave the precincts of the school unless they were in charge of either a grown-up or a prefect. This was where Margot literally lifted up her voice and wept. In plain English, she howled like a small child.

"I am glad to see you are sorry, Margot," the Head said severely. "It is quite time you realized that behaviour like yours on Saturday is wrong and babyish in the extreme. Now you may go, and please give me no cause to have to speak to you like this for the rest of the term."

Somehow they got themselves out of the room, though Emerence had to lead the sobbing Margot and both forgot their curtsies. The Head let it go. As she said later, they had enough to think about in any case.

Once outside, Emerence dragged her friend into the nearest form-room, gulped loudly and then said, "Stop bawling, Margot! It's bad, I know, but it might have been worse. Supposing the Head had said we weren't to go near the Sale?"

"I'd *rather*," Margot sobbed, "than be told she d-didn't t-trust me! Oh, what *will* Mamma say when she hears that?"

"The Head won't tell her," Emerence said sturdily. "She wouldn't do such a mingy thing as that!"

Lifting her head for a moment, Margot glared at her friend out of swollen eyes that were swimming in tears. "Of course she w-won't! I shall t-tell M-mamma myself!"

Emerence stared. "Say! Do you tell your mother *everything*?" she demanded.

Margot's head went down into her hands again. "I used to—we all always used to," she wept. "And then I got uppish and

I thought it was a baby thing to do and I wouldn't do it at all. And—and n-now—now I'm t-told I'm, unt-trustworthy!" She ended on a low howl.

Emerence was not given to caresses, but she put her arms round her sodden friend at this. "Oh, don't cry like that, Margot! I'm sure your mother will understand," she said earnestly. "I know it's a ghastly thing to have said to you. She said it to me, too. But we can try—and it's only for what's left of this term, dear. *Don't* cry, please don't, Margot!"

But Margot was not to be consoled. Miss Annersley's words had given her a real shock, second only perhaps to the shock she had had from her fall. She was very proud and she felt the disgrace far more keenly than Emerence whose early training had been along the lines that you should never say "No" to a child. Emerence managed to get her to stop crying before the others came back, but she remained red-eyed and subdued for the rest of the morning and it was some days before she was herself again. It was just as well, perhaps, that the Head had taken this line. Thereafter, she was restrained from many a mad prank by the memory of those stinging words and she really did begin to refuse to "listen to her devil".

Meanwhile, Prunella, walking with Barbara Chester as partner, was letting herself go so far as her limited French would allow, on the idiocy of Juniors in general and their own Juniors in particular.

Barbara heard her diatribes on the subject with more than one chuckle. "I'm afraid you'll have to put up with it, my dear," she said. "In fact, though of course *we* won't make asses of ourselves over it, we are fairly proud of having you in our form, Prunella. If you don't want the little ones"—how furious Len and Co. would have been had they been privileged to hear her!—"to treat you like a heroine, you shouldn't do heroic things. And it *was* heroic, you know. Oh, yes; you're a good swimmer. We all know that.

You've dinned it into us all day yesterday *and* this morning! But Nancy Wadham was quite right when she said you might have got cramp or something."

Prunella was so annoyed at this that she forgot her French and said in good, downright English, "Then I think you're a set of dunder-headed ninnies!"

"Taisez-vous, bête fille!" hissed Mary-Lou who was just in front of them. "C'est le jour pour parler en français. Voulez-vous d'avoir Mdlle—er—écouter a vous?"

Prunella decidedly did not. She said curtly, "Oh well—I mean eh bien, changez le sujet—and be quick about it!"

Luckily for her temper, the subject was changed very thoroughly by the announcement Miss Annersley made to the school after Prayers.

"You must remain in your common-rooms or form-rooms this evening, girls. The Welsen branch are coming up after Abendessen to have a dress rehearsal in Hall of their pantomime. So remember, everyone, that you may not go there at all. Prayers will be held before Abendessen and you can go on with your work in your own rooms."

After that, everyone was keyed up to the last degree with excitement. No one knew what the pantomime was to be, for the Welsen folk had kept it very dark indeed. Julie, as Head Girl, answered the anguished looks of entreaty from her confrères and rose to ask if they might know the title, but the Head laughed and disclaimed all knowledge.

"I'm sorry, Julie, but I am unable to tell you that," she said in her fluent French. "I really do not know. Even Miss Wilson has refused to enlighten me when I asked her. I am as curious as you are, but we must just wait and see, for no one will say anything. I can tell you one thing," she added. "She did say that it was to be quite unlike the one they did last year—in subject, at any rate."

That was all they had to go on and many and wild were the guesses made throughout the day when they had any time for it.

"Nothing like last year's," Mary-Lou said thoughtfully when they were all changing for the evening after Kaffee und Kuchen. "Now what could that possibly be? It was *The Sleeping Beauty* last time, wasn't it? What could be really different?"

"*Little Red Riding Hood*?" suggested Barbara as she put a burnish on her fair curls. "*That* would be different."

"*Could* you make a panto of that?" her cousin Vi Lucy queried doubtfully.

"Don't see how. I mean there isn't a prince or a princess in it," observed Catriona Watson from the opposite cubicle. "*I* was wondering if they were taking something like one of the *Alices* and doing that."

"They couldn't possibly!" came quickly from Mary-Lou. "A panto has all sorts of soppy songs and rags in it and you'd spoil either of the *Alices* if you did that."

"Perhaps it's *Ali Baba and the Forty Thieves*," suggested Verity-Anne's small, silvery voice from behind her curtains.

They all united to cry this idea down on the spot.

"How could they possibly?" Vi cried. "Ali and the Thieves would take up everyone they have. I believe there's only about forty of them at Welsen. Here, Barbara, has Nancy ever told you how many they have?"

"Forty-two, she said," Barbara replied as she returned her brush to its proper place and proceeded to strip her bed of its counterpane. "Oh, drat this thing! I never *can* get it into the proper folds! Mary-Lou, can you give me a hand? And I'll help you with yours."

"There you are then!" Mary-Lou emerged from her cubicle and began to help Barbara to fold the counterpane neatly. "That would leave one person for Morgiana and no one for anything else. Besides, where would they get the huge jars from?"

"I never believed that part of it," confessed Emerence who was herself again. "I mean, how could you *possibly* have jars big enough to hold a man?"

"Oil jars you could," replied Mary-Lou, the daughter of an explorer and herself inclining to archæology. "In some of the ruins in Crete and Greece and Troy that they dug up, they found jars six feet high and more. The thing is, I don't see how our girls could make anything like them."

"And even if they made it only *ten* thieves—one to count as four—and managed the jars," put on Vi, "how could you have a 'lived-happily-ever-after' ending? Or does Ali Baba marry Morgiana in the end? I forget."

No one could remember and Verity-Anne subsided into crushed silence.

"What about *Aladdin*?" Emerence asked, arriving with *her* counterpane. "Help me with this thing, someone, or Matey will make remarks about it when she sees it."

Catriona also appeared with hers and they set to work to fold the things in the laundry folds as insisted on by Matron.

"H'm! I believe you've got something there," Mary-Lou said. "It just *might* be! I shouldn't like to say."

"I'll bet it isn't!" Barbara said decidedly—they had all conveniently forgotten about speaking French—"Nancy did say that they were all out to do something that wasn't *usual*. There are dozens of *Aladdin* pantos every year."

As the bell rang for preparation at that moment, they had to give it up. They finished the counterpanes and went off downstairs still wondering.

Half-way through prep., they heard the arrival of the Welsen people who had had an early meal and were to have cocoa and buns when they returned after their rehearsal. As a result, more people had returned lessons next day than ever before. Upper IVB were the worst for their form-room door faced the upper doors of Hall and they could hear sounds of subdued laughter and snatches of song every now and then. Once, when Maeve Bettany opened the door to go and ask Miss Armitage a question about their home-work, they all distinctly heard Miss Wilson's voice saying, "Speak *up*, Bride! I can't make out a word you're saying!"

Maeve cast an agonized look back at her form; but she dared not stay. She went out, shut the door and turned in the direction of the staff common-room to see Miss Armitage herself coming along, a well-known notebook in her hand.

"Were you coming to ask me about your prep., Maeve?" she said with a smile as she reached that young lady. "I suddenly remembered that I didn't finish explaining it to you before you had to go, so I was coming to do so now. Come along!"

She opened the door and pushed Maeve through in front of her. The form rose to its feet even as peals of laughter sounded from the Hall. The mistress saw their faces and laughed. Then she said sympathetically, "Yes, I know. It's most tantalizing. But we can't do anything about it. Now pay attention to me."

Further laughter came to them when she went out and Prunella said, "It's cruelty to dumb animals! How can we work with *that* going on all the time?"

"French, please!" remarked Clem Barrass's voice from the doorway.

Prunella looked horrified; but there was never anything wrong with Clem's discipline, so she made an effort. "Er—c'est la cruelté à—I mean aux—des animaux—er—muëts. Comme travaillons-nous avec celà allant sur tout le temps?"

Clem bit her lips at this remarkable sentence. "If you use 'aux', you don't use 'des' as well," she observed. "As for the rest of your sentence don't use 'avec' like that. Yes; I know it means 'with', but the French use 'quand—when' in that connection. And never use a present participle like that, either. You'd better put it into decent French and bring it to me before Prayers to-morrow morning." Then she went to the mistress's table in search of the textbook Miss o'Ryan had sent her to find and departed to regale the rest of the prefects with the story.

Mary-Lou made a face after her before she said, "Pour moi, je pense bien d'expecter—is that the French for 'expect', anyone? Oh well, never mind. It'll do!—d'expecter nous à travailler quand ces filles dans Hall faisant toute ce bruit là et nous ne savons du tout quoi qu'elles faisent est plus que la crueltè!"

Everyone agreed with her, but there was nothing they could do about it. They applied themselves to their tasks with more or less success and then Mdlle came in to say that the Head wished to hold an exhibition of all their work on the coming Saturday and they must finish up everything before then.

"On the following Monday we shall all be busy preparing for the Sale on Tuesday," she said, "so all articles for the stalls must be finished on Friday night. Work hard, mes enfants. We wish to make our first Sale up here a great success, you know."

That hint did help them over the next few days, but they were thankful when Friday evening brought them a respite from German. Miss Dene arrived while they were at Kaffee und Kuchen to say that they must all change immediately after the meal and go straight to their common-rooms. All preparation would be excused that night; they were to sit up an hour longer; and, best of all to a good many of them, they might speak in whatever language they liked for the rest of the day.

"Thank goodness for that!" Betsy Lucy exclaimed when the door had closed behind the secretary. "Between pitching in at work and trying to make up sentences in German that will pass muster, I'm all of a dither!"

There was a good deal of giggling when they came racing down from their dormitories and began to take their work out of the form-room and common-room cupboards where it was kept. But time was too short for them to waste much of it and soon peace descended on the school as they settled down to hard work.

In the common-room occupied by the Upper Fourths, the girls looked as if they were about to open a bookshop. Piles of storybooks, both old and new, stood on one table and various people sat down to write out price tickets for them. At another, headed by Mary-Lou, half-a-dozen of them were busy with scrapbooks. The rest had pictures to frame, Easter and birthday cards to finish off, and Barbara, urged to it by Joey Maynard's example, was busy cutting out a jigsaw puzzle with a treadle fret-saw which belonged to the school. Joey had sent ten large puzzles herself and Barbara, who had made her first attempts the previous term, was able now to turn out quite well-cut smaller ones.

They worked in silence for the first few minutes. Then Mary-Lou broke the ice.

"Hand over those tiny scissors, please, Vi," she said. "You always try to hog them!"

"I don't!" Vi protested, pushing them at her. "Anyhow, I've finished for the moment." She regarded with admiration the handsome, chestnut horse she had cut out and then turned to her page to decide where she should place him. "I only follow your example," she said calmly as she made her decision and reached for a paste-brush. "How much have you left to do, by the way?"

Mary-Lou was diverted from the insult. "Three pages still to fill; but I've got centres for all of them and some of the scrappy things cut out already. I want to do all the cutting first. I find I work much faster that way. It'll be quite a decent scrapbook when it's finished," she added complacently as she finished her basket of flowers and turned back a page or two to glance down them. "I've made this a *pretty* one. And I've done three funny ones and two that are a sort of mixed grill."

"Come again?" remarked Lesley who was adorning sheets of note-paper with tiny flower-scraps.

"There's a bit of everything in them," Mary-Lou explained.

"Oh, I see. What's yours, Vi?"

"An animal one—dogs and cats and horses, mainly, though I've a gorgeous, raging tiger and a *wizard* group of lions! Oh, and an elephant on the ramp, judging by the way he's waving his trunk around," Vi said, "so I can't grumble. Wild animals are jolly hard to get hold of."

"Well, anyhow we have a nice lot of Auntie Jo's books," Barbara remarked with a glance at the goodly pile that stood to one side. "And every last one autographed!"

"Yes; they'll sell like hot cakes," Hilary Bennett said, coming from a corner of the room where she was busy with a pile of water-colour sketches, sheets of glass and cardboard and passe-partout. "Stop nattering a moment, you people and give me your advice. Would you frame this in black, or gold, or dark brown, or what?"

"Let's see!" Mary-Lou considered the dainty sketch Hilary obligingly held up, with her head on one side. "Gilt, I think. I say, that's a very nifty thing! Who did it?"

Hilary turned it round and examined the signature brushed in at one corner. "Someone called 'E. Conroy'," she said finally. "It must have come up with the Welsen things. We've never had an E. Conroy here, staff or girl, to my knowledge."

"It's Welsen," Maeve said with decision. "That's Elma Conroy. Peggy's talked of her. She was to have come to us for a week or ten days in the summer hols., and then Auntie Jo was coming here and that messed things up, so she never came. She's going to be married this summer and she's asked Peg to be chief bridesmaid."

The rest looked at her incredulously. "*Married?*" they chorused.

Maeve nodded. "She's twenty in August. She was at Welsen for a year and she's had a year at home. She comes into Peggy's second circle," she said mysteriously.

"What *do* you mean by that?" Mary-Lou demanded, picking up her pasting-brush.

"Well, Dickie Carey and Nell Randolph and Daphne Russell are her first circle of friends. Then comes the second circle and Elma's one of that crowd."

"Oh, I see. It sounded rather mad the way you put it—rather like a thriller novel, I mean."

Hilary stamped. "Do stop talking about things that don't matter. Mary-Lou says gilt frame. Anyone else got any other ideas? Mind the mount and your sticky fingers!" she added, hastily removing the picture out of reach of Heather Clayton.

"Well, I only wanted to see it," Heather replied, giving her fingers a rub on a handkerchief that had seen distinctly better days. "Let's have a dekko, Hilary."

Hilary went to the nearest wall and held the sketch against it. "Come on, everyone! Get an eyeful, for it's your last chance—for the moment, anyhow. I want to get it framed. There are piles more to do yet."

They crowded round, admiring it. It was very pretty—a duckpond at the end of a meadow with a flowering maybush reflected in the still water. The colouring was clean and the outlines given boldly and the whole thing was evidence of real talent—though certainly nothing more. But it had a freshness that was delightful.

"I like it," Vi said. "I think a gilt frame, Hilary. A black one wouldn't suit it nearly so well. Gilt, decidedly."

That settled it. Vi's mother was an artist and Vi herself was giving signs of artistic gifts of no mean order. They all chorused their agreement and Hilary took her picture and went back to her table while the others returned to their work.

"Is Elma Conroy still at Welsen?" Carol Younger asked.

"I *told* you she left last summer," Maeve scolded. "You never listen to anything a person says, Carol! She must have sent that picture from her home. Did she send any more, Hilary?"

Hilary and her co-adjutors looked hurriedly through the pile of sketches they were framing and found two others, equally charming. One showed a corner of a village with the church spire peeping over the tops of pink-flowered chestnut trees. The other was the sea on a summer day.

"Mother would like one of those. Are they priced yet?" Mary-Lou demanded.

"None of the pictures are priced," Lesley replied. "Herr Laubach is coming along early to-morrow morning to do it. He said that as we meant to frame them he would wait till they were all done—anyone got a cardboard strip eighteen inches long? Oh, thanks a lot, Ghislaine—so we've just *got* to finish up to-night. Don't dither, you folks; there simply isn't time. You know what he's like when things aren't ready for him!"

They all did. Herr Laubach was an excellent art master, but his temper was, to put it mildly, hair-trigger at any time. There was a legend afloat in the school that when Jo Maynard, then Joey Bettany and a Senior, was having a lesson from him on one occasion, she had so infuriated him, that he had picked up her work and flung it at her head before turning her, neck and crop, out of the art room. But then, as Jo herself would have been the first to admit, drawing and painting were not in her line. She might also have added that she had done her best to annoy him at the time.

Lesley's warning was timely. The framers stopped chattering

and wasting their time and set to work in grim earnest. The result was that when the bell rang for bed, there were piles of neatly framed pictures as well as rows of books all neatly priced, five trays of handmade Easter and birthday cards, and no fewer than twenty scrapbooks of every kind.

"We shan't have such a bad stall after all," Vi said, surveying the results with pride before they began to pack up for the night.

"I think it'll be a jolly decent one," Prunella assented, bringing a charming illumination to add to the collection. "Mind how you touch that, anyone. I don't think the gold paint is quite dry yet and it smudges frightfully easily."

"It's a wowser!" Heather said approvingly. "What are the words, Prunella?"

"An old sixteenth century prayer. Grannie had it on a card she kept in her Bible. I rather like it myself," Prunella replied before she read it aloud.

"'Oh, Lord, support us all the day long of this troublous life, until the shades lengthen, and the evening comes, and the busy world is hushed, and the fever of life is over, and our work done. Then, Lord, in Thy Mercy, grant us safe lodging, a holy rest and peace at the last through Jesus Christ Our Lord.'"

Heather, a scamp of the first water, remained silent a moment. Then she said quietly, "I like that. I can't buy the picture, of course, but I'd like a copy of the prayer some time if you can do it."

"Of course I can." Prunella looked sidewise at her illumination. "That's dry at last." She laid it down. "I say, if we sell all that, we ought to make quite a decent sum."

"I don't suppose we'll do as well as last year," Verity-Anne observed.

"That was a record," Mary-Lou reminded her. "How much did we make altogether?"

"Over £200, anyhow," Clare Kennedy chipped in. "Tom

made that wizard model village and we had £30: 5s. for that alone. A draw always does make a lot of money if it's anything decent."

"That doctor-man—Sir James Talbot—won it," Vi said reminiscently. "He said he was going to give it to a San. for T.B. poor children, Prunella. You should have seen it. Tom certainly did excel herself that trip!"

"She's doing a chalet this year," Catriona remarked.

"If it's anything like the Maynards' 'Maison des Poupées', it'll be marvellous," said Mary-Lou who had not been above playing with that wonderful toy herself.

"Look here," Prunella burst out, "what is that girl's *real* name?"

The others looked at her and each other and then giggled.

"'Wrop in mystery'!" Clare quoted. "No one knows *what* it is—oh, the Head, of course. But no one's ever called her anything but 'Tom' here. Her initials are M.L. I've always thought myself that it's something extra girly and there's nothing Tom despises more than girliness!"

"Oh?" said Prunella, rather stunned.

"Do you kids intend to clear up to-night or to-morrow?" asked an irate voice; and they turned to behold Madge Herbert glaring at them.

"We're just going to, Madge," Mary-Lou said, hurriedly picking up a pile of books.

"Well, hurry up about it, then!" Madge snapped. "Lower V have gone up already and the bell rang ten minutes ago!"

They fled to do her bidding and ten minutes later the common-room was clear. Madge took the keys to carry them to the office with a brief, "You'd better hurry if you don't want Matey to catch you!"

The Upper Fourths looked round to make sure that everything had been left in order. Then Mary-Lou saw them all out and switched off the lights and they went flying upstairs on tiptoe, reaching their dormitories in time to avoid a rencontre with Matron. Luckily for them, Miss Annersley had kept that lady talking rather later than usual so when she came up to go her rounds, she found everyone safely in bed and apparently sleepy, and never knew what a narrow escape of her wrath quite a number of them had had.

Chapter XIV

The Sale

IT was the day of THE SALE! The girls always spoke of it in capital letters and, as Miss Dene once said, with bated breath. The whole of the previous day had been given up to arranging Hall. The opening would be at noon as a good many visitors would want to leave the Platz early in order to catch their trains from Interlaken. Others were coming from the villages round about and had to reach home before dark. That, at this time of year, meant round about eighteen o'clock. Apart from that, the Welsen pantomime was to be given in Hall and was to begin at seventeen, so the stalls must be cleared away and the scenery rushed into place and that would take time. Therefore, it had been decided that the Sale would go on until half-past fourteen. That would give everyone time to clear up, set the stage, and have a brief rest before the curtain rose on *The Story of the Willow Pattern* which the Welsen folk had hit on long before the school had decided what form their own share of it would take.

"A case of great minds thinking alike!" as Dickie Christie of Welsen had remarked.

"If we and the two Sixths all turn to and help to clear and then leave it to the men and Welsen to cope, that ought to be enough," Miss o'Ryan remarked as she looked round the room. "They want the lanterns left, so that can be seen to to-morrow."

Lady Russell—Madame to the school—was to open it. She was staying at Welsen with her sister-in-law, Mrs. Dick Bettany, mother of Peggy and Bride at Das Haus unter den Kiefern and of

Maeve up at the Platz. In the days when Lady Russell had been Madge Bettany, she had begun the school on the shore of the Tiernsee in Tirol. Even after her marriage she had kept on with her teaching until David, the eldest of her family, arrived. Then she had had to give up, but she retained her interest in it, both personally and financially.

Joey Maynard had clamoured loudly for her, but Madge Russell had only laughed at her.

"From your own account," she had written in reply to Jo's frantic letter, "you'll be chock-a-block, anyhow, so you can spare me to Mollie this time."

Jo had written a scathing epistle in reply, but her sister who knew her, had only chuckled over her diatribes with the remark, "Oh, well, I expect she feels a lot better for having got all *that* off her chest!"

She turned up at an unconscionably early hour on the Tuesday morning, demanding Frühstück with the school, since she had had only coffee and a roll before she set out.

"Where's Mollie?" Miss Annersley demanded.

"How should I know? I left her comfortably in bed, so she may be there yet; or she may be up and dressed. She's coming up with the girls, anyhow. But I wasn't waiting till late morning to see everyone. Have you room for a little one at the staff table, Hilda?"

"If you mean you, of course we have," the Head said, laughing. "I hope you're prepared to receive an ovation, though."

"Oh, mercy! What horrid ideas you do get! Don't talk nonsense, for pity's sake! The girls will have more sense than that. After all, lots of them only know me by repute, more or less. I don't think I've ever taught any of the present lot."

"Have your own wilful way! But I have warned you!" the Head retorted.

As a result, when the staff filed into the Speisesaal, Lady

Russell followed the Head and when the girls had sat down, they all spied her and nothing prevented Julie from springing to her feet and crying, "Madame! Madame's at Frühstück! Three cheers, everyone!"

The girls were excited in any case and they all stood and cheered loud and long. Miss Annersley gave them their heads for about two minutes. Then she struck her bell sharply and the school suddenly realized where it was and sat down again. As for Madge Russell, she was crimson with embarrassment. The staff proved most unfeeling and told her it served her right and was her own fault.

"I *warned* you!" Miss Annersley said. "You *are* an idiot, Madge! You asked for it."

"Scathing as ever!" her guest sighed. "If I'd thought they'd behave like this, I'd have gone on to Jo and demanded breakfast from *her*."

"I rang up Jo just before we marched in and told her you were here," Miss Dene said. "She just raged at me! Haven't you seen her yet?"

Lady Russell shook her head. "I have not. We only reached Welsen at eight o'clock—oh, but you say twenty in these parts, don't you?—last night. I was up here early enough, as you'll all admit. I simply haven't had time to go to Freudesheim."

"Well, you're in for it when you do see her," Miss Dene said with satisfaction. "You should have heard her! 'Oh, is she, indeed? She'll hear all I think when we meet and you can tell her I said so!' You're for it, my dear!"

"Consider that I'm shaking in my shoes. But if she feels like that, I'd better make tracks for Freudesheim as soon as this meal is over and make my peace with her. I do *not* want her irrupting over here. You never know what she'll say next and I don't want the girls to hear anything they oughtn't."

"To hear you talk, anyone would think Jo was in the habit of embellishing her conversation with strange oaths," Miss Annersley said, laughing.

"No-o; she doesn't do that exactly," the lady's sister replied. "But you've got to admit that she can and does say the most outrageous things on occasion."

The staff could only agree to this, and as the Head had no wish to hear Lady Russell addressed in public as a "mean hunks!" or something even worse, she cordially endorsed her decision. The result was that when the girls poured out of the Speisesaal later on with the idea of catching the head of the Chalet School Ltd., they were disappointed. Lady Russell had vanished and no one saw anything more of her until, on the stroke of noon, Jack Maynard as Chairman, led her on to the daïs.

The school had all been at their posts an hour earlier, for a good many people were likely to turn up well before the opening. As they would all be fully occupied during the Sale proper, the Head had given permission for each girl to reserve any three purchases she liked and they had hurried to make the most of the permission.

It really was a charming scene. At the top end of Hall, behind the daïs, was hung the six-foot cardboard representation of a Willow Pattern plate which Herr Laubach had painted for the earlier effort. On either side of the daïs which had been enlarged for the pantomime with heavy boarding, stood the wings needed for the first scene. Being oriental in character, they fitted into the scheme very well, though the table and chairs placed for the Opener and her company were a misfit.

Facing this, at the back of Hall, was a canvas and wood representation of the willow tree and beneath it stood the largest of the stalls with its pagoda-like roofs, meant to represent the Mandarin's house. Here, the two Lower Fourths displayed their toys. These ranged from rag dolls and cuddly animals, both knitted and sewn, to small baskets piled high with whipping tops and willow whistles, all hand-made. Emerence, assisted by Margot and two others, beamed across a pile of home-made games, some of them most ingenious. One table croquet set had been manufactured out of stout hair-pins, slices of cork and large marbles, while the mallets were wine-corks, with wooden skewers for handles. Some of the elder girls had painted games of the *Snakes and Ladders* variety for them and Matron had already reserved one based on *Beauty and the Beast* for the school San.

Chang's Cottage stood in a corner, showing rows of pots of home-made jam, lemon curd, marmalade and potted meat, all the offering of Matron and Frau Mieders, the domestic science mistress. The cookery classes had baked piles of little cakes and scones and biscuits and the two Sixths had given up the Saturday evening to concocting sweets of every kind they could manage. The chef-d'œuvre was a huge, iced cake Frau Mieders had contributed, which was to be a competition prize.

Towards the centre lay *Chang's Boat* piled high with mysterious parcels and in charge of Len and Con Maynard, Isabel Drew and Connie Winter. The four were got up as Chinese boys, complete with pigtails which had been sewn into the crowns of their huge pointed hats, and were in a fine state of giggling pride.

The Upper Fourths had established their pitch on *An Island.* They had put together four old mistress's platforms and surrounded them with huge stones, lugged in from outside—Matron's face when she found how they had scratched the floor was a study!—and over these they had draped streamers of artificial moss. They had rigged up bushes with fir-boughs and wreaths of ivy, and among these were set piles of books. In the centre they had set up another canvas tree from the acting cupboards and decorated it with their pictures and cards. They had rigged up a smaller island nearby and on this Lesley Malcolm and Vi Lucy took charge of the jigsaw puzzles.

As for the Sixth forms, they had *Li-Chi's Balcony* and its railings were hung with needlework of all kinds, from baby frocks and knitted bootees to afternoon tea-cloths, tray-cloths and Zoé's scarves.

In the very centre of the room, *The Bridge* zigzagged across the floor from side to side in truly Chinese manner and was laden with handcrafts of all kinds, presided over by a selection of the Welsen girls while the rest had charge of refreshments in Upper IVB form-room, as that was just opposite.

Strings criss-crossed the upper part of Hall and from them dangled every Chinese lantern the school could beg, borrow or steal. The walls had been draped with big blue curtains and against this background the lanterns, all lit up by tiny, electric bulbs and the girls in their brilliant Chinese dresses, stood out with the glowing effect of an eastern picture.

As Lady Russell took her seat between her brother-in-law and the Head, she managed to whisper to the latter, "Really, I almost think it's the pick of all our Sales so far. How *did* you do it?"

"Dyetub, mainly," was the hissed reply. "You should have seen Joey's hands! She was responsible for most of it."

Then Dr. Maynard rose to introduce the Lady Opener with a few remarks on the reason for the Sale. Out of mercy for the younger portion of his audience, he cut them very short and then called on Lady Russell to open the Sale.

Madge stood up; but before she could say anything, there was a little stir at one side of the room and Nan Wentworth, nearly hidden under the great bouquet she carried, and Julie Lucy, bearing a big hamper, came forward. Nan presented her bouquet very shyly; but Julie, turning to Jo who was ornamenting the platform and who stared with all her eyes, had a few words to say.

"Ladies and gentlemen," she said, "we all feel that you ought to know that Mrs. Maynard has been responsible for a great deal of the scene you now behold. We are very grateful to her and we want to show our gratitude." She turned back to Joey. "Will you please accept this hamper and its contents. We all know how badly you've missed dear Rufus since he died two years ago, and we felt we'd like you to have your new dog from the school."

Amid breathless silence, Jo bent down over the big hamper and opened it. From it, she lifted a handsome St. Bernard pup, just two months old. "The darling!" she cried, cuddling him close. Then she looked at the audience. "Thank you all, girls, more than I can say," she said, her beautiful, golden voice reaching to the furthest corner. "I've been talking of another dog, I know, but I couldn't make up my mind to getting one. But I'm very, very glad to have this little chap now. Once more, thank you for your lovely thought—though I didn't expect it, you know," she added.

There was a burst of laughter which frightened the puppy into yelps and she added breathlessly, "I'll just run over home with him and leave him with Anna, poor little chap. He doesn't understand and he's frightened."

She disappeared on the word, and she was gone, Julie scuttling after her with the hamper. By the time they came back, having settled the little chap in a corner of the study with a big saucer of milk and a bone, the opening was over and Madge had left the platform and made straight for the *Mandarin's Pagoda* to admire Tom Gay's model chalet which stood by itself on a big stand.

"Oh, Tom!" she exclaimed, turning to the talented carpenter, a big six-footer, looking utterly British, despite her purple and yellow petticoats and enormous pigtail. "It really is a wonder!"

"Just look at the little stoves!" exclaimed her sister's voice behind her. "How ever did you get that shiny look on them, Tom?"

"Easy," said Tom, straightening her mandarin's hat. "Daph.

Russell painted the tiles effect on cardboard and then we stuck cellophane over that."

"It's simply wizard!" Jo said, surveying the chalet with deep admiration.

"Did you get your baby safely parked?" Lady Russell asked her.

Jo nodded. "Quite all right. I'll be slipping off presently to see how he's going on. Tom! Tell me: did you people join in, too?"

Tom nodded. "Rather! Glad you like him! What'll you call him? Rufus II?"

Jo shook her head, her eyes serious. "There could be only one Rufus. I don't know, but I rather think he'll be Bruno. I'll let you know later. In the meantime, what do we do to compete for this?—Oh, *Madge*! Do look at the cuckoo clock!"

"Whoever made that?" Lady Russell demanded. "See, Jo; even pine-cone weights! Who's the genius, Tom?"

"Your own niece. Peggy did the case and the weights—they're of plaited raffia. And look here." Tom unhooked the little clock and showed the back of it. "We got this out of an old wristwatch. I roved this crocheted chain over these cogs and when you wind them up like this," she suited her action to the word, "and hang it up, they unwind, very slowly."

She hung it up and sure enough, the tiny weights began to descend.

"It's marvellous!" Lady Russell said. "I must have a go at it. What's the competition this time? Have we to guess some awful German name?"

Tom grinned broadly as she said, "No. Bill—er—Miss Wilson, wouldn't hear of it. You take a minute's dekko at it—six of you at a time. Then you answer the question you'll find inside this envelope. Sign your name and address and hand it over to one of the kids when she calls time." She looked at the crowd pressing round to see the chalet, which was a magnificent toy, three feet high and two-and-a-half feet wide and furnished completely as a Swiss chalet. Then she picked out four more people and directed them to a table and forms set to one side, where six people were waiting importantly for them, headed by Betsy Lucy.

"Sit down," Betsy said hospitably. "Here are pencils. You have five minutes from," she glanced at her watch, "*now*!"

They tore open their envelopes and found inside a sheet of lined paper headed with the question, "How many of the articles in the chalet will work? Tell no one what this question is."

"Heavens!" Jo exclaimed. "What a ghastly thing! I didn't take particular notice of anything. The general effect was what I was after."

"No talking!" Betsy said severely, pointing to the "Silence" notice pinned on the curtain behind them.

Jo said, "Sorry!" and meekly bent her mind to the question.

It was one that no one seemed to like very much and the papers they handed in had very little added to their contents. Then they had to go to make room for others, for everyone was anxious to win the chalet.

Meantime, the other stalls were also very busy. Prunella and Clare, in charge of the pictures, were having a difficult time of it. Herr Laubach had wisely priced them very reasonably and quite a number of people wanted to buy.

Earlier in the day, Mary-Lou had visited them and begged Prunella to mark the duck-pond picture "reserved" as she meant to spend most of what she had on that as a gift for her mother. Prunella had written the word lightly across the back and thought no more of it. Several other people also liked it, however, and she had a hard time keeping it safe. Then, while she was busy wrapping up another, Clare, who had not noticed the scrawl, calmly sold it to Leila Elstob's mother!

Prunella saw that it had gone the moment she turned and a quick question to Clare told her what had happened.

"She can't have it! Mary-Lou reserved it and I promised to keep it for her!" she exclaimed. "What a blind bat you are, Clare! I *marked* it 'reserved'!"

Then she was off, chasing Mrs. Elstob all over Hall until at last she cornered her beside the Chalet. She gasped out her explanation to the lady.

"It's marked on the back," she wound up. "If you wouldn't mind coming back to the stall again, you can choose another. Or we'll give you your money back."

Mrs. Elstob looked disappointed. "Oh, are you sure?" she asked.

"Yes; I sold it myself," Prunella replied. "I'm so very sorry the mistake has happened," she added, returning with a bang to the prim Prunella they had known most of the term, "but it really is sold already."

"But perhaps if you told the purchaser—I want it for my little girl. It really is the one I like best and I'm sure Leila would be delighted to have it. Can't you explain this to whoever had bought it and ask *her* to choose something else and let me have this? I would willingly pay double to keep it."

Prunella was in a quandary. She had given her word to Mary-Lou and yet even she—and she was new that term—knew what the doctors feared for poor Leila. "We shouldn't dream of charging double for it," she said slowly. "That would be awfully unfair. But I know who bought it, of course. I'll go and ask her. If you go in for the Chalet competition, I'll find her now and come back here and tell you what she says. But I can't be sure that she'll agree," she added warningly, for Mrs. Elstob's face had lit up at this.

"I see. Yes; I'll do as you suggest and, meantime, I'll leave you to plead Leila's cause for me. Do put it strongly." Then she turned to look at the chalet. "I must certainly do my best to win this. Leila would be delighted to own it. And where is Sue, my niece? She must try, too. Then Leila will have two chances."

"Sue's on duty at the stall," Prunella explained. "I'll see if she can be spared, though."

She gave Mrs. Elstob a friendly nod and then went off to wriggle her way through the crowds which still thronged Hall, though people were beginning now to patronize the refreshment room. Arriving at *The Island* she neatly cut Mary-Lou out from a bevy of packers who were all making parcels safe and told her the story.

Mary-Lou's face fell at the news. "Oh dear! And I did want it for Mother! It's just exactly the sort of thing she loves!"

Prunella said nothing. She knew by this time that Mary-Lou made her own decisions.

That young woman stood frowning to herself for a full minute. Then she looked up. "O.K.! She'd better have it and I'll choose something else. After all—that poor kid! You go and tell Mrs. Elstob it's O.K. and she can keep it."

Prunella looked swiftly at the few pictures left adorning the tree. She had a sudden inspiration. "That's wizard of you, Mary-Lou! And look here! There isn't anything very decent left. If you like to wait, I'll do you an illumination of that prayer you liked instead. Will that do?"

"Oh, I'd love that!" Mary-Lou said instantly. "Of course I'll wait. Thanks a million, Prunella; you really are a—a peach!"

"I can't let you have it till after the hols.," Prunella warned her again. "But I'll bring it back with me and you can post it to her then."

"That'll do. I'll tell Mother I've *ordered* my present for her and she'll have to wait till it's done," Mary-Lou said with an appreciative giggle.

Prunella nodded and went off again to tell Mrs. Elstob that it was all right and she could have the picture for Leila.

"It's frightfully decent of Mary-Lou," she thought as she made an excuse for crossing *The Bridge* which had fascinated all the girls. "She'd said Leila could have it before ever I offered to do the illumination. She's rather a grand person."

She found Mrs. Elstob just leaving the competition table, looking very crestfallen. She cheered up when she heard what Prunella had to say.

"Oh, I'm so glad!" she said. "That makes ten things I have for Leila and I'm certain she'll like all of them. I wish I could think I'd any chance of winning the Chalet, but I'm afraid I've none. I could only think of three things that would work and I'm not sure of one of them."

"I'll send Sue along now to see if she has any better luck," Prunella offered. "People are going for refreshments, so we'll probably get a rest from selling."

"If you would." Mrs. Elstob suddenly looked anxious. "You—you know about Leila, don't you? I—I want to give her every single thing to please her that I can. She is all I have—" She stopped short and bit her lip and Prunella, not knowing what to say, looked round for inspiration. She found it in *Chang's Boat* which was just behind them with Con Maynard looking very serious beside it.

"Have you had a go at *Chang's Boat* yet, Mrs. Elstob?" she asked eagerly. "Oh, you must! Only ten centimes and the prizes are really decent. Here, Con! Pick out something nice for Leila, won't you? Have a go, Mrs. Elstob, and I'll go and send Sue."

She thought no more about it as she went to rout out Sue and send her to try her luck with the model chalet. In any case, she had no time, for Madge Herbert came up to ask if she had been to have anything to eat and hearing that she had not, shooed her off to the domestic science room where the school was having its sandwiches and cakes and coffee.

There was not a great deal of time left after that. The competitions and draws came at fourteen o'clock and they were the last thing. Most of the stalls were practically sold out and *Chang's Boat* had been emptied a good half-hour earlier. The visitors stood facing the daïs when Miss Dene rang the bell to announce that the lucky winners would now be named and there was an atmosphere of expectation in the room. Jo had returned from a visit to her babies—the twins and the puppy—and Mrs. Elstob, who had departed to take half her purchases to Leila, had come back. She had entered for everything and though she had no hope of the chalet, she might have a chance of one of the others.

Jack Maynard stood on the platform to announce the prizewinners and there were outbursts of applause for each name. Frieda von Ahlen had won Beth's twin set. When she saw it, she gave a gasp and then handed it over to Jo with the remark that she herself would swim in it!

"You're much fatter than I am," she added; and Jo was left to swallow the cheerful insult in silence, since you can't scrap with someone who has just made you a charming present!

Frau Mieders' cake went to Matron of the big Sanatorium at the other end of the Platz. The cake weighed eight pounds ten ounces and Miss Graves had guessed nearest with eight-and-three-quarter pounds. She was cheered by the girls, especially when she announced that she meant to give a tea-party with it for all those patients who were well enough to enjoy it.

A two-pound box of American candies was won by Clem Barrass and Miss o'Ryan came away with Julie Lucy's tea-cloth which had been voted much too handsome to sell cheaply so that they had had a raffle for it. The multicoloured blanket Anna from Freudesheim had knitted went to Miss Wilson and Lady Russell found herself the owner of a three-foot high stuffed elephant, very handsome in his covering of grey velvet.

The Welsen girls had offered a prize for the winner of a competition for guessing the number of separate articles crammed into a matchbox, and this went to a patient's sister and proved to be a pretty flowering plant. Jo was left horrified with a whole Gorgonzola cheese for which she had rashly entered, urged thereto by the donor, one of the doctors at the Sanatorium.

"But what on *earth* can I do with a thing like that!" she wailed. "It isn't as if any of us were mad on Gorgonzola! I'll have to share it out among everyone!"

However, she recovered when Gillian Culver, secretary at Welsen, won her own offering of an enormous jigsaw. Jo had set them all to guessing how many pieces made up the thing which measured thirty inches by twenty-five and Miss Culver had guessed exactly with 987 pieces.

Finally, they came to the Chalet. Tom and Barbara Chester's sister, Nancy, staggered up to the platform with it and set it down while Nell Randolph, Peggy Bettany's special chum, handed a sealed envelope to the doctor who took it with a grin.

"Who's going to be rent asunder for winning?" he demanded as he slit the envelope with his penknife and drew the folded slip of paper from it in his most leisurely manner.

"Open it—do!" urged his wife, standing near him. "You *are* a maddening man!"

He chuckled and opened it. Everyone watched him with interest and when his jaw dropped, there was a sensation.

"Who's won it?" Jo demanded. "Don't say—"

He waved her to silence and she subsided. "The model chalet," he announced, "has been won by—Con Maynard!"

There was a gasp from the girls, for two years before, Con had won another of Tom's wonderful models. Then there was a small scrimmage at the back of the room and Con, supported by her two sisters and very red in the face, appeared below the daïs.

"Please, Papa," she said clearly, "I only went in for the fun of it and we have two dollies' houses already. We don't think we ought to keep this." She waved to her two sisters who nodded instantly. "We've decided that we'd rather give it away—if Tom won't mind?"

"Oh, do as you like about it," Tom said bluntly. "The thing's yours!"

But Con had lost her tongue and it was left to Margot to finish what she had begun. "We want to give it to Mrs. Elstob for Leila," she announced simply.

Then she turned and ran, the other two going after her. They vanished out of Hall and Dr. Maynard checked any pursuit by saying through the loud speaker, "Then that's settled. Is Mrs. Elstob here?"

Mrs. Elstob, looking rather flustered, came forward. "Oh, Dr. Maynard, are you sure your little girls should do this?" she asked anxiously. "Leila would be overjoyed, I know. But oughtn't they to keep it for themselves?"

Jo stepped forward quickly. "Oh, no Mrs. Elstob. As Con said, they have two already and it won't be many years before, I'm afraid, they'll begin to think themselves too old to play with them. Luckily, Felicity will be wanting them by that time. But I'm very glad they want your little Leila to have this one. Please take it for her and tell her that we all hope she will have lots of fun with it."

While this was going on, some of the Welsen girls had been having a quick colloquy among themselves. As Jo ended, Tom stood forward.

"We'll pack the things and some of us will bring it all along to your place, Mrs. Elstob, and to-morrow, if I may, I'll come along with one or two of the others and help your kiddy put all the things in the right rooms for a start," she said.

Mrs. Elstob was incapable of replying. Jack Maynard gave her a quick look and promptly changed the subject. "Can anyone tell me how *many* articles my gifted daughter guessed?" he asked plaintively. "I had a shot at it myself and my limit was six."

Amid peals of laughter, Tom answered. "Every last one! There were fifteen and she got the lot! That kid ought to be an aeroplane spotter when she grows up! She doesn't seem to miss a thing!"

Prunella was surprised out of herself. "Three cheers for Con and her sisters!" she shouted. "They aren't here, so it doesn't matter. But I think they've deserved it! Hip, hip, hip—"

And with one voice, everyone present joined her in "Hooray!"

Chapter XV

Big Results

HALL was packed a good twenty minutes before it was time for the curtain to rise on *The Story of the Willow Pattern*. This, they had learned, was the product of the combined brains of Peggy Bettany and Bess Herbert. Three or four other people had written most of the lyrics and the school's own singing-master, Mr. Denny, known to them as "Plato", a name bestowed on him by Jo Bettany in her wicked youth, had composed most of the music for them as well as for one or two of the choruses. For the others, they had fallen back on well-known tunes.

As soon as the girls were settled, they eagerly scanned their programmes to see "who was what", to quote Mary-Lou. They were highly delighted to find that quite a number of their old friends had leading parts. Dickie Christy was *The Mandarin*. Daphne Russell who was small and dark was *Li-Chi* and Peggy Bettany would play the part of the Chinese Mother-goddess, *Kwan-si*. Her sister Bride was to be *The Gardener*, the father of *Chang*, and Hester Layng was to be *Li-Chi's* old *Nurse*. *Chang* himself was played by Peggy's great friend, Nell Randolph. There was a ballet, arranged by Lesceline St. Georges and her sister Ghislaine.

"Will it be a *Chinese* ballet?" Con Maynard asked Vi Lucy in awed tones. "I thought that in those days all Chinese girls had their feet bound when they were little to make them small? How could they dance like that?"

"Not the foggiest," Vi replied. "Mary-Lou, do you know?"

But for once Mary-Lou was not omniscient. She had to confess that she had no more idea than they had.

"It takes place in the Garden of the Gods," Barbara Chester read. "I've read the story, of course, but I don't remember *that* coming into it."

Len chuckled. "It sounds lavish all right," she said, borrowing one of her mother's favourite expressions. "Oo-oh! Here comes the orchestra. They'll begin in half a sec. Here, anyone, have some more cocoanut ice?"

She passed the box round and by the time everyone near was munching cocoanut ice, the orchestra was seated and Mr. Denny, who was conductor, was coming in and mounting his tiny rostrum amidst loud applause to which he replied with a jerk of his head before turning round, raising his baton and then swinging the instruments—two violins, a cello, a flute, a piano and the glockenspiel, played by Herr Laubach, the art master—into *The Pagoda Dance* from Tchaikovsky's *Casse-Noisette Suite*.

Verity-Anne, next to Mary-Lou as usual, was moved to murmur to that young lady, "I do hope he doesn't suddenly forget it's a play and stop a chorus or something to make them take a few bars over again. For he might, you know. Quite easily!"

"Phooey to that!" Mary-Lou retorted. "He's got *some* sense—though not a lot, I must agree," she added.

Madge Herbert just behind, tapped her on the shoulder at that moment, so both subsided. The dance came to an end and Mr. Denny gave the audience a minute for applause before he tapped his desk lightly. The orchestra came to the "ready", and a lovely air stole out as the curtains rose to show The Garden of the Moon Fairy.

The Welsen people had added to the old legend for their own purposes and now showed the garden where, the old Chinese legends say, babies wait till their time to go to Earth arrives. The babies were largely dolls, tied into the hearts of enormous paper flowers. But there were half-a-dozen small children as well who were staying at Welsen, Laubach, or the Platz and had been borrowed for this scene by the girls. They were in charge of Frances Coleman, an old Chalet School girl, who had small brothers and sisters at home and knew how to handle tinies. Moving about among them were radiant beings, clad in somewhat scanty rainbow draperies and singing the opening chorus: "Here in the Garden of the Moon". The *Moon Fairy* was played by Gabrielle Fournet, a pretty French girl, who was the owner of a very charming, soprano voice, not strong, but sweet and clear. The chorus ended, the music modulating and she came forward and sang the story of how the *Moon Fairy* takes care of all babies, sending them to earth when the right time comes. Just as she finished, there was a stir, off-stage, and then came a strong alto voice, singing The Boatman's Song: "Yeo-ho! Yeo-ho! Fly, Boat of Dreams!" and across the back of the stage, behind a balcony railing draped with sprays of artificial, wild roses, came the cardboard boat—somewhat jerkily, it must be admitted—adorned with crimson sails and with *The Boatman*, one Gwynneth Hughes, standing in it, using a long pole. He reached the opening in the railing and sang to the end of his song. Then the *Moon Fairy* began selecting the children and handing them over. As she did so, she bestowed on each a gift. One was to become a rich merchant; one to be a rice coolie; and so on. She came to twins, boy and girl, who clung together, but she carried them to the boatman who stowed them in. Then the music changed back once more to the Boatman's Song with a final verse in which everyone joined, waving good-bye as the boat was pulled slowly off with due regard for its fragility, though the girls had screwed silent domes into the bottom to ensure that it would move easily. The curtain fell as it vanished and the audience applauded rapturously.

"This is rather more than a pantomime, I should say," Lady

Russell said to Miss Annersley and Miss Wilson under cover of the clapping. "It's a lovely opening."

"I don't know what you'd call it," the Head of Welsen agreed. "Musical Play might fill the bill, I suppose. There *are* funny scenes, of course, but you're quite right. It *is* more than a pantomime."

They sampled the "funny scenes" almost at once, for when the curtain rose again, it was on a street scene, with *The Gardener* and two or three cronies of his enjoying glasses of lemonade while they gossiped. *The Gardener* informed everyone that he was standing treat in celebration of the arrival of a son. One of the others instantly told him that that was a pity, for that morning, his master had been presented with a daughter.

"The Moon Fairy's done it this time!" he added. "What will your boss say when he hears that you've got the boy and he has nothing but a miserable girl?"

The Gardener promptly swooned at this horrifying news and the others rushed to bring him to. The various suggestions they made caused the audience to rock with laughter and by the time he had come to, they were all shrieking. He sat up to demand feebly that they should say that again, which they did, playing the part of Job's comforters with gusto.

"Oh, drat that Moon Fairy!" he remarked, getting to his feet. "A nice mess she's made of it this time! Oh, what *will* become of me?"

Here, the orchestra broke into a jolly tune and he sang a song which began:

"Here's a nice todo!
Misery, misery me!
A girl has come to the Mandarin;
The Mandarin's son to me!"

He went on to number all the awful punishments he expected when his master should hear what had happened and his friends joined in the chorus:

> "Sorrow will be my lot
> Woes will hound me down!
> I'm in a mess—a horrible mess!
> I'd better depart from town!"

At the end of this, *The Mandarin* arrived, gorgeous in blue and scarlet, to demand to know if what he had been told was true.

The four fell on their faces and a very funny scene ensued as *The Mandarin* raged up and down the stage, promising his servant all sorts of horrible punishments for daring to have a boy when he, the great man, had only a miserable girl. *The Gardener* kept on muttering apologies which were constantly interrupted by his master in a series of cross remarks and crooked answers which reduced the audience to such shrieks—for a good many school events were touched on—that they might have been heard to the big Sanatorium at the other end of the Platz!

Finally, *The Mandarin* strode out, falling over the four, one after the other, in his passage, and the curtain fell—just in time to prevent one or two people from having to be removed in hysterics.

This ended Act I and while the spectators gradually recovered themselves, the people backstage rushed round, removing the last dolls from the paper flowers and making sure that the willow tree which had been fixed centre-back, was quite safe. Ten minutes later, the orchestra, which had retired to help, returned to their seats. To the tune of *Funiculi Funicula* the curtain rose to show The Mandarin's Garden with various servants moving about and singing a chorus which announced that to-day *The Mandarin's* daughter was to be formally betrothed to a wealthy Mandarin—who never once appeared throughout the play—and also that this was going to be hard lines on both her and *Chang* since everyone knew that they were in love with each other. *The Nurse* stalked on as this ended to demand what they thought they were doing. *The Gardener* came forward to complain that it was all very unfair on the two young people, to which she retorted that a Mandarin's daughter could hardly marry a Gardener's son. It was all *Chang's* fault for putting ideas into her darling's head. Whoever heard of a Chinese lady falling in love with someone who was no better than a coolie?

He replied that his boy was as handsome a young man as you could find anywhere and anyhow, such ideas were out of date. They went for each other, she trying to grab at his pigtail and he fending her off. It ended in their tripping up and falling full length—this was an entirely unrehearsed effect—and rolling over and over until some of the others managed to part them, when he was lugged off in one direction by an arm and she in the other by a foot, by which time the audience was once more in convulsions of laughter.

Music broke out again and the servants sang a chorus, bemoaning the sad state of things that caused a lovely girl to be married willy-nilly to an ugly, old miser while she was in love with a fine young man. They drifted off, still singing and then *Li-Chi* came in, her hands full of flowers. She reached a stool at one side and sat down, dropping her flowers, and spoke a soliloquy in which she stressed her own miserable fate. The boat—which was holding together remarkably well—was pulled along, denuded of its sails, and *Chang* leaped out, climbed over the balcony railings with due care for their fragility, and came to take *Li Chi* in his arms and ask if the news he had just heard of her betrothal was true.

She told him mournfully that it was only too true. Her father was determined on it and had vowed that she should never marry *The Gardener's* son. Nell Randolph was a very tall girl, and she made a good foil for the slightness of Daphne. A very pretty love-scene followed, which ended with a charming duet, for soprano and alto.

Chang opened it, singing:

"When the whispering willow blooms and Spring is come again
Oh, little Moon of love's delight, my heart is thrilled with pain."

She answered,

"When the night is powdered o'er with silver stars and gold,
My being aches to hear again your tale so sweetly told."

Their voices blended in the refrain:

"Come what may!
Let Spring forget her day;
The willow fade; the night stars pale and fly.
Let this mend all;
That I will love you till I die."

When the applause that greeted this died away—there was no time for encores—*Chang* told *Li-Chi* the plan he had made. He would seek the Garden of the Gods and beg their help. She pleaded that her father might marry her to the mandarin he had chosen before her lover could return from such a journey. He pointed to the willow—on which Gaudenz, the man at the school who was working the limes, had flung his deepest amber light—and said that now it was autumn. The willow was withering. Let her insist that she could not wed until the willow was in leaf again. He would set out when he had bidden her farewell and he would return before the willow budded.

After a little demur, she promised him and then, clasped in each other's arms once more, they sang the last verse of their duet.

"Through the weary winter days my heart will long for you.
I will think of you always; I will still be true.
When the spring wind brings the rain; when the ripples sing
In the river flowing fast, look for Love's bright wing."

"Come what may!
Let Spring forget her day;
The willow fade;
The night stars pale and fly.
Let this mend all;
I love you till I die."

The curtains whispered down on the pair standing carefully spot-lighted by Gaudenz. They rose again as the applause thundered out to show *Chang* in his boat, taking up the oars while *Li-Chi* stood waving from the balcony. Then they descended again and the storm of clapping rose once more. In fact, it only ceased when Mr. Denny rapped with his baton to bring the orchestra to attention and they broke into the old sea-shanty, *What shall we do with the Drunken Sailor*. The curtain rose to show a backdrop with *The Mandarin's* kitchen in full swing and *The Nurse* hectoring everyone though she dropped her ladle when *The Gardener* arrived, staggering under the weight of a clothes-basket piled high with vegetables of as many kinds as they could muster at that season. He dumped this down in the middle of the floor and was at once embroiled in a quarrel with *The Nurse* who ordered him to take it away and not dirty *her* nice, clean kitchen with his earthy vegetables. The quarrel grew, with the kitchen folk taking sides, and ended when *The Nurse*, pursuing *The Gardener* with her ladle, fell on top of the basket, whereupon, two husky men picked it up and carried it out—they dropped it almost before they reached the wings, for Hester was no mean weight!—and the scene ended with the audience, some members of which had felt quite choky over the love-scene, nearly weeping with laughter.

The next scene was a magnificent effort—The Garden of the Gods. They had used the wings and backdrops of The Moon Fairy's Garden, but in addition, they had built up a staging on which, in a gorgeous row, sat the Gods in state—six of them. Below their feet had been set school tables, covered with every flowering plant they could beg, borrow or steal, while the nature of the supports was hidden by green baize, liberally bestrewn with sprays of creepers and artificial flowers. The orchestra gave a great chord and the Gods, ably supported by the chorus off-stage, broke into a thunderous song: "We are the Gods!"

As it was sung at fortissimo most of the time, and never dropped below a good forte, there was some excuse for Jo's whispered comment to Biddy o'Ryan, "I'll bet those kids have sore throats at the end of this. I wonder Plato puts up with it!"

Miss o'Ryan's lips quivered, but she contrived to suppress her chuckles as she whispered back, "You hold your tongue, can't you? Setting a poor soul on to laugh at what's most likely the wrong minute!"

There was no time for more, for fresh music stole forth, refreshingly piano, and *The Moon Fairy* led in a troupe of ballet dancers and Con's question was answered as they circled round the stage and then broke into a dance which mainly consisted of drifting about the stage, taking up graceful postures, breaking them to move again, all as charmingly as they could to a Chopin waltz. It merged into one of his mazurkas, and the two St. Georges ran forward and performed a pas de deux which nearly brought the house down. Then *The Moon Fairy* joined them and to the music of another waltz, they danced a pas de trois which ended with the whole band joining in, whirling round in a mazy dance which ended when they flung themselves into groups and single poses all arranged with an eye to their rainbow draperies.

"Amazingly good!" said a strange voice behind Madge Russell. "Who are those two that did the pas de deux? They are excellent—such a beautiful sense of line and almost perfect movement."

Madge hardly liked to turn round; but Miss Wilson, who had also overheard, did, and peered through the gloom of the house to see if she could glimpse the speaker. She was not very sure, but she thought the lady's face seemed vaguely familiar. She turned back in time to see the entry of *Chang*. Advancing, he fell on his knee before the Gods and sang his request to them. *The Father of the Gods* rose when he had ended with *Kwan-si* and together they sang a reply. If it could be done, *Li-Chi* and *Chang* should wed. But if anything intervened, they would be changed either into twin stars to shine together in the evening skies, or else twin turtle-doves to nest in the willow as each spring came round. *Chang* sang his thanks and backed off and a final chorus brought the scene to a close.

The next one was as frankly funny as the last had been beautiful. It took place in *Li-Chi's* room, with *The Nurse* bustling about, scolding vigorously, the servants falling over each other, and the women spreading out curtains of every kind or size, exclaiming that this or that would make a beautiful bridal dress.

The Welsen folk had had to use what they could, and it was proposed to dress the luckless bride in crimson plush and heavy green damask among other things. However, when she entered and they showed everything to her, she shook her head at them all. *The Nurse* brought a tunic of royal blue with gold butterflies appliquéd and gold trousers and *Li-Chi* said that would do. Then she left and *The Gardener* bounced on with a bouquet of paper flowers nearly as large as himself. He proceeded to try to put it down, but whenever he found a place, *The Nurse* found some good reason why it could not go *there*. It ended in their landing down centre to sing a quarrelling duet and the curtain fell to show him flinging the bouquet at her and racing off, while she followed waving a huge towel to pin to his tunic.

Next came another balcony scene with *The Mandarin* trying to insist that his daughter must wed her bridegroom without more delay while she refused on the grounds that the time he had promised her was not yet up.

"The willow tree has budded!" yelled her indignant father.

"But not blossomed," she replied.

"Are you still thinking of that miserable wretch Chang?" he shouted. "The last I heard of him he was in gaol for committing arson, bigamy, forgery and trigonometry! You'll do as you're told!"

"If he committed murder, theft and embezzlement, I wouldn't care!" she retorted. "I'm going to my room. I won't marry that horrible man until the willow is in bloom." She departed and he was left to shake his clenched fists over his head and bellow that he didn't know what the world was coming to when daughters were so refractory. Here he had found a really rich husband for his daughter and she refused to have him! If she didn't look out, she'd be left on the shelf!

The orchestra swung into the tune of *Here we come*

gathering nuts in May and all the servants danced in to sing:

"Left on the shelf! She'll be left on the shelf!
All alone! All by herself!
Unless she wed she'll be left on the shelf
On a cold and frosty morning!"

The Nurse waddled forward to croak,

"Poor little bird, she'll be all alone!
All alone! All alone!
And then she'll wish to her wedding she'd gone
On a cold and frosty morning!"

The chorus was repeated and *The Gardener*, who always declared that she had very little voice and therefore more or less declaimed her words to the tune, sang:

"As for my son, he'll be in his grave!
If he's alive now, he'll soon be in his grave!
And there'll be an end of my Chang so brave
On a cold and frosty morning!"

It was *The Mandarin's* turn and he gave the assembled company something they never forgot. Dicky Christy had a good robust voice but not much ear. She started in by pitching the tune too high and bawled:

"If she doesn't take care she'll be left behind
And that's a thing that a girl will mind!
And she'll wish she'd obeyed her father so kind
On a cold and frosty morning!"

Dicky squeaked up to the end of the first line. Then, finding she couldn't keep it up, she abruptly descended two full tones lower and as the orchestra were too stunned to follow the lead of Miss Lawrence at the piano and transpose it at once, but kept on with the key in which Dicky had started them, the result had to be heard to be believed! They did what they considered the next best thing and played the tune as loudly as they could in an effort to drown her shouts. Dickie merely roared the louder and it ended with *The Mandarin* bawling his head off while the orchestra, faint but pursuing, went all out, and still failed to cover up her howls. As for the audience, they were mostly quite helpless with laughter. Jo clung to her husband, laid her head on his shoulder and shrieked with the tears of mirth rolling down her cheeks. Lady Russell and the two Heads clung together moaning feebly. As for the girls, when the curtain fell, Len and Con in the front seat, collapsed on the floor, and Margot at Con's other side was only kept from following suit by the strong arm Mary-Lou behind flung round her, though Mary-Lou's own face was streaming and she was on the verge of hiccoughs.

Luckily for all concerned, the setting of the final scene took a little time and when the curtains were raised, most people were more or less recovered. This was the elopement scene and the girls had shoved the balcony further to the back of the stage to make a little room for the actors to manœuvre. They had been unable to do the actual chase over the bridge, so they had left that to the cries of the crowd. They opened with *Li-Chi* sitting on her balcony, attired for her bridal. She rose and went to stand by the rail to look at the willow tree which glowed greenly in the green limelight thrown on it and was clearly in full bloom, or very nearly. She sang another of the songs Mr. Denny had composed to a sad little minor air.

"Oh willow, in the garden that I was wont to love,
Let fall your budding leaves and bloom no more.
For if you blossom, willow, then my weeping heart will break.
Oh, bid your flowerets slumber! Let them never, never wake
Till my Chang shall row his boat again to shore.

"Oh birds that wanton in the skies and sing of love and joy,
Be still and hush your songs that swell my pain!
Kind Death, come quickly, quickly and take me to your breast!
Bid aching heart and throbbing brain be still in endless rest,
For my Chang will never come to me again!"

She ended and stood gazing down the river. Then a tall man in a long cloak and enormous straw hat appeared and bowed low to her, saying, "Gracious lady!"

She turned and asked how he came there. "Depart!" she added. "The willow blossoms and Chang has never come!"

"Chang is here!" cried the stranger, tossing aside his hat with such reckless lack of aim that it skimmed across the footlights and obliterated the first violinist completely. He threw off his cloak and held out his arms. *Li-Chi* looked, gave a cry and flung herself bodily into his arms. He staggered and nearly went over with the impetus, but luckily this had happened at rehearsals and he was more or less prepared. He saved himself and they remained on their feet.

"Oh, when can we be married?" *Li-Chi* asked with an amazing lack of maidenly modesty.

"Now," he said. "Are you ready? For we must go now."

"One moment," she replied. "I must not be a dowerless bride. Here; take these jewels. I will carry my distaff. Now let us go!"

Carefully he helped her over the balcony—and the river must

have changed its course, for they began to run. *The Mandarin* suddenly appeared bellowing with rage and carrying a whip. *He* nearly brought the balcony railing down as he got over. The servants crowded in after him and began exclaiming.

"There they go!—Li-Chi and Chang have reached the bridge!—So has the Mandarin! He's nearly on them!—Oh look! He tried to clutch Chang's shoulder!—He's caught him!—They're caught!"

Then the tune changed. "They've vanished! There goes something into the water—Oh, what a splash!—That must be the big casket of jewels!—There goes her distaff!—Where are they?—Everything's gone!—Only the Mandarin is left!"

Then *The Nurse* gave a shriek. "Look—see! Where did those two doves come from? They weren't there before! Look at them, circling round! Oh, where is my precious baby?"

The Gardener added, "And what's got my son? There's magic at work here—that's what it is! Magic!"

On his last word, the stage was suddenly blacked out. When the lights came on again, it was on the Garden of the Gods who were seated on high, the dancers grouped below them and the servants skipping in while the orchestra played Edward German's *Torch Dance* until they were all in their places. Then the music changed into a song of triumph and welcome as *Chang* entered with *Li-Chi*, led her up to the Gods and both bowed down, the throng on the stage swinging as far back to the sides as they could manage to give them room.

The Gods rose and sang a welcome to them. Then *The Father of the Gods* sang a few lines, bidding the lovers nest each year in the willow and be an example to all true lovers of constancy and faith. *Li-Chi* and *Chang* had a brief duet in reply to this. Then the music slipped into the strains of a very old song and the entire chorus and principals—including *The Mandarin* who had slipped in among his servants—ended the play with a delightful rendering of the old English song, *Love will find the way*.

The curtains fell on the last victorious note and the pantomime was over except for the calls for the principals, and, finally, the gifted writers.

*

"Well, it was a jolly good show!" Clem Barrass observed later on when the visitors had departed and the two branches of the school were crammed round the tables in the Speisesaal, enjoying a meal that had begun with chicken salad and was ending with ices. "I almost think it's one of the best I've seen any of us put on."

"Jolly good Sale, too, if you ask me," Peggy Bettany replied. "I'm only sorry I can't stay another year and be in another panto."

"Well, why don't you?" Julie Lucy suggested; but Peggy laughed and shook her head until her linty curls flew and said it couldn't be done. She was going to be badly needed at home after the summer term.

"Besides, I was nineteen in January," she added. "I can't stay at school forever! Not that Welsen is 'school', exactly; but it comes to the same thing in the end."

Later on, when Jack and Jo Maynard, accompanied by Lady Russell, came over to superintend the counting of the takings, Clem repeated her comment.

"Don't you think it's been a jolly good show, Aunt Jo?"

"Super!" was Jo's unparliamentary reply.

"It's been a jolly good term all round," Julie Lucy said. "What's more, it's been quite a peaceful one—for us, that is."

"I'm glad you added that!" Jo said severely. "What about my young Margot's escapade at Lucerne? You couldn't call that exactly peaceful, could you?"

"No-o," the Head Girl said. "But in a way it all helped, you know."

"'*Helped*'? How did it help?" Jo gasped.

"Well, it ended Prunella's primness which was beginning to set everyone in her own crowd by the ears. I mean it really was awfully plucky of her to go in as she did and once she'd done that, the rest began to see there was more to her than just a sickener of a new girl," Julie explained.

"What English!" cried Miss Annersley. "Still, you're quite right, Julie. But it's a good thing we decided to have only representatives of you prefects *and* Welsen in here while we counted. Well, you folk?" she turned to the people headed by Miss Wilson, who had been absorbed in counting the notes and coins they had amassed that afternoon and evening.

"Quite well," Miss Wilson replied, standing up and stretching. "Here's the total. Go and ring the bell, someone, and get everyone into Hall and we'll announce it. Then we Welsen people will have to fly or we'll miss the last train down and I don't suppose anyone would be overjoyed at having to put us all up for the night!"

"You could always walk down," Jo suggested.

"With no moon? Really, Jo! Have you *no* sense?"

Jo subsided and Miss Dene went off to ring the bell. When the school *and* Welsen had pulled all the forms into position and were sitting waiting, the two Heads led the way on to the stage where the curtains had been pulled back. The visitors followed and when everyone was in place, Miss Annersley stood forward.

"Girls, I congratulate you!" she said. "We have made 1404 francs altogether. For the sake of those of you who find the exchange rate difficult, that means about £140: 4s. And now, Welsen, we're sorry to lose you, but you must run if you're to catch your train. School, it's bed for you—all of you. Clearing-up can wait till the morning. Good night, everyone and, once more, congratulations!"

"Mayn't we have three cheers first?" pleaded Peggy.

The Heads laughed and nodded and the three cheers were given with great effect.

But when the girls had all gone and the weary staff and their three visitors were drinking a final cup of coffee with the Head, Jo had the last word.

"This term has seen big results on the whole," she said seriously. "We've given the free ward at the San. a decent lift with to-day's little efforts. My bad Margot has, I hope, begun to realize that you can't go monkeying about just as you please without unpleasant results for someone. Finally, a girl has come to us who needed straightening out and she's got just that. Prunella obviously had to reform and she's doing it. I don't mind betting that some day she'll be one of the girls we shall be proud of having as a Chalet School girl. In short, and I hope you all agree with me, the Chalet School has done it again!"

And with one voice, everyone agreed.

STRANGER AT THE PLAY

a short story by Katherine Bruce

"Amazingly good!" said a strange voice behind Madge Russell. "Who are those two that did the pas de deux? They are excellent—such a beautiful sense of line and almost perfect movement."

Madge hardly liked to turn round; but Miss Wilson, who had also overheard, did, and peered through the gloom of the house to see if she could glimpse the speaker. She was not very sure, but she thought the lady's face seemed vaguely familiar. (p234)

The *Story of the Willow Pattern* was of the same high standard St Mildred's had established with their *Sleeping Beauty* the previous year, but Miss Wilson—who had seen the dress rehearsal—still found moments during the show to ponder the identity of the mysterious stranger. The more she thought about it, the more certain she became that she knew the lady sitting behind her. Not an Old Girl, she felt almost positive, mentally reviewing the generations of former pupils, although the darkness made it difficult to tell.

The performance finished with the obligatory happy ending as the two lovers were welcomed into the Garden of the Gods and the entire cast sang a final song. Miss Wilson, as head of St Mildred's, was called up on stage to thank the audience for coming, but with the footlights shining she had no chance to make out individual features of those in the seats below her. To crown it all, no sooner had she spoken her few words and reached the bottom of the stairs than she was stopped by one of the visitors.

"Oh, Miss Wilson," Mrs Elstob exclaimed, "that was simply delightful. Your girls are to be complimented for a most enchanting performance! I don't suppose," she added rather wistfully, "the chorus could come tomorrow and perform some of the songs for Leila? She would so love to hear them!"

It was impossible for Miss Wilson to peer over Mrs Elstob's shoulder to look for that mysterious visitor without seeming terribly rude, so she had to put off her search for the moment and answer the question that had been put to her.

"I'm afraid not, Mrs Elstob," she replied, as patiently as she could manage under the circumstances. "Tomorrow is the last day of term and the girls must tidy everything up before going to the train, so they won't have time. You must encourage Leila to get well as soon as she can so that the doctors will let her come to the pantomime and the Sale next year."

"Oh, dear." Mrs Elstob's face fell. "I had so hoped to have something for Leila to look forward to tomorrow. She found the Christmas holidays so dull without news from the school and the friendly little notes and messages she receives from everyone."

"It won't be as bad as you fear, Mrs Elstob," Miss Wilson said soothingly. "Leila has Sue to entertain her in the holidays, and if you remember, Tom Gay has promised to come along with a few of the Seniors to help set up the little chalet. I'm sure the triplets will be round to play with it and her as soon as they can."

"But she's going to the Sanatorium after Easter for her treatment and she's already begun to fret," Mrs Elstob explained, tears welling up in her eyes.

"Then you will have to make her see that it is for her own good," Miss Wilson said sternly, for she, like all the Chalet School staff, knew that Mrs Elstob was inclined to spoil and pet her daughter. "You know she will have the best chance if she is given the proper treatment, and she can't have that at home."

"I do know." But Mrs Elstob's expression remained one of utter misery. "She's all I have, though, and it's so difficult to see her like that."

"At least you can tell her all about today," Miss Wilson said in consoling tones. "Come and talk to Lady Russell, Mrs Elstob, and then Dr Maynard will be ready to drive you back to the Élisehütte with all your prizes and purchases."

Mrs Elstob, her disappointment clear, nevertheless allowed herself to be led across to the corner of the room in which the school's founder was talking to several other members of the Chalet School staff. Lady Russell broke off her conversation to talk to Mrs Elstob and finally Miss Wilson could escape.

She turned to look round the large room, groaning inwardly at the sight of the greatly diminished audience, for many people had already left to catch the train down to the lower shelves or to Interlaken itself. How could she possibly hope to find the stranger now?

She was about to confess herself beaten when she heard light footsteps and a voice spoke quietly from close beside her. "Excuse me—Miss Wilson?"

The Head of St Mildred's turned to find herself face to face with a young woman with mousy brown hair, while an older woman with features sufficiently similar to proclaim them sisters stood not far away. Miss Wilson smiled as she recognised the speaker. Now she was able to identify the mysterious stranger and could understand why her face had seemed familiar.

"Dorcas Brownlow!" she exclaimed. "How lovely to see you!"

The girl who had once been a mystery to the Chalet School beamed. "It's lovely to be here," she said; then, gesturing to her companion, "and I would like to introduce my sister. Eunice, this is Miss Wilson. Miss Wilson, my elder sister. I've told her all about you."

"She has," Eunice laughed as she shook Miss Wilson's hand. "All about you and the School."

"Well, she told us a great deal about you, too," Miss Wilson said, smiling in response. "I'm delighted you could take the time to come and visit us today."

"Only good things I hope," Eunice replied, glancing at her sister before returning her attention to Miss Wilson. "I've been longing to come to one of the Chalet School plays ever since I first read about them in Dorcas's letters."

"I hope it was worth the wait." Miss Wilson looked at the famous actress curiously, unable to help asking, "What did you think of our little play?"

"The whole pantomime was wonderful," Eunice enthused. "I can scarcely believe that the girls wrote it themselves, lyrics and all."

"And made the costumes, didn't they?" Dorcas added. "I think that's what Gill said."

"Oh, you've heard from Gillian Culver?" Miss Wilson enquired, referring to her secretary, a former Head Girl of the Chalet School. "I must admit I wondered how you knew which day to come."

"Yes, I told Gill I would be nearby and she told me about the Sale and the panto," Dorcas replied.

"At the moment we're down in Interlaken working on a film," Eunice added, "so Dorks suggested we come up for the afternoon."

"I hoped we could make it to the Sale," Dorcas explained with a rueful sigh. "But unfortunately we went on rather longer than I'd hoped and so we had to catch a late train up to the Görnetz Platz."

"Still, the pantomime was the real reason for our visit," Eunice reminded her sister before turning to Miss Wilson. "Dorcas has told me how important plays and performances have always been to the Chalet School, and I wondered about giving a prize for the best actress or dancer. But Dorcas had a feeling that might not be suitable for the Chalet School, so I thought about providing a scholarship of some sort for those girls who want to pursue that avenue in the future."

Miss Wilson gazed at Eunice in astonishment. "Do you mean it, Miss Brownlow? Of course, we would be delighted to have something like that for girls who have an inclination towards acting or dancing. And it would be particularly appropriate to St Mildred's, with its focus on the girls' future and the opportunity for them to take specialised subjects like drama or musical appreciation. We have several girls at the moment who have an interest in dance, as you may have seen in the pantomime."

"Yes, I noticed the dancers." Eunice looked interested.

"She loves dancing," said Dorcas by way of explanation. "She did ballet when we were at school together in Boston and she's always eager to see other people dancing."

"That's part of where this idea came from," Eunice confessed. "I've been so fortunate and I would love to help other girls who want to follow in my footsteps."

"I would be delighted to accept your offer," Miss Wilson told her warmly. "I can think of at least one girl who would benefit from being the first recipient of the Eunice Brownlow Scholarship."

"Thank you." Eunice glanced at her sister out of the corner of her eye, and added, "Perhaps it should just be the Brownlow Scholarship though. I'm not the only actress in the family."

Miss Wilson wondered at the tone in Eunice's voice, but felt that it was not the right moment to ask about it. Instead she changed the subject. "What film are you working on at the moment?" she enquired.

"It's called *Werner of the Alps*," Eunice replied, and Dorcas added quickly, "Mrs Maynard's latest title."

"Oh, yes, the one that came out last Easter," replied Miss Wilson. "Mrs Maynard wrote it to celebrate the Chalet School—the St Mildred's branch, at least—returning to the Alps." She caught the attention of one of the girls who happened to be passing. "Clem, go and ask Mrs Maynard to come here, please."

"Yes, Miss Wilson," agreed Clem, and scuttled off in search of her quarry, who arrived in short order to greet the newcomers with shrieks of delight.

"Why, Dorcas Brownlow! And is this Eunice? Of course, I've seen your picture all over the place, but it's a real pleasure to meet you at last. I'm delighted you've come to pay us a visit."

"Actually, Jo," Miss Wilson interrupted, "the girls have come here to offer a new type of scholarship to St Mildred's."

She explained about the offer Eunice had made and Jo expressed her enthusiasm for the idea. "That will provide opportunities for some of our girls who could never have managed them otherwise," she declared.

"Yes, that was my thought when Dorks first suggested it," Eunice nodded. "And when we found we'd be working in the area, it seemed like a good time to come and tell you."

Jo cast a curious glance in her direction. "Does this mean work has begun on the film already?"

"Three days ago." Eunice smiled gratefully at the author. "I'm delighted that you were willing for it to be filmed. It's such an exciting tale, but I understand how difficult it must be to hand your precious story over to others."

"Well, if it hadn't been for your sister, I can assure you it would never have happened," Mrs Maynard replied, with a quick smile at Dorcas. "She was the one who made me change my mind over *The Leader of the Lost Cause*, and if it hadn't been for that, none of my other historical stories would have been filmed either."

Miss Wilson happened to be looking at Eunice at the moment that Jo made this remark and saw a guarded expression on the elder girl's face. She began to feel that there must be more to this situation than met the eye and wondered if she could do anything to help.

Mrs Maynard, seemingly oblivious to this, continued, "I'm delighted that this film will have such a special connection to the school, with you in the starring role and your sister having been a pupil at the school."

"Oh, I'm not the only one of us acting in it, Mrs Maynard," Eunice said, giving her sister a nudge. "Dorcas has a small role as well. She's playing the maid who helps Werner escape. Those smaller character parts are her *forte*."

"It's my first film," said Dorcas rather shyly, glancing at the story's author. "I've been doing theatre, but Mummy thought I would be well suited to that character and she asked Eunice to help me get the role."

"Good for you, Dorcas!" Joey beamed at her. "I know you'll do it wonderfully well." She gave the younger girl a thoughtful glance. "I think you'll be perfect as the maid. But we've always known you were good in that kind of part."

Dorcas smiled shyly. "I am enjoying it," she admitted, glancing at her sister. "And it's lovely to work together with Eunie on a film. She's far more occupied with it than I am, of course, playing the female lead, but we still have plenty of chances to spend time together. Well, us and …"

"Dorks!" A pair of arms was flung round Dorcas's shoulders and Gillian Culver irrupted into the group, eagerly embracing her friend. "You did come after all! When I didn't see you at the Sale, I thought you might not have been able to make it."

"Ahem." Miss Wilson coughed gently to remind her secretary

that they were not alone and Gillian's cheeks flushed scarlet as she remembered where she was.

"Sorry, Miss Wilson," she apologised, stepping back to study her friend from head to toe. "Only it's been so long since I saw Dorcas and—hello, what's this, might I ask?"

"Oh, that." It was Dorcas's turn to go bright red and her eyes fell as Gillian picked up her left hand, on the fourth finger of which sparkled a brilliant diamond ring.

"You never told me!" Gillian exclaimed accusingly.

"Well, it only happened last week," Dorcas protested feebly. "I have a letter all ready to send you, but I thought, if I saw you here, I'd tell you in person instead."

"Congratulations, old thing!" exclaimed her friend.

"What wonderful news," Jo beamed. "When will the wedding be?"

"And who is your future husband?" asked Miss Wilson with interest.

"His name is David," Dorcas told them.

"David Murchison," Eunice added, managing a somewhat wry grin as she went on to explain, "He's my leading man."

"Oh, yes, he's been in a number of films with you, hasn't he?" Jo said.

"Wasn't he in *Tedder's Cove*, that film we saw when we were still at school?" Gillian asked curiously.

"Yes, that was the first film we starred in together," Eunice agreed. "We've done several films together now. The last one was a year or so ago and Dorks came to visit me, so that was where they met. Now we're all three of us doing this film together."

"He's 'Werner', too, isn't he?" asked Jo. "I'm sure I was told something about it."

"That's right." Eunice nodded. "We did some filming last week in Paris—and that's the result," she added, lifting Dorcas's left hand in her turn so that the pretty ring sparkled in the light.

"The wedding will be in July," said Dorcas, finding her voice at last. "Please tell me you'll be able to come, Gill."

"So soon?" Gillian looked surprised. "You don't want to wait a while?"

"We meant to at first, but—have you heard from Gay?"

"Gay Lambert?" Gillian shook her head. "Not a word, or at least not since Christmas. We exchanged cards then, as we always do, but she didn't hint at anything—she isn't engaged as well, is she?" she demanded in astonishment.

"Not as far as I'm aware." Dorcas smiled. "No, she's been accepted to go on a teaching exchange—to Australia."

Her audience exclaimed at this, for not even Eunice had heard the news, and she had met Gay several times so she was as interested as everyone else.

"Good for her!" Jo exclaimed.

"That's wonderful news," Miss Wilson chimed in. "The school will be delighted to hear it. There are still a number of girls who remember her, of course."

"Well, I can quite see why you're bringing your wedding forward," Eunice told her sister. "You couldn't possibly get married without Gay!"

"What about Jacynth, though?" Gillian asked anxiously. "Do you know if she will be able to make it?"

"Why shouldn't she?" Dorcas looked puzzled. "I haven't heard from her since January when we met up, and she said nothing about her plans then."

"Oh, she wrote the other day to tell me that she has a tour arranged for Canada and America. I don't remember when she said it would begin though—should we go and see if we can put a call through to her to find out?"

"What, 'phone her?" Dorcas asked in astonishment. "Really?"

"Certainly—then you can tell her all about your wedding yourself—that is, if it's all right with you, Miss Wilson," asked Gillian rather contritely, suddenly remembering that the decision was not properly in her hands.

Miss Wilson smiled. "Oh, go on, the pair of you," she agreed. "I don't imagine Miss Annersley will mind when I explain things to her."

"Thanks, Miss Wilson. Come on, Dorks!" Gillian grabbed her friend's hand and all but towed her through the room to the door that led to the study.

"Say hello to Jacynth for us," Jo called after them.

Miss Wilson glanced at Dorcas's sister and surprised a tense expression in her forget-me-not-blue eyes. Eunice looked up in time to see Miss Wilson's gaze on her and managed a smile. "Thank you so much," she said rather primly.

"Jacynth will be delighted to hear of it, I'm sure," Miss Wilson replied, adding thoughtfully, "As happy as you are."

"She certainly will," rpelied Jo. She glimpsed her husband approaching the group along with Mrs Elstob, and offered her hand to Eunice. "It was lovely to meet you and I'm so glad you decided to come and visit the school."

"You must come down and watch the filming one day," replied Eunice, shaking hands, her relief at the change of subject obvious. "I think you'll like what we've done with the story and the setting."

"That would be lovely." Jo moved away to join the others who were waiting for her and Miss Wilson turned to Eunice, her curiosity piqued.

"Just what *are* you doing with the setting?" she asked. "I don't imagine you could fill the streets of Berne with people in French military uniform, even for a film."

"No, we certainly couldn't do that," Eunice replied with a

slightly forced laugh. "Berne doesn't look right for that period now in any case. We're filming all over the place, actually—which gives us a wonderful chance to see lots of different parts of Switzerland. Luckily we were nearby today so we were able to fit the visit here in with the filming schedule."

"Do you enjoy working with your sister?" Miss Wilson asked curiously, wondering where the sore point in Eunice's soul lay.

"Oh, yes." Eunice nodded, her enthusiasm unmistakeable. "Of course," she continued, "she hasn't been acting for as long as I have, and she's only playing a small role, but it's nice for her to be able to see all the things I've told her about."

"It must be interesting," Miss Wilson suggested carefully, "to think that Dorcas is about to have an adventure you haven't."

"What do you mean?" Eunice demanded, a sharp edge to her voice.

Miss Wilson hesitated for a moment. After all, this matter was no business of hers. Dorcas was no longer a schoolgirl, and in any case, she had not asked for help. Perhaps she had not even noticed Eunice's feelings. Still, now that Miss Wilson understood the root of the matter, she felt it would be a good thing if she could help to ease the difficult situation before it drove a wedge between these sisters.

"Are you so unhappy about her getting married first?"

"Well, she is my *younger* sister," Eunice said, a frown marring her lovely features.

"A younger sister who has given up a great deal for her elder sister," Miss Wilson replied quietly, having heard much of the Brownlow family's story, first from Lady Russell when Dorcas was still at school and later from Gillian.

"She had the chance to travel a lot more than other girls of her age," Eunice pointed out rather resentfully. "I sent her to dancing-school, too."

"From what I've heard," Miss Wilson retorted, her indignation at Eunice's seemingly low opinion of her sister rising, "she was left behind in England because you insisted on signing a contract that took you and your parents back to America. You didn't even tell anyone about it until afterwards so that nobody could try to change your mind or offer any reasons for you not to take it."

Eunice opened her mouth to interrupt, but Miss Wilson gave her no chance to speak.

"Thanks to the fact that she shares your last name, she was made miserable at the school she had to attend in England," she hurried on. "She couldn't tell anyone about it in case word got back to your mother and she felt she had to leave America and you. She even talked Mrs Maynard into letting them film *The Leader of the Lost Cause*, since she knew how much you wanted to do it, although it involved letting people know who she is."

For a long moment, Eunice stared at the floor of Hall in silence. "I—I never thought about it like that," she admitted at last.

"No, I suppose not," Miss Wilson commented rather coldly. "After all, *you* are the star of the family, aren't you? Dorcas merely followed in your footsteps."

"Yes, she did," Eunice agreed uncomfortably, her foot tracing a line on the floor and her shoulders hunched. She thought for a few minutes before turning her eyes in Miss Wilson's direction, as shamefaced as a Middle caught in mischief. "You've given me a lot to think about, Miss Wilson," she admitted. "I hadn't considered how Dorcas might feel."

"How did she and her future husband *really* meet?" Miss Wilson asked pointedly. "I don't think you introduced them, did you?"

"Not exactly, no," Eunice admitted. "Dorcas did come to see me, but they met by chance. I wasn't very happy about it," she added, suddenly deciding to make a clean breast of it. "Now that I look back, I suppose I was jealous that David was paying Dorcas more attention than he was me. I tried to keep them apart for as long as I could, perhaps because I always knew secretly that they would be such a good match for one another. I didn't want Dorcas to have all the excitement and attention of a wedding. You should have heard Mummy as soon as Dorcas told her about being engaged!"

"I can imagine," Miss Wilson said gently. "But it's important for you to remember that, for most of Dorcas's life, the focus has been on you. *You* have had the starring roles, and been the prettier one, and been the person getting all the attention, and around whom other people have arranged their lives. Just because Dorcas gets married and perhaps later has a family of her own, that won't affect you. I don't imagine Dorcas will continue acting after her wedding, so this time for the two of you together working on that film should be very special."

"And I shouldn't ruin that by being all silly and selfish," Eunice suggested, and Miss Wilson nodded.

"I think you would come to regret it later if you did," she said understandingly. "One day," she went on, "perhaps when it was too late, you would see how your behaviour had driven the two of you apart. I think you would be sorry to lose the special bond you have as sisters."

"She's asked me to be her bridesmaid," Eunice admitted, as if confessing to a shameful secret.

"So she wants to share this special moment in her life with you," said Miss Wilson, greatly encouraged by this. "That's good to hear, Eunice. Perhaps it's not too late."

"I hope not." Eunice looked rather more cheerful as she steadily met Miss Wilson's gaze. "I'll make certain of it," she promised. "I *will* remember what you've said."

Miss Wilson smiled at the young actress. "I'm very glad to

hear it," she said; then, gesturing at the doors of Hall, "Shall we go and join your sister now?"

Eunice cast her a grateful glance as she followed her out of the room. "Thank you so much, Miss Wilson. I'll always be glad I came to visit the Chalet School."

Dedicated to the memory of the dearly loved and much missed Pat Willimott, who loved the Chalet School so much.

ERRORS IN THE FIRST EDITION

In republishing *The Chalet School Does It Again* we have kept to the text of the first edition. We have neither edited nor updated it, but have corrected obvious typographical errors wherever it was possible to be sure what the author intended. In accordance with our usual policy we have not corrected French or German usage. We hope we have not allowed any new errors to creep in.

Punctuation

We have changed full stops to commas and vice versa, as appropriate; inserted missing full stops and deleted some for consistency; removed spurious commas and added missing ones; removed spurious quotation marks, changed a single to double and added missing ones; replaced a comma with an em dash; moved an apostrophe, and deleted a repeated word.

Misspelled words

As stated above, we have corrected obvious typos:

Annersey/Annnersley to Annersley
chockful to chockfull
dont to don't
exlaimed to exclaimed
Frau Helder to Frau Helden
Fraülein to Fräulein
Frühstüch to Frühstück
girlness to girliness
Julie Lacy to Julie Lucy
Luckly to Luckily
Marnard to Maynard
nonchalent to Nonchalant

o'clcock to o'clock
obseved to observed
polygot to polyglot
twentyfive to twenty-five
Welson to Welsen

Variant usages

We have standardised these where there is a clear majority usage:

Middle-School not Middle School
Turtle-doves not turtle doves
St. Georges not St Georges
Zoë not Zoé
willow tree not Willow Tree or willow-tree
Willow Pattern not willow-pattern or willow pattern
daïs not dais

Missing or incorrect words

We have added a missing word or replaced with an alternative in order to make sense:

page 54, paragraph 3, line 6: 'the only think I could see'—'the only thing I could see'
page 132, paragraph 6, line 9: 'in the town there they all lived.'—'in the town where they all lived.'
page 137, paragraph 2, line 5: 'she had learnt'—'she has learnt'
page 175, last paragraph, line 7: '*loved* you all long'—'*loved* you all along'

Claire Bell and Alison Neale

DISCOVERING THE CHALET SCHOOL SERIES

In 1925 W & R Chambers Ltd published *The School at the Chalet*, the first title in Elinor Brent-Dyer's Chalet School series. Forty-five years later, in 1970, the same company published the final title in the series, *Prefects of the Chalet School*. It was published posthumously, EBD (as she is known to her fans) having signed the contract three days before she died. During those 45 years Elinor wrote around 60 Chalet School titles, the School moved from the Austrian Tyrol to Guernsey, England, Wales and finally Switzerland, a fan club flourished, and the books began to appear in an abridged paperback format.

How Many Chalet School Titles Are There?

Numbering the Chalet School titles is not as easy as it might appear. The back of the Chambers dustwrapper of *Prefects of the Chalet School* offers a simple list of titles, numbered 1–58. However, no 31, *Tom Tackles the Chalet School*, was published out of sequence (see below), and there were five 'extra' titles, of which one, *The Chalet School and Rosalie*, follows just after *Tom* in the series chronology. In addition, there was a long 'short' story, *The Mystery at the Chalet School*, which comes just before *Tom*. Helen McClelland, EBD's biographer, helpfully devised the system of re-numbering these titles 19a, 19b and 19c.

Further complications apply when looking at the paperbacks. In a number of cases, Armada split the original hardbacks into two when publishing them in paperback, and this meant that the paperbacks are numbered 1–62. In addition, *The Mystery at the Chalet School* was only ever published in paperback with *The Chalet School and Rosalie* but should be numbered 21a in this sequence.

Girls Gone By are following the numbering system of the original hardbacks. All titles will eventually be republished, but not all will be in print at the same time.

Apart from *The Chalet School and Rosalie*, Chambers published four other 'extra' titles: *The Chalet Book for Girls*, *The Second Chalet Book for Girls*, *The Third Chalet Book for Girls* and *The Chalet Girls' Cookbook*. *The Chalet Book for Girls* included *The Mystery at the Chalet School* as well as three other Chalet School short stories, one non-Chalet story by EBD, and four articles. *The Second Chalet Book for Girls* included the first half of *Tom Tackles the Chalet School*, together with three Chalet School short stories, one other story by EBD, seven articles (including the start of what was to become *The Chalet Girls' Cookbook*) and a rather didactic photographic article called *Beth's Diary*, which featured Beth Chester going to Devon and Cornwall. *The Third Chalet Book for Girls* included the second half of *Tom Tackles the Chalet School* (called *Tom Plays the Game*) as well as two Chalet School short stories, three other stories by EBD and three articles. (Clearly the dustwrapper was printed before the book, since the back flap lists three stories and two articles which are not in the book.) It is likely that *The Chalet School and Rosalie* was intended to be the long story for a fourth *Book for Girls*, but since no more were published this title eventually appeared in 1951 in paperback (very unusual for the time). The back cover of *The Second Chalet Book for Girls* lists *The First Junior Chalet Book* as hopefully being published 'next year'; this never materialised. *The Chalet Girls' Cookbook* is not merely a collection of recipes but also contains a very loose story about Joey, Simone, Marie and Frieda just after they have left the School. While not all of these Chalet stories add crucial information to the series, many of them do, and they are certainly worth collecting. All the *Books for Girls* are difficult to obtain on the second-hand market, but most of the stories were reprinted in two books compiled by Helen McClelland, *Elinor M. Brent-Dyer's Chalet School* (out of print) and *The Chalet School Companion* (available from Bettany Press). Girls Gone By have now published all EBD's known short stories, from these and other sources, in a single volume.

The Locations of the Chalet School Books

The Chalet School started its life in Briesau am Tiernsee in the Austrian Tyrol (Pertisau am Achensee in real life). After Germany signed the Anschluss with Austria in 1938, it would have been impossible to keep even a fictional school in Austria. As a result, EBD wrote *The Chalet School in Exile*, during which, following an encounter with some Nazis, several of the girls, including Joey Bettany, were forced to flee Austria, and the School was also forced to leave. Unfortunately, Elinor chose to move the School to Guernsey—the book was published just as Germany invaded the Channel Islands. The next book, *The Chalet School Goes to It*, saw the School moving again, this time to a village near Armiford—Hereford in real life. Here the School remained for the duration of the war, and indeed when the next move came, in *The Chalet School and the Island*, it was for reasons of plot. The island concerned was off the south-west coast of Wales, and is fictional, although generally agreed by Chalet School fans to be a combination of various islands including Caldey Island, St Margaret's Isle, Skokholm, Ramsey Island and Grassholm, with Caldey Island being the most likely contender if a single island has to be picked. Elinor had long wanted to move the School back to Austria, but the political situation there in the 1950s forbade such a move, so she did the next best thing and moved it to Switzerland, firstly by establishing a finishing branch in *The Chalet School in the Oberland*, and secondly by relocating the School itself in *The Chalet School and Barbara*. The exact location is subject to much debate, but it seems likely that it is somewhere near Wengen in the Bernese Oberland. Here the School was to remain for the rest of its fictional life, and here it still is today for its many aficionados.

The Chalet Club 1959–69

In 1959 Chambers and Elinor Brent-Dyer started a club for lovers of the Chalet books, beginning with 33 members. When the club closed in 1969, after Elinor's death, there were around 4,000 members worldwide. Twice-yearly News Letters were produced, written by Elinor herself, and the information in these adds fascinating, if sometimes conflicting, detail to the series. In 1997 Friends of the Chalet School, one of the two fan clubs existing today, republished the News Letters in facsimile book format. Girls Gone By Publishers produced a new edition in 2004.

The Publication of the Chalet School Series in Armada Paperback

On 1 May 1967, Armada, the children's paperback division of what was then William Collins, Sons & Co Ltd, published the first four Chalet School paperbacks. This momentous news was covered in issue Number Sixteen of the Chalet Club News Letter, which also appeared in May 1967. In her editorial, Elinor Brent-Dyer said: 'Prepare for a BIG piece of news. The Chalet Books, slightly abridged, are being reissued in the Armada series. The first four come out in May, and two of them are *The School at the Chalet* and *Jo of the Chalet School*. So watch the windows of the booksellers if you want to add them to your collection. They will be issued at the usual Armada price, which should bring them within the reach of all of you. I hope you like the new jackets. Myself, I think them charming, especially *The School at the Chalet*.' On the back page of the News Letter there was an advertisement for the books, which reproduced the covers of the first four titles.

The words 'slightly abridged' were a huge understatement, and over the years Chalet fans have made frequent complaints about the fact that the paperbacks are abridged, about some of the covers, and about the fact that the books were published in a most extraordinary order, with the whole series never available in paperback at any one time. It has to be said, however, that were it not for the paperbacks interest in the Chalet series would, in the main, be confined to those who had bought or borrowed the hardbacks prior to their demise in the early 1970s, and Chalet fans would mostly be at least 40 and over in age. The paperbacks have sold hundreds of thousands of copies over the years, and those that are not in print (the vast majority) are still to be found on the second-hand market (through charity shops and jumble sales as well as dealers). They may be cut (and sometimes disgracefully so), but enough of the story is there to fascinate new readers, and we should be grateful that they were published at all. Had they not been, it is most unlikely that two Chalet clubs would now be flourishing and that Girls Gone By Publishers would be able to republish the series in this new, unabridged, format.

Clarissa Cridland

ELINOR M BRENT-DYER: A BRIEF BIOGRAPHY

EBD was born Gladys Eleanor May Dyer in South Shields on 6 April 1894, the only daughter of Eleanor (Nelly) Watson Rutherford and Charles Morris Brent Dyer. Her father had been married before and had a son, Charles Arnold, who was never to live with his father and stepmother. This caused some friction between Elinor's parents, and her father left home when she was three and her younger brother, Henzell, was two. Her father eventually went to live with another woman by whom he had a third son, Morris. Elinor's parents lived in a respectable lower-middle-class area, and the family covered up the departure of her father by saying that her mother had 'lost' her husband.

In 1912 Henzell died of cerebro-spinal fever, another event which was covered up. Friends of Elinor's who knew her after his death were unaware that she had had a brother. Death from illness was, of course, common at this time, and Elinor's familiarity with this is reflected in her books, which abound with motherless heroines.

Elinor was educated privately in South Shields, and returned there to teach after she had been to the City of Leeds Training College. In the early 1920s she adopted the name Elinor Mary Brent-Dyer. She was interested in the theatre, and her first book, *Gerry Goes to School*, published in 1922, was written for the child actress Hazel Bainbridge—mother of the actress Kate O'Mara. In the mid 1920s she also taught at St Helen's, Northwood, Middlesex, at Moreton House School, Dunstable, Bedfordshire, and in Fareham near Portsmouth. She was a keen musician and a practising Christian, converting to Roman Catholicism in 1930, a major step in those days.

In the early 1920s Elinor spent a holiday in the Austrian Tyrol at Pertisau am Achensee, which she was to use so successfully as the first location in the Chalet School series. (Many of the locations in her books were real places.) In 1933 she moved with her mother and stepfather to Hereford, travelling daily to Peterchurch as a governess. After her stepfather died in November 1937 she started her own school in Hereford, The Margaret Roper, which ran from 1938 until 1948. Unlike the Chalet School it was not a huge success and probably would not have survived had it not been for the Second World War. From 1948 Elinor devoted all her time to writing. Her mother died in 1957, and in 1964 Elinor moved to Redhill, Surrey, where she died on 20 September 1969.

Clarissa Cridland

COMPLETE NUMERICAL LIST OF TITLES IN THE CHALET SCHOOL SERIES

(Chambers and Girls Gone By)

Dates in parentheses refer to the original publication dates

1. *The School at the Chalet* (1925)
2. *Jo of the Chalet School* (1926)
3. *The Princess of the Chalet School* (1927)
4. *The Head Girl of the Chalet School* (1928)
5. *The Rivals of the Chalet School* (1929)
6. *Eustacia Goes to the Chalet School* (1930)
7. *The Chalet School and Jo* (1931)
8. *The Chalet Girls in Camp* (1932)
9. *The Exploits of the Chalet Girls* (1933)
10. *The Chalet School and the Lintons* (1934) (published in Armada paperback in two volumes—*The Chalet School and the Lintons* and *A Rebel at the Chalet School*)
11. *The New House at the Chalet School* (1935)
12. *Jo Returns to the Chalet School* (1936)
13. *The New Chalet School* (1938) (published in Armada paperback in two volumes—*The New Chalet School* and *A United Chalet School*)
14. *The Chalet School in Exile* (1940)
15. *The Chalet School Goes to It* (1941) (published in Armada paperback as *The Chalet School at War*)
16. *The Highland Twins at the Chalet School* (1942)
17. *Lavender Laughs in the Chalet School* (1943) (published in Armada paperback as *Lavender Leigh at the Chalet School*)
18. *Gay From China at the Chalet School* (1944) (published in Armada paperback as *Gay Lambert at the Chalet School*)

19. *Jo to the Rescue* (1945)
19a. *The Mystery at the Chalet School* (1947) (published in *The Chalet Book for Girls*)
19b. *Tom Tackles the Chalet School* (published in *The Second Chalet Book for Girls*, 1948, and *The Third Chalet Book for Girls*, 1949, and then as a single volume in 1955)
19c. *The Chalet School and Rosalie* (1951) (published as a paperback)
20. *Three Go to the Chalet School* (1949)
21. *The Chalet School and the Island* (1950)
22. *Peggy of the Chalet School* (1950)
23. *Carola Storms the Chalet School* (1951)
24. *The Wrong Chalet School* (1952)
25. *Shocks for the Chalet School* (1952)
26. *The Chalet School in the Oberland* (1952)
27. *Bride Leads the Chalet School* (1953)
28. *Changes for the Chalet School* (1953)
29. *Joey Goes to the Oberland* (1954)
30. *The Chalet School and Barbara* (1954)
31. (see 19b)
32. *The Chalet School Does It Again* (1955)
33. *A Chalet Girl from Kenya* (1955)
34. *Mary-Lou of the Chalet School* (1956)
35. *A Genius at the Chalet School* (1956) (published in Armada paperback in two volumes—*A Genius at the Chalet School* and *Chalet School Fête*)
36. *A Problem for the Chalet School* (1956)
37. *The New Mistress at the Chalet School* (1957)
38. *Excitements at the Chalet School* (1957)
39. *The Coming of Age of the Chalet School* (1958)
40. *The Chalet School and Richenda* (1958)
41. *Trials for the Chalet School* (1958)

42. *Theodora and the Chalet School* (1959)
43. *Joey and Co. in Tirol* (1960)
44. *Ruey Richardson—Chaletian* (1960) (published in Armada paperback as *Ruey Richardson at the Chalet School*)
45. *A Leader in the Chalet School* (1961)
46. *The Chalet School Wins the Trick* (1961)
47. *A Future Chalet School Girl* (1962)
48. *The Feud in the Chalet School* (1962)
49. *The Chalet School Triplets* (1963)
50. *The Chalet School Reunion* (1963)
51. *Jane and the Chalet School* (1964)
52. *Redheads at the Chalet School* (1964)
53. *Adrienne and the Chalet School* (1965)
54. *Summer Term at the Chalet School* (1965)
55. *Challenge for the Chalet School* (1966)
56. *Two Sams at the Chalet School* (1967)
57. *Althea Joins the Chalet School* (1969)
58. *Prefects of the Chalet School* (1970)

Extras

The Chalet Book for Girls (1947)
The Second Chalet Book for Girls (1948)
The Third Chalet Book for Girls (1949)
The Chalet Girls' Cookbook (1953)

COMPLETE NUMERICAL LIST OF TITLES IN THE CHALET SCHOOL SERIES

(Armada/Collins)

1. *The School at the Chalet*
2. *Jo of the Chalet School*
3. *The Princess of the Chalet School*
4. *The Head Girl of the Chalet School*
5. *(The) Rivals of the Chalet School*
6. *Eustacia Goes to the Chalet School*
7. *The Chalet School and Jo*
8. *The Chalet Girls in Camp*
9. *The Exploits of the Chalet Girls*
10. *The Chalet School and the Lintons*
11. *A Rebel at the Chalet School*
12. *The New House at the Chalet School*
13. *Jo Returns to the Chalet School*
14. *The New Chalet School*
15. *A United Chalet School*
16. *The Chalet School in Exile*
17. *The Chalet School at War*
18. *The Highland Twins at the Chalet School*
19. *Lavender Leigh at the Chalet School*
20. *Gay Lambert at the Chalet School*
21. *Jo to the Rescue*

21a. *The Mystery at the Chalet School* (published only in the same volume as 23)

22. *Tom Tackles the Chalet School*
23. *The Chalet School and Rosalie*
24. *Three Go to the Chalet School*
25. *The Chalet School and the Island*

26. *Peggy of the Chalet School*
27. *Carola Storms the Chalet School*
28. *The Wrong Chalet School*
29. *Shocks for the Chalet School*
30. *The Chalet School in the Oberland*
31. *Bride Leads the Chalet School*
32. *Changes for the Chalet School*
33. *Joey Goes to the Oberland*
34. *The Chalet School and Barbara*
35. *The Chalet School Does It Again*
36. *A Chalet Girl from Kenya*
37. *Mary-Lou of/at the Chalet School*
38. *A Genius at the Chalet School*
39. *Chalet School Fête*
40. *A Problem for the Chalet School*
41. *The New Mistress at the Chalet School*
42. *Excitements at the Chalet School*
43. *The Coming of Age of the Chalet School*
44. *The Chalet School and Richenda*
45. *Trials for the Chalet School*
46. *Theodora and the Chalet School*
47. *Joey and Co. in Tirol*
48. *Ruey Richardson at the Chalet School*
49. *A Leader in the Chalet School*
50. *The Chalet School Wins the Trick*
51. *A Future Chalet School Girl*
52. *The Feud in the Chalet School*
53. *The Chalet School Triplets*
54. *The Chalet School Reunion*
55. *Jane and the Chalet School*
56. *Redheads at the Chalet School*
57. *Adrienne and the Chalet School*

58. *Summer Term at the Chalet School*
59. *Challenge for the Chalet School*
60. *Two Sams at the Chalet School*
61. *Althea Joins the Chalet School*
62. *Prefects of the Chalet School*

NEW CHALET SCHOOL TITLES

In the last few years several authors have written books which either fill in terms in the Chalet School canon about which Elinor did not write or carry on the story. These are as follows:

The Chalet School Christmas Story Book edited by Ruth Jolly and Adrianne Fitzpatrick—featuring short stories by Helen Barber, Katherine Bruce, Caroline German, Heather Paisley and more (Girls Gone By Publishers 2007)

The Bettanys of Taverton High by Helen Barber—set immediately before *The School at the Chalet*, covering Joey's last term at her English school (Girls Gone By Publishers 2008; out of print)

The Guides of the Chalet School by Jane Berry—set in the gap between *Jo of the Chalet School* and *The Princess of the Chalet School* (Girls Gone By Publishers 2009)

Juliet of the Chalet School by Caroline German—set in the gap between *Jo of the Chalet School* and *The Princess of the Chalet School* (Girls Gone By Publishers 2006; out of print)

Deira Joins the Chalet School by Caroline German—set in the gap between *Jo of the Chalet School* and *The Princess of the Chalet School* (Girls Gone By Publishers 2010)

Visitors for the Chalet School by Helen McClelland—set between *The Princess of the Chalet School* and *The Head Girl of the Chalet School* (Bettany Press 1995; Collins edition 2000)

Gillian of the Chalet School by Carol Allan—set between *The New Chalet School* and *The Chalet School in Exile* (Girls Gone By Publishers 2001; reprinted 2006; out of print)

The Chalet School and Robin by Caroline German—set after *The Chalet School Goes to It*. The 2012 edition includes a short story: 'Joey and Jean'. (Girls Gone By Publishers 2003; new edition 2012)

A Chalet School Headmistress by Helen Barber—set during the same term as *The Mystery at the Chalet School* (Girls Gone By Publishers 2004; out of print)

Peace Comes to the Chalet School by Katherine Bruce—set in the gap between *The Chalet School and Rosalie* and *Three Go to the Chalet School*; the action takes place during the summer term of 1945 (Girls Gone By Publishers 2005; out of print)

A Difficult Term for the Chalet School by Lisa Townsend—set between *Three Go to the Chalet School* and *The Chalet School and the Island* (Girls Gone by Publishers 2011)

New Beginnings at the Chalet School by Heather Paisley—set three years after *Prefects of the Chalet School* (Friends of the Chalet School 1999; Girls Gone By Publishers 2002; reprinted 2006; out of print)

FURTHER READING

Behind the Chalet School by Helen McClelland (essential)*

Elinor M. Brent-Dyer's Chalet School by Helen McClelland. Out of print

The Chalet School Companion by Helen McClelland*

A World of Girls by Rosemary Auchmuty*

A World of Women by Rosemary Auchmuty*

*Available from:
Bettany Press, 8 Kildare Road, London E16 4AD, UK
(http://www.bettanypress.co.uk)

Girls Gone By Publishers

Girls Gone By Publishers republish some of the most popular children's fiction from the 20th century, concentrating on those titles which are most sought after and difficult to find on the second-hand market. Our aim is to make them available at affordable prices, and to make ownership possible not only for existing collectors but also for new ones, so that the books continue to survive. We also publish some new titles which fit into the genre.

Authors on the GGBP fiction list include Margaret Biggs, Elinor Brent-Dyer, Dorita Fairlie Bruce, Patricia Caldwell, Gwendoline Courtney, Winifred Darch, Monica Edwards, Josephine Elder, Lorna Hill, Clare Mallory, Dorothea Moore, Violet Needham, Elsie Jeanette Oxenham, Malcolm Saville and Evelyn Smith.

We also have a growing range of non-fiction titles, either more general works about the genre or books about particular authors. Our subjects include Girl Guiding, Monica Edwards and her books, Elsie Oxenham's books, and Geoffrey Trease. The non-fiction books are in a larger format than our fiction, and some of them are lavishly illustrated in colour as well as black and white. For details of availability and when to order, see our website—www.ggbp.co.uk—or write for a catalogue to GGBP, 4 Rock Terrace, Coleford, Radstock, Somerset, BA3 5NF, UK.

Some of our titles are available as eBooks. These are only available from our website: www.ggbp.co.uk